DATE DUE	BORROWER'S NAME	ROOM NUMBER

Mitch got up slowly, as if he had grown taller and needed to feel his new height. He moved close to Carlie and took her arm.

"Look," he said, pointing down to the valley and up at the green hills. "Look at those trees. They shine. Look at those mountains! Just being here makes you feel so alive. When I look around I keep thinking of the words in the psalm we say every Friday night: 'The rivers will clap their hands. The mountains will sing together.' Carlie, I want to be where the mountains can sing."

Carlie scarcely moved, hardly breathed. She had never loved him so much as at this moment. "A singing mountain," she whispered. "That's so beautiful."

—from *The Singing Mountain*

The Singing Mountain

Sonia Levitin

Simon & Schuster Books for Young Readers

With special thanks to my editor, Stephanie Owens Lurie, for helping me climb this mountain. And for Rabbi Richard Levy and Rabbi Chaim Menz, with gratitude for their tireless and gentle teaching.

Special thanks to the following people:
John Cohan, for telling me his personal story of Ymuiden, which became the inspiration for an incident in this book; my friend Jeremy Eichenbaum, for teaching me about skateboarding; Aron Hirt-Manheimer, for his generous help and advice; John Hofman, in memoriam, for his confidence and inspiration; Adaire Klein, for her generous help in reading and correcting the manuscript; Gloria Miklowitz, for her continued encouragement and faith in this project.

SIMON & SCHUSTER BOOKS FOR YOUNG READERS
An imprint of Simon & Schuster Children's Publishing Division
1230 Avenue of the Americas, New York, New York 10020

Book design by Lucille Chomowicz
The text for this book is set in Bembo.
Printed and bound in the United States of America
First Edition
10 9 8 7 6 5 4 3 2 1

Library of Congress Cataloging-in-Publication Data
Levitin, Sonia, 1934–
The singing mountain / Sonia Levitin.
p. cm.
Summary: While traveling in Israel for the summer, seventeen-year-old Mitch decides to stay and pursue a life of Jewish orthodoxy, forcing him to make some important decisions about the family and life he is leaving in southern California.
ISBN 0-689-80809-7
1. Jews—Israel—Juvenile fiction. 2. Jews—California—Fiction. 3. Israel—Fiction. 4. Cousins—Fiction. 5. Family life—Fiction.] I. Title
PZ7.L58Sh 1998
[Fic]—dc21
97-33365

For my good son, Dan, who stands beside me always;
for Lloyd, steadfast and loving husband;
and for my wonderful daughter, Shari

THE SINGING MOUNTAIN

"The rivers will clap their hands,

the mountains will sing together before the Lord,

for He has come to judge the world . . . "

Psalm 98: 8-9

CHAPTER 1

MAYBE IT WAS a premonition. Carlie had spent the last twenty minutes debating with herself, annoyed that something as trivial as going to the beach with Melanie was keeping her on edge. She wanted to go—no, it was too hot. Too noisy and dirty. Melanie would argue, reminding Carlie that she was the one who always wanted to swim in the ocean. . . .

The telephone on Carlie's desk rang. She grabbed the receiver. "Hello!"

"Mrs. Green? Mrs. Harry Green?"

"No, they've gone out. This is Carlie, their niece." Through the window Carlie noticed the dirty, hazy sky—smog.

The man on the phone breathed hard into the receiver. "Okay, look. This is Sy Rosen. From the temple."

Carlie was confused. She knew Rosen vaguely. He was a youth counselor from the Valley Temple, a thin man with wild, kinky hair, always yelling. She stammered, "I thought—where are you, Mr. Rosen? I thought . . ."

He said, "I'm calling from Israel. We've got a little problem. When will your aunt and uncle be back?"

"I'm not sure. They're playing golf." Carlie's heart began to pound faster. Her gaze took in the grass and the bougainvillea outside, placid in contrast to Sy Rosen's frantic voice and the dread that was creeping over her. "What's wrong? Is something wrong with Mitch?" Her mind raced over possibilities—the time he broke his wrist skiing, the time he got food poisoning. She wanted to shout. Enough! Am I my cousin's keeper? But she only stammered, "I thought you were all coming home tomorrow."

The man took a deep, labored breath. "Look, this is important. Can you take a message?"

"Of course." A quiet numbness settled over Carlie while her mind began reciting with utter clarity: *Sy Rosen calling from Israel. This is important. Something happened, get it straight, get it right . . . don't panic.*

The man's voice was shrill, almost explosive. "We can't find Mitch. He left the hotel last night, left a note saying he'd gone with a friend. Now it's early evening, and he hasn't returned. We fly back to L.A. on the midnight flight. Has Mitch called you?"

"No. We haven't heard from him. But—I don't understand, Mr. Rosen. Who's the friend? How come Mitch has a friend in Israel?"

"I don't know!" shouted the man. "I thought maybe you'd heard. If you hear something . . . "

"I'll call you right away at the Ramada. That's where you are, isn't it? The Ramada Hotel in Jerusalem." Carlie's mind clicked off the facts as if she were a computer, while inside a familiar ache began to spread, a gnawing feeling. She had a name for it—*the lion*—a roar inside her, a huge emptiness.

"I'm going to send some of the boys out to look for him," Sy Rosen said. "We'll call you if we hear anything."

"Wait!" Carlie shouted into the receiver. "Have you told the police?" Did they have police in Israel, she wondered, or only soldiers? She saw them all the time on the TV news, with their rifles and their tense faces, always in confrontation.

"Yes, yes, of course," Rosen said. "They said it's too soon to do anything. They think he's just gone sight-seeing."

"Mitch wouldn't just go off like that," Carlie objected. "Let me talk to Ari. Or Jonathan."

"They've gone to look for Mitch. Listen, don't get hysterical, Carlie, I'm sure . . . "

Hysterical? Look who's talking! she thought angrily. "Call us," she said, making her tone authoritative. "Please, the minute you hear."

"Of course I will. Take it easy. It's probably nothing. I was just checking."

Carlie put down the receiver. For a long moment she sat staring out the window at the hazy sky. Already the heat was stifling. August was almost unbearable in the San Fernando Valley. For a moment Carlie's mind flipped back to other summers, when she and Mitch had gone to the beach to cool off. The summer Mitch and his pals were lifeguards, Carlie and Melanie and some of their friends had gone out there almost every day. That was two summers ago, and Carlie had felt awkward in her bathing suit and kept a towel wrapped around her body most of the time.

Carlie glanced at the clock. Only three minutes had passed since Sy Rosen's call. In minutes, the world can change. She knew that as well as anyone. Now as Carlie picked up the receiver and punched in the automatic dial, she forced herself to focus, to breathe deeply, the way she'd learned from her yoga tape.

Melanie answered right away. "Hey, Carlie!"

"How'd you know it was me?"

"Familiar ring. Also, you said you'd call about the beach."

"Ha, clever," Carlie bantered. As long as she didn't say the words, things still seemed normal. Then she steeled herself and said, "Mitch has disappeared. Sy Rosen called from Israel. I don't know what to do."

"What?" Melanie cried. "Where would he be? What could have happened?"

Carlie heard Melanie murmuring to her mom. "Mitch has disappeared. I don't *know*!" Then to Carlie she said, "My mom's all upset. She wants to know what happened."

"I don't know. I'm just calling to tell you."

Carlie could feel the tightness in her own face. Her body was tense, already building a wall against terrible words, bad news that could change everything in a moment.

"Do you want me to come over?" Melanie asked.

"No. Thanks. I'll call you later."

"Wouldn't you rather have company? Why do you want to be alone at a time like this?"

"*Melanie!* I'm okay. Really. I have to go. *I can handle it!*"

"Okay." Melanie sighed. "Call me later. When you know."

He'll call back, Carlie thought. Sy Rosen will call back in a minute and say Mitch just came in. He got stuck in an elevator. Or he fell asleep at the friend's house, or they went out somewhere . . . a million things could have happened, none of them bad. And if it *was* bad, she could handle it. Sure.

"She's a strong girl," Aunt Vivian would tell friends in that low tone, as if Carlie couldn't hear. "If she could overcome that tragedy, she can do anything."

It sounded great. Except it wasn't true. Inside, *the lion* was always waiting, kept at bay by her shrug, her casual grin, her refusal to cry.

Now, she opened her diary to past entries, needing something to occupy her mind. Melanie had given her the journal for her fifteenth birthday, along with a pair of beautiful silver and turquoise earrings.

So, Mitch is going to Israel for the summer. Great! I can hang out with anyone I want, nobody to criticize.

Mitch had been gone for nine weeks now, most of the summer, and Carlie still seemed to see his shadow and hear his voice. Mitch took up a lot of space, in more ways than one. At first the house had seemed so empty. Now, she had to admit, her feelings were mixed. She'd gotten used to the extra space, to being listened to at the dinner table—no Mitch to pop out with a joke, to steal the attention, to get his dad fuming. With Mitch around, Carlie always felt like the bit actor in a movie. Mitch, of course, was the star.

Well, he was their child, wasn't he? Their own, while she . . .

When the trip to Israel had come up, things were settled pretty quickly. Apparently Aunt Vivian had already made up her mind that some "cultural experience" was what Mitch needed before starting college. Also, as Carlie had overheard, "It will be good for Carlie to be on her own, to get used to Mitch being away at college. She hangs on him too much."

Hangs on him? Carlie had felt humiliated and furious. But

she'd swallowed down her anger and written in her journal:

The continuing problem is, I can't be myself. I'm not their child, not their guest, but something in between. I'm constantly aware of how much I owe them. Everyone tells me how wonderful they are, how lucky I am. And it's true. That's what hurts—I've got the obligation, but not the feeling. Maybe I'm some kind of a monster, ungrateful. I don't want to open up all this stuff. I really don't want to talk about it.

Carlie picked up the telephone, called for information for the Valley Golf and Country Club. She dialed, feeling that ache again. She pulled a pillow from her bed, holding it in her lap against her stomach. At last someone answered and told her sharply, "There's no way for us to reach them if they're out on the courses. We have a strict rule against disturbing our members. Is this an emergency?"

"No," Carlie said. She put down the receiver. "Not yet."

Emergencies come swiftly, with violence. Like a car crash or an earthquake. In a real emergency, words disappear, nothing matters except getting through the next minute, getting to the other side of the abyss.

Carlie flipped back the pages of her journal.

Big earthquake—6.4 on the Richter scale—it actually threw me out of my bed. I heard this terrible roar, like a train was coming through the house. I remember holding on to Mitch, both of us down under the dining room table. Arnie kept pawing at my arm, howling, trying to dig under the rug. "Keep down! Don't move!" Aunt Vivian screamed. "Oh, my God! Where are the kids?" Glass was breaking all around us, things were crashing down. I thought we'd die. I tried to think what you're supposed to do before you die, but all I could think of was a train, a train. . . .

Carlie skimmed through her journal once more, glancing

at the notation she had just made. "Sy Rosen called from Israel. The folks are out. Mitch is gone. I had a bad feeling about this trip from the start . . .

When the shaking stopped, and the crashing and the swaying, Carlie and Mitch had crept out from under the dining room table. Arnie, the dog, gave a yelp and ran out to the yard, digging himself in among tall ferns that grew by the side of the garage. Tremors persisted. The earth was heaving like an ocean.

"Careful," Carlie said as they picked their way among the splinters of glass and crockery. "Aunt Vivian!" she called upstairs. "Get some shoes. It's a mess down here."

"Be careful!" Uncle Harry shouted down. "Mitch! Where's Mitch?"

"I'm here, Dad. I'm okay."

"Don't touch anything!" his father warned.

"Okay, Dad."

"Go outside," Uncle Harry yelled. "Get out of the house, into the backyard. We're coming down."

"It's so dark!" Aunt Vivian's voice was a whisper, a kind of wail.

"Where's the flashlight?" Carlie asked.

"Can't find anything," Mitch said, his tone muffled. "All the liquor slid out of the cabinet. It's a mess. The whole floor—"

"Get out! Get out!" cried Harry as another tremor set the house rolling.

Then the four of them were out on the patio, watching the palm trees swaying eerily in the darkness, their spiky fronds looking like grotesque heads lit only by a faint moon.

With the dawn, they began to move about, peering inside at the devastation. "Is there food?" Harry wanted to know. Inside the pantry bottles, cans and packages lay smashed and oozing.

"Of course there's food," Aunt Vivian said. Her tone was tight, a kernel of outrage deep inside, threatening to explode. "I always have food in the house!"

"I mean . . ."

"We shouldn't eat anything that's broken open," Mitch said. "I read it could be contaminated."

"With what?" Harry demanded. He looked angry. "Mitch, for God's sake, will you help me with these boards?"

Afterward, when they had swept up and dumped out the debris, when they had called out to neighbors with feigned good cheer, "Hey, is everything okay over there?" they all sank down once again on the grass, feeling the strange ripples underground, a series of aftershocks.

"I don't think we have enough water," said Aunt Vivian in a dull tone.

"I thought you always get water delivered," Harry said.

"We ran out."

"I'll go get some," Carlie said. "I'll take the Jeep."

"I don't know," said her aunt, frowning. "What if . . ."

"Please," Carlie said. "I need to get out of here. I want to see . . ." She hesitated, not wanting to say it: Was the world still functioning? Was the town still standing? Nothing worked, no radios or TV; the battery-powered radio had been smashed when the bookcase fell down on it.

"Don't go alone," Aunt Vivian said.

"Mitch will come with me," Carlie said.

They went, Mitch driving the Jeep, Carlie squinting out at the wreckage, reporting, "House is collapsed over there—oh, my God! The roof is all caved in. Be careful—there's water all over the street, broken hydrant. Look at that car. There' s a telephone pole on top of it."

At the small mall on Ventura, people milled about, clutching at each other with their eyes. Strangers talked to strangers. They pushed their shopping carts with a certain fury, like tanks.

"Get water and soda," Carlie told Mitch.

"Yes, boss," Mitch grunted.

"Get stuff we can eat without cooking," Carlie said. "Bread and cheese and bananas." Carlie glanced at Mitch. He was scared, too. She could tell by the tilt of his shoulders, the way he frowned at the food. It could happen again. Harder. The big one. What they'd been through might just have been a warning.

Carlie slowed down, walking beside Mitch, both of them holding the handle of the shopping cart. At the bakery aisle she grabbed a bag of cookies and a chocolate cake in a box. "Might as well enjoy," she said, making her tone light.

Mitch said, "How about ice cream?"

"Sure. We'll eat it right away. Can't keep it; the power's out."

They ate almost a whole quart of pistachio ice cream while sitting in the Jeep, watching people scramble and hurry as if they could outrun another quake.

Then they went home. "What took you so long?" Mitch's parents were furious. "We were so worried!"

Harry glowered at Mitch. "Where's your brain? Didn't you know we needed you here?"

"Sorry, sorry," Mitch said. "Next time I'll plan an earthquake more conveniently."

"Don't give me that sass!"

"Stop it! For God's sake, Harry . . . "

"We brought stuff for sandwiches," said Carlie. Carlie, the peacemaker. "And cake. Chocolate cake."

Now Carlie braced herself as she heard the Jeep coming up the driveway and into the garage. She dreaded telling them, mentally rehearsing the right words to make it less frightening, to keep them calm.

There were no such words. She went to meet them at the door. "Aunt Vivian! Uncle Harry, there's something I have to tell you."

CHAPTER 2

MITCH STOOD WITH the others, his eyes closed, his body swaying slightly to the low chanting. The sound reminded him of summer camp, with the wind blowing through the aspen trees. At camp he'd felt the same sense of peace and love he felt now.

The soft hum of Hebrew was soothing, even though he did not understand the words. About fifty male voices rose together in responsive prayer. Mitch felt the soft cloth of the white prayer shawl enfolding him, keeping him close and sheltered from the world outside.

The Jerusalem streets were almost empty of traffic, for it was Saturday, the Sabbath. Tal and his friends called it *Shabes.* Still, the air was filled with sounds as people strolled along the sidewalks, calling out greetings.

Beside Mitch, his new friend, Tal, took a few steps backward, made several weaving, bowing motions, then he sat down. "It's nearly over," Tal whispered. "Then we have lunch."

Mitch nodded, glancing at Tal's calm face, those lively and

sparkling eyes. He had met Tal during his first week in Israel.

Mitch and his friends had been walking across the courtyard of the *Kotel*, the Western Wall, a main attraction for tourists. Tal sauntered up. "Hello! You're from the States, aren't you?" Tal walked with Mitch for a few minutes, talking amiably. Tal told Mitch that he, too, was from California. San Diego. He'd been in Israel for four years now.

"Aren't you ever going home?" Mitch had asked.

"This is my home," Tal replied with a smile. "My parents joined me last year. My sister, Halle, came first, nine years ago. Now, we've all made *aliyah*."

"What's that?"

"Literally, it means going up—higher."

"I see." Mitch had frowned. "Like, every other place in the world is inferior to Israel. The rest of us are lowlifes."

"Is that what you think?" Tal had seemed startled rather than annoyed.

"No," Mitch had snapped. "But I guess it's what *you* think."

Sy Rosen, the counselor from the temple back home, had warned them before they left about various "elements" in Israel, especially in Jerusalem. "These people are fanatics," he said. "Ultra Orthodox, which is okay, except that they want everybody to think the way they do. Be careful, especially when you go to the *Kotel*. They hang out there, try to engage you in conversation. Remember, you don't have to talk with anybody you don't want to. Just walk away."

Mitch's buddies, Ari and Jonathan, had done exactly that. "Come on, Mitch," they called over their shoulders. "Let's go."

But Mitch hung back, and eventually he and Tal sat down on a low wall intersecting the courtyard as Tal spoke quietly about his life.

"When I decided to stay here," he said, "I felt as if a kind of weight had been lifted from me. For the first time in my life I knew what I wanted to do, and that it was exactly right. Everything in the past seemed to point me in this direction. Have you ever felt that, Mitch?"

Mitch hesitated, but only for a moment. "Once," he said, "when I first went to camp in the mountains. They taught jewelry making and wood carving. I loved it." He glanced at Tal, suspicious. "So, what do you do here? Are you a sort of missionary?" He looked around for his friends, but they had vanished into the throng at the Wall.

Tal laughed. "I'm just a student. My sister's husband, Richard, is a teacher at the *yeshiva*. I like it a lot. Sometimes I do meet people who want to visit, guys from the States, like you."

"I don't think so," Mitch had said abruptly, standing up.

"Well, it's been nice talking to you," Tal said. He held out a small card, like an ordinary business card. "Call me if you have any questions later, or if you want to visit."

"I won't," Mitch said.

"Okay." Tal smiled and extended his hand. "*Shalom.*"

"*Shalom,*" Mitch had said grudgingly. Peace. Ha. There was no peace, certainly not here, in Israel.

Back home Mitch had watched the TV news and read an occasional newspaper article about Israel. Riots seemed commonplace, with Arabs and Jews at each other's throats all the time. American diplomats shuttled back and forth; world leaders pleaded for peace or threatened war; nothing ever seemed to change.

Once, he and his family had watched a TV special about

Israel, and Mitch was mesmerized by the music, the sight of Bedouins still living in tents, and the ancient architecture. That night he dreamed of spired cathedrals and Roman ruins. But when he first heard about the trip to Israel, he hardly gave it a thought. The trip was sponsored by the temple, and his friends Ari and Jon were going. Jon's parents were always wrapped up in temple activities; Jon's mom was on the board.

Mitch had been to Sunday school for the obligatory two years, just long enough to skim through a *Bar Mitzvah* ceremony. He'd gone through the *Bar Mitzvah* for his family, not for himself.

"It means a lot to your grandmother," his father had said.

"It doesn't hurt to know something about your own religion," his mother told him seriously.

After the *Bar Mitzvah* ceremony, his parents gave him a party at the Valley Inn, with all his friends and a three-piece band. Everyone was proud of him, they said, and he received lots of presents, even some cash.

Rabbi Hoffman wanted Mitch to continue and study for confirmation, but Mitch hated it. He clowned in class, his behavior "so rambunctious," according to the principal, that everyone agreed he should quit.

"Well, you can lead a horse to water," his dad had said good-naturedly, "but you can't force him to eat oats."

His mother shook her head, laughing. "Once again, Harry, you've mutilated a metaphor. Well, it's okay with me," she said. "Mitch doesn't need to be confirmed."

His dad said, "Going to temple doesn't make you a good person, or a good Jew. Manny Snyder, big shot at the temple, doesn't pay his taxes. When he did my electrical work, he asked me to make out the check in his name, so he wouldn't have to report the income. Big hypocrite!"

So it was settled. Mitch was off the hook.

When the trip to Israel came up, Mitch's mother urged him to go. "Look, life has a way of moving pretty fast. You don't have any real obligations now. Go and have a good time."

Ari and Jon were excited about the trip. "We'll have a blast, Mitch! We're going to London first—discos, girls, the Tower, the palace. Hey, it'll be great."

So Mitch withdrew the eight hundred dollars he had saved, and his parents chipped in the rest, as a graduation gift. At first he had thought Carlie might go, too. But his mom had come into his room one night, talking very softly about Carlie, how she needed to become more independent and not rely on him so much. Mitch had felt sort of surprised; he didn't think Carlie relied on him at all. She was the tough one, getting through her parents' death the way she did, hardly ever talking about it.

The last night, Carlie gave him a canvas knapsack for the trip. He used the knapsack every day, and he thought of home without any regrets. If he'd stayed home, his dad would have had him working at the store. Most of his friends were away for the summer. He was sick of tennis, tired of the valley—the mountains were dry and dense; the air sometimes seemed to suffocate him. Here, in Jerusalem, it was hot, too, but different. There was a sense of freshness and freedom here. It was both exhilarating and—Mitch had to admit—disturbing. He didn't want to leave. So he had decided to prolong the last weekend by spending it with Tal at the *yeshiva*. He and Tal had met again by chance outside Steimatsky's bookstore, and they sat up late at a sidewalk café over ice cream and coffee, and Tal had said, "Why don't you come to the *yeshiva* once for a real *Shabes*?"

"We had *Sabbath* at our temple," Mitch said, grimacing.

"Well, that's a start. Watered-down Judaism. Why not try the real thing?"

"Look, I'm just not into religion," Mitch said with a shrug.

"Don't you want to see what it's all about?"

"I know what it's about. I went through the whole *Bar Mitzvah* jazz. That was enough."

"Proof of what I'm saying." Tal smiled genially. "Why don't you come and be with some guys who are really turned on to Judaism? Are you afraid?"

"What's there to be afraid of?"

"You tell me."

So Mitch had gone the following Friday night to the service and the dinner. It was the singing that captivated him, the unanimous spirit of joy. Then he'd wondered, am I only being drawn in by the crowd? A kind of mass exhilaration? But later, back at the hotel, lying in bed, Mitch had felt something different. A kind of stirring, like a twig snapping in distant memory, the sense that he had experienced this before, that he belonged. So he had decided to give himself this last *Shabes* in Israel with "turned-on Jews," as Tal said.

Now everyone rose. Rabbi Nachum murmured several words, and Mitch caught the word "Kiddush," the blessing over the wine that preceded every ritual meal.

He joined the others, calling out a hearty "Amen!" The rabbi poured a trickle of wine from his silver challis into small paper cups that had been set out. Tal handed a paper cup to Mitch. "Wait," he whispered, "for the blessing."

Now Rabbi Nachum held everyone bound with his gaze, his smile. He was a short man, but well built, with a full, dark beard and deep-set eyes that seemed to hold infinite wisdom and compassion.

Rabbi Nachum gestured toward Mitch. "We welcome our new friend, Mitch Green, who is joining us for *Shabes*, and we thank Tal for bringing Mitch to us. Mitch comes all the way from California. He told me last night about that terrible earthquake they had last January. And he said to me—may I tell them, Mitch?" Rabbi Nachum smiled at Mitch, who nodded slightly.

"He said, 'Rabbi, I don't really believe in God—that is, I don't say there is one or there isn't—but I'll tell you, when that whole house was heaving underneath me and I thought I was going to die, all I could think of was the prayer my grandma taught me when I was a little kid. And I said it. I said the *Shema*.' "

A chorus of voices erupted as one, *"Boruch Hashem!"* Praise God!

Mitch felt his face flush, and he smiled wanly.

"So, even in the wasteland that is Southern California," quipped Rabbi Nachum, and everyone laughed, "that small spark still glows. Welcome, Mitch! Now, let's go wash, then eat lunch. Nobody should go away from here hungry!"

That evening, Ari and Jonathan came to talk to him. "We figured you'd be here," Ari said. "Rosen is beside himself."

Mitch took them into the parlor. Ari sat down on the old sofa, leaning forward toward Mitch. Beside him, Jonathan crossed and uncrossed his legs, sighing as if the room were too small, too close to contain his large frame.

"I told you I was coming here," Mitch said. "Weren't you listening?"

Ari said, "Look, we were all talking to those girls—we didn't pay attention. Besides, I didn't think you were staying over night. I'm sorry. I should have listened."

Jonathan stood up, hands in his pockets. "Come on," he said. "We'd better get going. The flight leaves at one A.M."

"I'm staying," Mitch said. "I discussed it with the rabbi. He said I could stay here for a while and learn. Just leave my stuff at the hotel. I'll pick it up tomorrow."

Ari's mouth hung open.

"You've gotta be crazy!" Jonathan exclaimed. "You want to stay here? Look at this dump!" Jonathan scowled at the worn carpet and the ragged brown sofa. "What would you do here?"

"What do you care?" Mitch retorted. "Why are you yelling at me?"

"Because you're nuts," Jonathan said. "You meet this guy, Tal, and suddenly it's like you're on a different planet."

"Take it easy, Jon," said Ari, but he, too, frowned as he leaned toward Mitch. "We're your friends," he said. "Come on, Mitch. This is a joke, right?"

"You know better."

"Come on, Mitch! We're your *friends,*" Ari said again.

"Then why are you bugging me?"

"Because you're making an ass of yourself," Jonathan said.

"We don't want you to get hurt," Ari said. "Look, come on home with us. If you want, you can come back here next year. But Sy Rosen's going to be in deep shit if you don't come home. Rabbi Hoffman's going to cancel all trips. It's not fair. You're giving the group a bad name."

"So blame me for everything!" Mitch cried. "Look, I'm sorry. But if I don't stay here now, I'll never have a chance again. I'm not rejecting anyone—not Rosen or my friends or—anyone. Anyhow, it's just for a few weeks."

Ari shook his head. "You'll get sucked in. Rosen says he's heard of guys getting picked off the wall—that's what they call it, you know—and never coming back."

"Nobody's forcing me to stay," Mitch said.

"You don't belong here, Mitch," said Ari. "My dad's Israeli—even he, after twenty-five years in America, says it's a different world."

Mitch smiled. "Maybe that's why I like it."

Jonathan exploded. "Mitch, if you stay here, they'll draft you into the army. You'll be in some foxhole in Lebanon. What's wrong with you? You trying to be a damn martyr or something?"

"I just want to study," Mitch said.

Ari leaned toward Mitch. "What is it that you're looking for? Tell me, buddy."

Ari's sudden gentleness startled Mitch. He felt overloaded with visions and emotions. "It's a feeling," he began, his voice quavering. "Didn't you ever feel like you had to do something?"

"Yeah, sure," said Jonathan with a grin. "When I was at the beach at night with Brenda Silverman. . . ."

"Shut up, Jon," said Ari with a wave of his hand. "This isn't funny. Tell us about the feeling, Mitch." Ari's eyes were penetrating, demanding.

"It's like—that first time we all went to the Wall."

Mitch paused. The two boys nodded. "Well, I went up

there, and time seemed to stop for me. It was like a shock. Like some current going through me, a sudden feeling of *knowing* that there's something going on here. Something important. Listen, do you remember when Joel Bradshaw died?"

"Sure, sure," they said, nodding. "What's Joel got to do with it?"

Mitch sighed. "At the Wall, I suddenly thought of Joel, as if he was *there*. Poor Joel. I mean, he had nothing to hang on to. And I told you about that awful service his folks had at the beach. Well, I thought of Joel, and I saw . . ."

"You're saying you had a vision?" Jonathan exclaimed.

Mitch gritted his teeth; his entire body felt rigid. Why was it so much easier to talk to Tal? Ari and Jonathan had been his friends for years.

Mitch cried, "Why can't you listen?" He sat down again at the edge of his chair, hands braced.

Jonathan raised up his arms in a gesture of surrender. "I just can't understand what happened to you. You were one of the guys. Now you sound creepy."

Ari gave Jonathan a warning look. "Shut up, Jon," he commanded sternly. "Mitch isn't creepy. He had—an experience. Tell us about it," he said earnestly. "Tell us what happened at the Wall."

"I don't know. I felt—connected. Kind of solid. Like, this was exactly where I wanted to be. Where I belonged. It was just like—well, getting someplace and knowing it was a place you've been looking for all your life."

"So, what is it you want to do?" Ari asked.

"I want to study. I want to find out what makes these *yeshiva* guys so—so certain. I want to figure out what to do with my life, what it means to be a Jew."

Mitch heard himself saying the words, but they seemed to be coming from someone else. He saw himself as he was, wearing old jeans and a Dodgers T-shirt, and he felt like an impostor.

"So, you want to be a rabbi?" Jonathan asked, copying Ari's posture and his gaze.

"No. I just want to figure it out. I always thought that God was sort of a—you know, a myth. An idea to keep people in line. Now, I don't know. That's all I'm saying. I want to learn. . . ."

Somewhere in the distance a door slammed. Ari glanced at his watch. He said, "Look, Mitch, you can study back home. I think there's a *yeshiva* in L.A. You could maybe take classes there part time and still go to UCLA."

"It's different here," Mitch said. "Rabbi Nachum's a saint. He's brilliant. And it's not just the classes. It's a whole way of living."

"You've got to get back for orientation," Jonathan said.

"I already made out my class schedule last spring," Mitch said. "I don't need orientation. It's just a bunch of bullshit."

"When will you come home, then?" Ari asked.

"Soon. Don't pin me down! What if I started UCLA a semester later? Lots of guys take time off. Why is everybody so freaked about this?"

"Because you're letting this rabbi brainwash you," Ari cried.

Mitch stood up. "Look, I really appreciate you guys coming here. Don't worry, I'll call Rosen and explain. I'll square it with my folks. Don't worry. You're not responsible for me. This has nothing to do with you guys."

Ari lifted his hands. "So much for friendship," he said disgustedly. "Come on, Jon," he said, standing up. "We've got to go." He gave Mitch a penetrating look. "It's your life, pal," he said. "But I'm really disappointed in you. I thought you were always so cool."

"Look, I didn't even want to come on this trip!" Mitch burst out. He was astonished at his own vehemence and the sudden bitterness he could no longer contain. "You guys talked me into it; my mother kept pushing. Just like that summer you decided we should all be lifeguards, and I did it and I got that second-degree sunburn. And the time we all went kayaking and I was sick in that damn tent all week."

Ari tensed, his chin thrust out toward Mitch. "So now you're blaming me?" he cried. "You could have said no."

"Well, that's what I'm doing now. No! No!"

Ari turned, furious. "Come on, Jon. Let's go. We've got a plane to catch."

For a long time after they had left, Mitch sat alone in the shabby parlor. Books, cabinets, dark chairs seemed to loom over him. He knew exactly what the others would say about him. "He's flipped. He's been brainwashed."

And it struck him now how it appeared, how it actually *was*, maybe, that once again he'd been persuaded, twisted and turned around by someone else's notions of what was good for him. Why couldn't he have a mind of his own? Why was he such a wimp?

Maybe they'd reeled him in, like a fish taking bait. Now, even if he wanted to go back, how could he? He had made his absurd declarations, gotten everyone upset. What could he possibly say now that wouldn't sound ridiculous? *I changed my mind?*

Mitch heard the last slight shuffling on the floor above, of students settling down into their beds or to their books. The quiet enshrouded him. He took a prayer book from the shelf and turned to the evening prayer. Slowly now he formed the Hebrew words in his mind, saying them over and over like a mantra: *"Ribono shel olary . . ."* "Master of the universe . . ."

Strange, he thought, as he became calm and light and peaceful, how soothing those few words could be.

CHAPTER 3

FOR A WHOLE hour after Carlie told them about Mitch, Aunt Vivian had sat in the breakfast nook, the telephone by her side. Again and again she asked, "Why doesn't he call?"

Carlie had waited beside her aunt, thinking of other times—Mitch home late from a school trip to San Diego, and everyone sitting up worrying, ranting. Mitch calling from Alaska, needing a prescription; the bugs were eating him alive. When he came home, grinning, they all surrounded him, forgiving, hungry to hear about his adventure.

Aunt Vivian squeezed a tissue in her hand. She kept asking, "Did Rosen say anything else? Think, Carlie! Are they still leaving tonight? What if Mitch doesn't return? Would they just leave him?"

Uncle Harry paced, muttering, "I never wanted him to go on that trip. You know that, don't you?"

"No, I don't know that!" Aunt Vivian cried. "You agreed."

"I always agree. That's the damn trouble." Harry slapped at a mosquito, rare intruder into the immaculate kitchen. The dog, Arnie, growled softly at the commotion.

Now it was noon. Vivian had gone out back to busy herself with some paint swatches. Carlie stood at the kitchen counter, fixing avocado-and-tomato sandwiches. She froze when the phone rang.

"Get the phone, Carlie!" Aunt Vivian called from the back porch. "Get the phone!"

Carlie leaped over Arnie, lunged for the receiver, and picked it up. "Hello."

"Hey, Carlie!"

It was Mitch, exuberant, as if nothing had happened. Carlie's heart raced. "Mitch! Where are you? What are you doing? Do you realize we've been . . . ?" Bits of tomato clung to her fingers; she felt doubled over, as if she'd been hit with cramps.

"Hey, I'm fine, Carlie. How are you?"

"Sy Rosen called. He said you were missing. We thought you were kidnapped."

"No. I'm here." Mitch laughed. "I know where I am," he said, their childhood joke, copied from some cartoon, "but I won't tell you!"

Carlie pulled over a chair and sat down, her legs suddenly weak. "Where are you? The folks are livid. You're supposed to come home tonight. What time is it there? Did you miss the plane?"

"Stop yelling at me, Carlie, and I'll tell you. I'm with my friend, Tal. He is standing right here beside me. It's nighttime here. Carlie, I'm not coming home with the group. I'm staying for a few weeks."

"They're going to kill you this time, Mitch. You've gone too far."

"Oh, Carlie, please. Don't be mad."

"I'm not mad. We were worried. What are you doing there, Mitch?"

Aunt Vivian ran in; a paint smudge covered her cheek. Her eyes were wide. "Is that Mitch?"

"Yes. It's your mom," she told Mitch. She glanced up. Uncle Harry stood in the doorway, watching, his face frozen into a nonexpression.

Mitch spoke urgently, "Listen, Carlie, please explain to them, it won't cost them a cent. I'm getting a scholarship from this—this school. I just want to learn. . . ."

Aunt Vivian was beside her, panting, her hands stained with paint, reaching for the telephone. "Carlie, let me talk!" She grabbed the receiver, turning, seeking privacy with her son.

"Mitch! My God, are you all right?" she cried.

Uncle Harry's hands were braced high in the doorway, as if he'd been hung there. He muttered, "Tell him he better get his ass on that plane! I'm not putting up with this. Damn it, he's supposed to report for orientation at UCLA in two weeks."

"Hush, Harry! For God's sake, let me talk!" cried Aunt Vivian. "Mitch, darling, we were so worried about you." Aunt Vivian's voice was a whisper. She was crying in earnest now.

Carlie wanted to grab the phone and tell Mitch—tell him what? That he was a bad and ungrateful son? That he had no right to cause everyone to worry? That she secretly envied him? The truth struck Carlie like a blow. Yes, Mitch could do anything, get away with anything. He was their boy, their flesh and blood, aggravating but always wonderful and adored.

Aunt Vivian wiped her eyes with the edge of her shirt.

She was nodding now, breathing easier. "How long do you think you'll be?" she asked, her tone once again steady. "Three weeks? Well, that doesn't sound . . . too unreasonable . . . but . . ."

Carlie realized she was twisting the ring on her right middle finger, the way she always did when she was upset, that amethyst ring of her mother's.

"You want to talk to your father?" asked Aunt Vivian.

"I don't want to talk to him," said Harry.

Vivian held out the phone and mouthed the word, "Talk."

Harry grabbed the receiver. "Mitch! Listen, I'm glad you had a good time, but you've got to come home now. You've got to get yourself in gear for college. We've already paid your tuition."

There was a pause while Carlie imagined Mitch standing there, upset, misunderstood. That was it; they loved him, sure, but they never really understood him.

Uncle Harry's face hardened, his voice became brittle. "Look, I want you on the next plane home. And if there's a penalty for changing your ticket, that's coming out of your bank account."

Carlie winced. She wished Uncle Harry hadn't made it a matter of money.

Something changed in Uncle Harry's posture; he slumped down against the kitchen counter, his back to Carlie, as if suddenly his own weight was too much to bear. "His name was Max."

Another pause, and Carlie saw Uncle Harry's arm raise up, then drop to his side. "It was Mordechai. Look, Mitch, I don't understand why you want to go back into all that. . . ."

Uncle Harry shuffled his feet, slapped at the counter. "Damn! The line's breaking up. Mitch? Mitch?" Harry put down the receiver and turned to Vivian. "Damn."

"What is it?" Aunt Vivian moved nearer to Harry. "What happened?"

"He wants to know his grandfather's Hebrew name."

"What for?"

"Who knows? Then the line went dead," said Harry.

"Your father's Hebrew name?" Aunt Vivian repeated, blinking, as if to clear her vision. "Did you know it?"

"It was Mordechai. I don't know how I remembered that. It just—it just popped into my head. Mordechai. His real name was Max. That kid's gone off the deep end." Harry opened the refrigerator, looking for something, then he slammed it shut again. "We should never have sent him, Vivian. He doesn't appreciate . . ."

"Harry, all his friends were going. Why shouldn't he . . . ?"

"He isn't like his friends! His friends are coming home with the group, like they're supposed to."

"But—it's just for a few weeks," Vivian said.

Carlie could see her trying to hang on, grasping the sleeves of her shirt, her hair. "Isn't it just for a few weeks?"

Harry whirled around, his face dangerously mottled. Harry yelled, "I give him a two-month trip! All I ask is for him to come home with the rest of 'em. Now he pulls this on me. Why does he have to study over there? He's all set to go to UCLA! The kid's goldbricking. He's always into something weird."

"When was he ever weird?" Vivian cried.

"My God, remember that summer he wanted to go

kayaking in Alaska? And that time I had to buy him a kiln? Remember that?"

Carlie stood in the corner, waiting for the storm to abate. On the counter the avocado was beginning to darken at the edges; the bread slices were drying out. Arnie lay under the table, avoiding the clash, eyelids fluttering.

At last it was still. Aunt Vivian looked down at the beginnings of their lunch. "Were you making sandwiches, Carlie?" she asked. Her tone sounded almost normal again.

"He's just asking for a couple of weeks more," Carlie said. She felt the reaction of her aunt and uncle, a stiffening, as if they were turning into statues. She went to the counter and began putting the sandwiches together with mayonnaise and lettuce. "It's no big deal," Carlie continued, her tone mellow. "He just wants to feel like he's old enough to make some decisions on his own. You know. He's turning eighteen."

Aunt Vivian nodded slightly. "I met you when I was eighteen," she murmured to Harry.

"What's that got to do with anything?" he cried, and for the first time Carlie saw the pain in his eyes.

Vivian said, "I think Carlie's got a point. The boy needs to grow up. This is a small thing, just a few weeks."

"Classes at UCLA don't start for a month," said Carlie. "By then, Mitch will be home. He'll have had a—an adventure."

"Adventure," repeated Uncle Harry. "Adventure, he wants."

Aunt Vivian sighed, gazing at Carlie. "I think Carlie's right," she said at last. "It's not a big deal."

"Everyone will wonder what happened," said Harry.

"So, you'll tell them we let him stay a little longer."

"They'll say he's rebelling."

"So?" said Vivian with a small smile. "What else is new?"

"Mitch loves you," Carlie said. "He never really does anything bad. This kid in our class? Dirk Stevenson? Got caught by the police for breaking into a house. He stole a bunch of rare coins and stamps. He's on cocaine. Two hundred dollars a day for his habit."

Aunt Vivian and Uncle Harry glanced at each other.

"I'm not saying Mitch is bad," said Harry.

"We were just worried about him," said Vivian.

"But he's fine," Carlie said. "He phoned. He doesn't want you to be upset. Hey, I'm in a tennis tournament this afternoon. Did anyone remember? Aren't you coming? I'm partnered with Kip Warner."

"Kip Warner? Hey, that's great." Aunt Vivian put her hand on Carlie's shoulder. "Harry, she's playing with the pro! Kip Warner!"

Carlie knew they would come and cheer for her, just as she knew they would tell their friends, "Oh, Mitch? He's staying in Israel a while. Yes, we thought he might as well enjoy himself, take a few more weeks. Why not? He's a good kid, and soon enough he'll be back at the old grind."

Telephone calls came from Israel, with odd pauses, syncopated delays. Voices ran together, like watercolor paint; you had to stop and wait that extra moment for things to settle. Carlie couldn't get used to it. She never knew quite what to say. Beg him to come home? Scold him? Urge him to discover all he could while he had the chance? She envied him his courage. She'd never be able to do what he was doing.

Mitch said, "I can't leave yet, Carlie. I'm in the middle of . . ."

"Oh, Mitch. What about your tuition?"

"They can apply it to next semester."

"Your father's upset."

"He's always upset. Carlie, I've got to do this."

"How long?"

"A couple more weeks. That's all."

Two weeks later, another call. Vivian answered. "What are you talking about?" she cried. "We always go to the temple on the high holy days!" This time she sounded offended, beyond anger.

She told Carlie and Harry, *"He wants to go to synagogue in Jerusalem."* Her voice was low, desperate. "He says it's a holy city. He says he wants to—to experience—God's presence."

Carlie and Uncle Harry stood motionless, staring at Vivian. Carlie's mouth felt dry. "Mitch said that?"

Her aunt nodded.

Carlie felt the sinking, empty feeling. "What's happened to him? Melanie says they brainwash people. Like a cult. Like the Moonies."

Harry grunted and sat back on the sofa, rubbing his hands over his thighs. "I don't like the sound of it," he said.

Aunt Vivian seemed to waver. She shook her head. "Maybe after all that praying he'll change his mind. He used to be bored to death in synagogue. Never wanted to go. He said the holidays aren't over until the end of the month."

"Oh, he's talking about *Sukkot,* too. That whole thing," said Harry.

"What's that?" Carlie asked. It was like a new language, suddenly, that everyone knew a few words of; she alone was ignorant.

"Like a harvest festival," said Harry grimly. "They build a hut."

Vivian attempted a smile. "My son, the rabbi."

"This isn't funny," said Harry. "Marv Gross told me about a cousin of his—the kid went into some group, grew a beard, wears a little cap on his head all the time. The boy quit school. He was going to become a lawyer. Just quit cold. These groups are dangerous. They're extremists."

"What can we do?" Vivian asked.

"Well, I've canceled his credit card," Harry said.

Vivian recoiled. "When did you do that?"

"Couple of weeks ago. When he missed his first commitment. He thinks he can take the easy way out. Well, I'm not supporting him. Let him go and work, find out what it is to earn a dollar. He spends more money on CDs and movies than he can earn in a week. You better believe he'll sober up fast when he has to take responsibility for himself."

"What if there's an emergency?" Vivian cried. "What if he needs something?"

"Tough. He should have thought of that."

Carlie said, "Maybe he doesn't need money there."

"Oh, you can bet he does," Harry said. "This scholarship thing is to lure them in at the start. There's no free lunch, Carlie. You better believe it."

Carlie believed it—no free lunch. Echoes of it swept through her mind later that night as she lay in bed trying to figure out what Mitch was doing. Looking for God, His presence? How weird! No free lunch. What does it cost to look for God?

No free lunch. The words made her feel guilt. Everything she got was a freebie here; they had taken her in out of the goodness of their hearts—or out of necessity, because there was nobody else. She already owed them more than she could ever repay.

"We want you!" Aunt Vivian had said. And Carlie had gone with them, silent, like stepping over into another life, all in a single day. And now Mitch, who had everything—friends, parents, a great future—was obviously trying to step into another life, too. She couldn't imagine why.

Carlie and Melanie raced to the bus, panting, making their way to the back. "For once," Melanie gasped, "I'd love to catch this bus without almost breaking my neck."

Carlie laughed. "It's our morning workout. Clears the brain."

They clattered into their usual seats, last row from the back, across from Scott and Barry. The boys were all excited about Career Day. "Look, I'm tired of all this 'Perfect Planet' jazz," Barry said. "How many careers can you get out of ecology?"

"About a million," Scott said. "Why are you so narrow-minded? Ecology is where it's at. The future."

"I'm going to the genetics workshop," Barry insisted. "That's the wave of the future. My dad said." He called out to Carlie. "What are you going to, Carlie?"

"I don't know."

"What about you, Mel?"

"Performing Arts, of course," said Melanie. "They've even got a section on set design and promotions—it's not just drama. It's everything having to do with performance and media and . . ."

The boys groaned and rolled their eyes. "Okay, okay."

Carlie laid her head back, as if she were dozing. Talk billowed all around her. Everyone seemed to know exactly where they were headed—social work, politics, law, business. Career

Day was a big event; every year the *Times* did a piece on it.

Carlie had seen her counselor last week. "Have you decided on your Career Day choice?" Ms. Oliver blinked from behind her oversized red-framed glasses. Her pen was poised over Carlie's file.

"I don't know, Ms. Oliver," Carlie said. "I can't decide."

"Well, what are you good at?"

"Tennis, I guess."

"Sports, then? Have you thought of teaching?"

"Tennis is just—for fun," Carlie said. "I don't think I'd want it for a career," Carlie said. She sighed. Obviously something more was expected of her, and she simply couldn't deliver.

Ms. Oliver pursed her lips. She glanced at Carlie's file. "I understand it might be more difficult," she said. "I mean, when there is a trauma . . . four years is not such a long time."

Carlie nodded, her throat tightening. They always got around to *the accident*, as if that explained everything about her.

"What did your mother do?" the counselor asked, her tone conciliatory, no longer hurried.

Carlie spoke carefully. At times like these, it was a little hard to breathe normally. She said, "My mother was in banking. International banking. She was manager of her branch."

"Ah. But you are not interested in a business career?"

Carlie said, "I'm terrific on a skateboard."

Ms. Oliver lifted her brows. A jest? She seemed uncertain, caught off-guard.

Carlie sighed. "Well, actually, my mom always said I had innate grace. She wanted me to take ballet."

"Did you?"

"Yes. Later. I took ballet one whole summer."

The counselor looked away. She closed the file. "After your parents died, you did take ballet."

"Yes."

"But you aren't really interested in performing arts."

"No."

"Well, there is a section," the counselor said brightly, "for 'undecideds.' Let's put you there. How about that?"

"Fine." But it wasn't fine, Carlie thought as she went grudgingly into the room where people came straggling in, sullen, obviously not the brightest kids in school. The girls wore outrageous get-ups; one had purple hair, another wore two gold rings through the side of her nose. Some boys shuffled in, their baggy pants dragging on the floor; they were punching each other, hooting and bellowing.

Carlie hurried out the door to the office. "I want to change," she said. "Is it too late?"

"Depends on what you want," the man said. "Some seminars are closed, like performing arts and ecology. . ."

"Health services," Carlie said.

He glanced at his list and gave her a smile. "Okay. Done."

The seminar made Carlie think of Mitch again. Everything seemed to lead to the same road—Mitch. After the earthquake, Mitch's Grandma Rose, Harry's mother, stayed with them because her apartment in Sherman Oaks had been demolished.

"There's a lot more to healing than just being a nurse or a doctor," the lecturer was saying. "Today we're going to talk about all sorts of medicine, both conventional and alternative, including nutrition, acupuncture, massage . . ."

Grandma Rose had had her own routine—a glass of hot

water every morning and night, before bed. "No caffeine," she said. "Bad for arthritis." Everything was influenced by Grandma Rose's arthritis—the food she ate or refused to eat, her bath, her daily walk. "My blood circulates better when I walk," she said. "Circulation helps my arthritis."

Uncle Harry had brought a cot into the room for Carlie. "Let Grandma have the bed," he said. "Her arthritis . . ."

For two months Carlie and Grandma Rose had shared the small room. It was the first time in Carlie's life that she heard another person's breath in the night and felt their vibes. It was strange, like sleeping outdoors for the first time, seeing the shadows of things and hearing trees.

In the morning, Grandma Rose was pert as a bird, ready to talk. She made plans. She asked about Carlie's day. "You are like my own granddaughter, Carlie," Grandma Rose said, hugging her. She was a great one for hugs. "If you ever have a problem, come to me."

"I will," Carlie said. At night she helped Grandma Rose climb into bed. Then gently she lifted Grandma Rose's legs and knelt down, rubbing them lightly, her fingers seeming to know a secret language.

"Ah, you have healing hands, Carlie," Grandma sighed. "It's a gift. Nobody can teach it."

Sometimes Rose took Carlie's hands into hers and pressed them. Grandma Rose's fingers were slim and surprisingly supple; she had always used them to knead and press and shape the dough for her sculpture. She was an artist, self-styled, self-taught.

"In the old country I baked bread," she said with a chuckle. "Now I bake flowers and small figures—not to eat, only to admire. Friday nights, my mother had me bake the *challah.* Mine was always the best, she said. Five loaves I made, every *Shabes*."

One Friday night Carlie and Mitch had begged Grandma Rose to bake the bread she was always talking about, and its fragrance filled the house. "We should light candles," Grandma Rose said.

Vivian brought out the silver holders and two tall red candles. They all stood around the table, suddenly shy as Grandma Rose placed a napkin over her hair and struck the match and lit the wicks. She circled her hands three times over the flames, and Carlie had a quick vision of fairy godmothers, incantations, childhood things. . . . She watched Grandma Rose close her eyes and murmur a prayer in Hebrew, and when she opened her eyes a brightness lay on her cheeks and in her eyes.

Grandma Rose reached out and gently touched Carlie's cheek. "*Shayne maydele,*" she murmured.

"What's that?" Carlie said, smiling, because she knew but she liked to hear it again.

"That's Yiddish," Grandma Rose said, speaking softly from the depth of satisfaction now, and ease. "Pretty girl. *Shayne maydele.* Pretty inside *and* outside."

Carlie brought in the mail. The pale blue envelope with the strange stamp felt like a living thing, trembling in her hand. Vivian opened it carefully with a knife and read aloud:

"Dear Family:

The high holy days were magnificent. It's like—I was parched. Now I feel nourished. I learned so much, and for the first time I fasted on Yom Kippur. Afterward we all danced in the courtyard. It was so joyous! We built a *sukkah* and decorated it with leaves and flowers and fruit. We ate all our meals in it for a week; some of us even slept in it one night.

I'm sharing a small room at the *yeshiva* with three other guys. David is from Texas, Guy from Cincinnati, and Bernie from Toronto. People come here to study for various periods of time. Nobody pressures you to stay. Believe me, everything they do for us is out of kindness.

Jerusalem has to be the most exciting city in the world. Don't worry about me. I feel great. I wonder whether you went to services with Rabbi Hoffman. I wish you all could have had the experience I did here, the intensity of it. For the first time in my life, I really felt connected."

"Parched," "nourished," "connected . . ." Mitch had never used such words before. It sounded almost as if someone else were dictating this.

"Please try to understand what it means to me to be here and to learn. It must be the way you feel, Mom, when you decorate a house and see it all done and beautiful, or the way Dad felt when he first opened his own store."

Carlie stiffened. Mitch sure knew all the right buttons.

"Don't worry about me. I haven't called because of the holidays. Also, there's only one phone here and it's hard to get a line out. The classes keep me very busy. Sometimes our study sessions don't end until after midnight. Did you ever think your son would be such a scholar? Ha-ha. I know you are wondering when I'll come home, and I realize that today is the day I'd have started classes at UCLA. What I'm learning here, I'd never exchange for anything else. I'll be home when—when I've learned enough. Please write. Carlie, you, too. Give my love to everyone, including Grandma Rose.

Your loving son and cousin,
Mitch"

It was awkward having Rabbi Hoffman in their living room. He sat on the large sectional sofa all by himself, his legs crossed and arms folded over his chest. Aunt Vivian sat on the round-backed white chair; Uncle Harry continued to pace. Carlie, not knowing quite what to do with herself, stood leaning against the wall, her hands clasped.

She had never seen Rabbi Hoffman up so close before. At the temple, where they went for the Yom Kippur service, they always sat in the back. Uncle Harry wanted to be near the rest rooms; Aunt Vivian liked to watch everyone coming in. Afterward, people stood in the courtyard, smiling, making small talk. It was always the same, partly pleasant, often boring, and when it was over Carlie felt a certain sheen of virtue: She had done her duty.

Now she listened as Aunt Vivian presented the problem to Rabbi Hoffman. "He said he only wanted to study there for a few more weeks. It's been six weeks already. What do you know about this group, Rabbi? Are they—legitimate?"

Rabbi Hoffman nodded soberly. "Well, there are all sorts of groups, you know. This one is a small Orthodox group devoted to outreach, that is, to gaining adherents to their mode of worship. They teach. They bring boys in and house them, make it all very stimulating. Young people," he said, "crave stimulation."

Uncle Harry stopped short, stared at Carlie, then turned away, his face contorted. Carlie couldn't tell whether he was angry or amused.

"These things do happen," the rabbi was saying. He stroked his clean-shaven cheeks with his long, delicate fingers. "Of course, we try to give our young people briefings before they leave. Did Mitch attend the meetings?"

"I'm sure he did," said Aunt Vivian. She gave Carlie a quick glance. "Didn't he, Carlie?"

"Yes," Carlie said. She wished they hadn't sent for the rabbi. It seemed almost—pagan, in a way, like getting the witch doctor in to exorcise some demon. "But what, exactly, are they teaching him?" Carlie asked.

Rabbi Hoffman pursed his lips and recrossed his legs. "Well, you see, these people believe, literally, that the Torah was handed to Moses by God. That every word in it is sacred and true. So"—he lifted his arms, dropped them down again—"they are still living in the first century. Many things that the rest of us have long since abandoned, they accept and practice without question."

"Like what?" Carlie asked. "Like—sacrifices?"

The rabbi chuckled. "Not quite. But—they won't mix meat and milk. They won't even turn on a light on the Sabbath. They observe countless rituals that we—uh—Reform Jews no longer believe are applicable. Don't get me wrong. The Torah is a wonderful, brilliant document. How did we get it? Nobody knows for certain."

"What do you think, Rabbi?" Carlie asked. She felt stupid, embarrassed, yet Vivian was nodding approvingly, and the rabbi seemed glad to tell her.

He leaned forward. "Well, I personally believe the Torah was written by many people over a long period of time. Or maybe it was written by Moses, *inspired* by God. But in my opinion it *should* be redefined as times change. For example, it no longer makes sense to ban pork; we have refrigeration nowadays, trichinosis isn't an issue. You get the point."

Vivian nodded.

Carlie said, "So Mitch is learning all those rituals? In the Torah?"

The rabbi nodded. "Rituals, prayers, and philosophy, I suppose. An old-fashioned Jewish education."

"But do they let him go places, Rabbi Hoffman? Can Mitch leave if he wants to?" Carlie asked. *Brainwashing.* The word kept ringing in her mind—had they done something to Mitch? Had they changed him, turned him into some kind of freak?

Rabbi Hoffman frowned and stretched his neck. "Every group is different," he said. "Some are more strict than others." He looked at Vivian, then at Harry. "Don't worry. I'm sure Mitch will be fine."

Rabbi Hoffman rose to his feet. "When you talk to your son on the phone, let him know you still love him. Tell him he can study religion at UCLA if he wants to."

"He was going to study business administration," said Harry gruffly.

"Well. Yes. Look, I wouldn't overreact. Sometimes young people do these things to gain attention." The rabbi nodded and smiled congenially. "As I recall, Mitch was always pretty good at drawing attention to himself. But, Mitch is a good kid. He's not abandoning his family. He's just working out some late adolescent problems. And if it were my son," Rabbi Hoffman said, reaching out to Uncle Harry in a comradely gesture, "I'd much rather he get over his rebellion in Israel than in Tijuana, if you know what I mean."

Carlie moved away from the wall.

Rabbi Hoffman bent toward her. "Good to see you, my dear," he said. And to Vivian he added, "Your son will be back here at home before you know it—a little older and a little wiser. When he comes back, I suggest that you simply accept this detour for what it was. An excursion into himself."

"Thank you, Rabbi," Aunt Vivian said stiffly.

They all saw Rabbi Hoffman to the door.

When they had closed the door behind him Aunt Vivian sighed and said, "I expected something more."

"The man's a rabbi, not a magician," said Harry. "He can't bring Mitch home. Why did you even call him?"

Vivian sighed again. "Maybe he's right. He should know. This is his area."

Carlie said nothing. Rabbi Hoffman liked to tout his "good relationship to our youth." It was obvious he didn't know her name. But then, why should he? Carlie only went to temple once a year, on high holy days, when Uncle Harry said every Jew needs to be seen and counted. He had a reason: "To show the *goyim* that Hitler didn't kill us all."

Uncle Harry tossed up his car keys and caught them smartly in his hand. He gave a snort. " 'Excursion into himself.' That pompous old fart!"

CHAPTER 4

IT WAS SOMETHING like summer camp, Mitch thought, up at six A.M., groggy, fighting the urge to get back into bed. But at camp the strict routine had brought plenty of complaints. Here students seemed to compete for piety and perfection. David was always the first one up and ready for prayers. Bernie was the last in bed at night, studying by the thin beam of a tiny reading lamp, murmuring to himself. Sometimes Bernie called out in his sleep, and Mitch awakened, startled and confused, thinking, what am I doing here? I'm not a scholar . . . but, what am I?

Guy was the most relaxed of Mitch's roommates, but he also corrected Mitch now and then, being tactful but firm. "Look, this is how you put on the *tallit*—you've got it backward. It's disrespectful."

"Okay. Show me."

And again, "For bananas it's a different blessing, not *fruit of the tree,* but *fruit from the earth*. This is important, Mitch. You don't want to make a vain blessing."

"Sorry, sorry," said Mitch.

Guy gave him a grin. "It's okay. I'm only a few months ahead of you. You'll get there."

And Mitch wanted to ask, "Where? What's 'there'? Will I become a carbon copy of a thousand other guys, with nothing of my own?"

He had never been a real groupie. Not deep inside. Oh, he pretended, and maybe he looked like a groupie, but he always kept a secret part of himself separate, thinking his own thoughts and having his own opinions.

Here, there were definite requirements, traditions, rituals. There were words like "respect" and "duty" and "obedience," which seemed almost foreign and undemocratic. And the more he learned, the more was expected; it seemed like an endless climb.

People on the streets looked at him differently now that he wore a *kippah* on his head. They expected things—women nodded, assuming he was "deeply religious," and would help them with their toddlers and their packages. Some people looked away. One man, rushing past him, turned back and spat. "It's guys like you," he charged, "who are ruining the country!"

Mitch told his roommates, shocked and angered. "All that hostility over a *kippah*!"

"Wait till you wear the *tallit katan,*" said Bernie, indicating the fringes that hung at his waist. "That really pegs you as a kook to some people."

"I wish we didn't have to be labeled," Mitch said.

"Everyone has labels," Guy replied. "And everyone claims not to want them. They're part of civilization, like it or not."

"Forget about other people," David said tensely. "They don't count. It says in the prayer book, 'Do not rely on man, for he has no power to save . . .' "

David's parents had sent him a letter, typed on business stationery. David had handed the letter around; the *yeshiva* held few secrets. In astonishment, Mitch read: " 'Son, we regret to inform you that as long as you choose to identify with this group and participate in their outlandish and reactionary behavior, you will not share in our estate. We have found, to our distress, that the deeper people go into these religious extremes, the more intolerant they are of others, and this we cannot condone.' "

"They are disinheriting you?" Mitch gasped.

"That's right," said David. "They're disinheriting me because *I'm* intolerant. I begged them to come to class with me, to open their minds. . . ." He shrugged. "Who needs them?"

But in the night Mitch awakened, hearing the stifled sobs. He had lain in bed wanting to go to David, but unsure about what to say or do. It would embarrass David to realize he'd been heard crying. On the other hand, wasn't it right to comfort one's friend in need? It struck Mitch then that he had grown accustomed to this process, the endless chain of questions and answers, degrees of behavior, consequences—in fact, the entire dialectical process that the *yeshiva* called, simply, learning.

This was what he loved—the mental probing, questions piled upon questions, all having been asked before, millennia ago, answered by the sages. What about creation? How did it happen? How did Maimonides know hundreds of years ago what scientists now believe, that before the "big bang" the entire universe was the size of a mustard seed? How else could he have known that, except by revelation?

Such thoughts were what kept Mitch glued to his seat—the mental exercises, the study of Talmud, matters of law. If a man lends his neighbor his ox, and the beast is killed, who pays? If a neighbor refuses to lend you his plow, what shall you do when he asks to borrow your shears? What can we expect of each other? What can we expect from God? What must we expect of ourselves? Judaism, he found, was a system not only of beliefs, but of laws, strict justice blended with caring and forgiveness.

Mitch's favorite teacher was Tal's brother-in-law, Richard. He had a gift for mimicry and a passion for teaching. "Kindness!" he declared. "That is the wellspring of all Torah. Out of kindness God created the world. By being kind, we imitate our maker. But what is kindness?"

He turned, made his expression goofy, shoulders hunched up, and in a high tone he simpered, "But, Rabbi, you don't have to be Jewish to be kind! I know lots of kind people. . . ."

Richard turned again, becoming the rabbi, and he bellowed, "I am talking about *specific* acts of kindness. *Mitzvot.* What are *mitzvot*?"

Again he turned, becoming the simpering pupil. "Oh, Rabbi, I know that—a *mitzvah* is a good deed."

"No!" A roar, a ferocious expression that sent the students into gales of laughter. "What does the Hebrew word mean? Do you know? Can you guess?"

"Commandment," said David, Mitch's roommate.

"Right! A gold star for you, my lad. Commandment! But the root of this word—and this is why you *must* study Hebrew, my friends, the root means the same as *to bind*. Ah. There it is. A *mitzvah* is a *commandment,* which, when we do it, binds us closer to God! Ha! Simple? Complicated? Think about it."

Richard sat back, stroking his well-trimmed beard. With

his blond hair and tan face he looked more like a California surfer, Mitch thought, than a rabbi. Now Richard made his voice deep, as he often did when he began a story.

"In this small Polish town the rabbi was very worried. The *shochet* had died. Of course, a new *shochet* was needed. What's a *shochet*? A ritual slaughterer. So, from everywhere came the contestants, and each was learned in the ways of *kosher* laws, the method, the prayers, the attitude of humility. But days went by. Weeks. After each trial, the rabbi stood there sadly, shaking his head, until the congregation lost patience. The elders came to him, complaining. After all, how long can a person go without eating meat? They confronted the rabbi. 'What's wrong with you? Why don't you pick a slaughterer? What was wrong with that last fellow? Didn't he know the prayers? Wasn't he humble? And wasn't his blade properly sharp, so that the animal felt no pain?'

" 'Yes, yes,' said the rabbi, wringing his hands. 'All that was fine. But he isn't like the old *shochet*, the one who died. The old *shochet* used to wet the blade with his tears.' "

Mitch's roommate Bernie went back to Toronto; he left Mitch his books and his *tallit katan,* the fringed undergarment that pious Jewish men wear next to their skin.

"Why are you giving me this?" Mitch asked. He didn't want to wear it; the fringes were too dramatic, too strange. They, more than a beard and *kippah,* implied a label.

"Because you're on the way in," Bernie replied, his hand on Mitch's shoulder. "And I'm on the way out."

"I thought you're just going home for a visit."

"That's what I said. But I know, deep down, I won't be back. I can't hack it. Too much to learn. I'm too restless.

Besides, my brother's getting married."

"So, come back after the wedding," Mitch said. "Look—I thought we were buddies."

"We were," Bernie said, nodding wearily. "But after a while you won't want me for a buddy anymore. Trust me. I know."

"How can you say that?" Mitch exclaimed. "I want to keep in touch with you, Bernie. We can still . . ."

"No." Bernie shook his head. "This is a pretty exclusive club you're in, and I don't belong. Don't get buried in this stuff, pal," Bernie advised Mitch, clapping him on the back. "I burned out. Do something else, too."

"What would I do?"

"Whatever you did before," Bernie said.

The empty bed in the small room was like a hole, a constant reproach to Mitch. Bernie had been brilliant in class. If Bernie couldn't make it, what chance did Mitch have?

In class the teachers talked about Creation and the Creator. "Man," said the teacher, "is the creative animal. In that respect man is like God."

And Mitch remembered long winter afternoons with Grandma Rose, when he was small—five, six, seven years old. She would mix her special sculpting dough: flour, water, a pinch of salt, and soda. Then she and Mitch made little gnomelike figures, and Grandma put them on a cookie sheet and baked them in the oven. After they were done, they painted on faces and clothes.

Then Grandma made roses. Sometimes she made an open bloom and painted on a face. It was her way, he now realized, of saying, "Here I am!"

Now he wondered again exactly what he was doing here.

Yes, there were moments of exultation, like being called to the Torah on Saturday mornings, standing beside the rabbi as he read the ancient scroll. The rabbi called out Mitch's name, his new Hebrew name, "Mordechai ben Harry!" and Mitch felt tall and proud. But that was his Sabbath self, the higher self that the rabbi said descended upon all Jews on that special day. What about ordinary days? He yearned for more, for sports, running, pitching, and especially for art.

Maybe he could find a place here to work, even a small studio.

"The sages tell us, a man must be the single-hearted, the same within as without. . . ."

At sixteen, disgusted with wasted summers, Mitch had decided to follow his heart. His dad had other ideas. "How about that lifeguard program? You loved it last summer."

But Mitch made himself a workshop in part of the garage, brought out some old soldering tools, and went to work with chunks of silver, rolls of copper, and enamel. He bought a used stone-polishing machine and a small kiln. That summer Carlie was into ballet, spending six to eight hours at the studio, so there was nobody to bother him. He woke up at dawn, exhilarated, and he jogged until the sweat poured from his body. Then he grabbed some bread, a quart of juice, and went out to his workshop.

There he stayed, sketching, pounding, pouring, molding, polishing; all his senses seemed to converge into his fingertips, and it was the way it had been with Grandma Rose so long ago, and he was happy. He was no longer pretending. Inside and outside, he was the same.

For his father's birthday, he made beautiful cuff links, silver and tigereye, his own design. When he opened Mitch's present, Harry's eyes glittered. He looked at Vivian, then at Mitch. "Thank you," he said. He gave Mitch an awkward half hug, murmuring, "You made these? What do you think something like this would sell for?"

It occurred to Mitch that if he could make jewelry and sell it, he could pay his way here. Excitedly he asked Rabbi Nachum whether it would be all right for him to pursue art along with his studies.

The rabbi seemed surprised at the question. "Why not?" he exclaimed. "The sages tell us that a man should not spend all his time on Torah study. We are commanded to work, to participate in the physical world, to improve it with our skills and talents. If you have a talent," the rabbi charged him, "you must use it!"

Two weeks after Bernie left, a newcomer took his bed. Joshua. He followed Mitch around, asked countless questions, made pronoucements: "I'm only staying for a week or two, you know. Just to find out what this is all about."

"That's fine, Josh. You're welcome to stay or to leave."

Josh came to breakfast in shorts. Mitch took him aside. "Modesty," he whispered.

"What?"

"The shorts."

"Okay, okay," Josh grumbled. "Why are you whispering?"

"I don't want to embarrass you," Mitch said. " 'He who embarrasses another publicly,' " he quoted, " 'has no place in the world to come.' "

"You mean heaven? Do you believe in heaven?"

"Don't you?"

"I don't know. That's what I'm here to find out."

"Me, too, Josh," said Mitch. "Me, too."

On Friday night Josh stood beside Mitch at the table. "Why do they cover the *challah*?" he whispered.

"Tradition," murmured Mitch. "The wine is blessed first. The bread is covered so it won't feel offended by being second."

"You've got to be kidding," Josh said.

Mitch smiled to himself at his new role. "The rabbis say," he began, "that if we are sensitive to the feelings of a loaf of bread, how much more so we will be considerate of other people."

When the news first broke, one of the older students ran through the halls like a wild man, screaming, "They've done it again! Oh, God! God! Twenty-one people—suicide bomb. Hamas. Pieces of bodies everywhere . . . the bus . . . twisted metal . . ."

Mitch sat frozen for a moment, then he ran with the others into the hall. Students shouted and gestured. "Damned Hamas! Bloodthirsty cowards! We have to blast them out of the country! Damned Hamas!"

"Sha! Sha! No more talk of killing. . . ."

"Forty-five wounded. Old people. Children, too."

Josh and David came running to Mitch. "Some of the guys want to go out into the streets. They say we can't just sit passively while our people are blown up."

"So you want to blow up someone else?" Mitch demanded. "Is that the way to settle things?"

"What do you know?" cried a student from Iran. "You're from snow-white America. You think things can be changed with a handshake? You think three thousand years of hatred can be mended in a day? They hate us!"

"This happened in Tel Aviv. Our city," said Tal. His face was white, his fists clenched. "They're animals."

"Nobody's safe," said Josh. "Not anywhere. My parents want me to come home. They'll be on my case now, for sure."

Mitch sat watching the scene, hearing the sounds of rage and frustration. Who needs it? he thought, visualizing home, Venice Beach, where he and Carlie jogged on the strand on fall days like this. He thought of his pals Ari and Jonathan, stretched out on the lawn at UCLA, watching the girls and eating French fries.

He picked up his backpack and went out. Jerusalem, Jerusalem. Some days this city was harsh and gray; even the rock faces of buildings seemed cold and unforgiving. Everything about Jerusalem was buried under layers of struggle. Why this land? Why this very sky and these stones and those copper rooftops?

Mitch walked and walked, watching the last rays of the sun touch the copulas of mosques, the windows of churches and homes. Everywhere one heard the sounds of life—laughter and music, the pounding of construction and traffic, people shouting, buses blasting their horns. Now and then a person passing by gave him a glance, a smile. These faces were somehow familiar. Was there an ancient, tribal identity that they shared? Did it show, or was it only a feeling?

The old people with their lives clearly stamped on their faces always made him pause and feel an instant of emotion, pain or shame or love, he couldn't quite tell. He was caught. Caught between two worlds: the simple world of home, and this complicated city that somehow held him trapped, too in love to leave, too confused to know how, really, to belong.

Rabbi Nachum was watching from the doorway. Mitch finished his recitation, a simple Hebrew lesson, and turned away self-consciously.

"Good," called the rabbi. "Very good."

Mitch chuckled. "Third-grade Hebrew, quite an accomplishment for an eighteen-year-old!"

"You've only been here for two months. You're making excellent progress. By the way, would you stop by my office after class?"

The casual invitation made Mitch's heart race. It was a privilege to be summoned to the rabbi's study, for the usual *yeshiva* affairs kept him busy from early morning until late into the night.

Later, when he stood in the doorway of Rabbi Nachum's office, the rabbi called heartily, "Come in! Come in and have a seat."

Mitch sat down beside a desk piled high with books, magazines, letters, and a perplexing array of mementos—a large bird feather, several seashells, rocks, and a sleek, wooden kaleidoscope. The rabbi followed Mitch's gaze, took up the kaleidoscope, and handed it to Mitch.

Mitch held the viewer to his eye. "I love these," he said. He moved the instrument to make the pattern change.

"My wife gave me this," said Rabbi Nachum. "She always had reasons for things. She said this teaches us that with many small, insignificant fragments you can build a beautiful pattern."

Mitch set the kaleidoscope down. He was weary of lessons.

"How's it going?" Rabbi Nachum asked.

"Fine, just fine." Mitch gazed out the window; rain pattered onto the dirty pane. He knew in California it would be warm and dry today, as always in October.

"Your Hebrew teacher told me you're the best in the class," said the rabbi.

"Thanks. Actually, I like Hebrew. It's very precise."

"Whereas"—the rabbi waved his hand—"the rest of it can be rather puzzling. Confusing."

"To say the least." Mitch held himself back, his body tense against the chair. He had not come here to complain. There was no point in arguing with the rabbi, anyhow; he had all the answers.

The rabbi said, "Tradition tells us that the confusion, the seeming inconsistencies are there for a purpose."

"What purpose?" Mitch was aware now of his posture, arms folded across his chest, a gesture of shielding and defiance. He let his arms drop down.

"They make us ask questions, delve deeper." Rabbi Nachum picked up the kaleidoscope. "Little specks, separately, just junk. Together, they make a beautiful pattern." He looked up. "Are you finding everything you need here?"

"Yes, thank you."

"The food?"

"It's fine."

"The students are friendly? Yes?"

"Everything's fine, Rabbi Nachum."

"I see. That's good. And you can ask questions of your teachers, and of Tal?"

"Yes. Plenty of questions. It's just that . . . ," he didn't want to say it, but the words came. "All this detail, blessings and commandments, do's and don'ts. Everything seems so regulated. And the things we are reading—sacrifices, slaughtering bulls and sheep, bringing grain to the temple—how is any of this relevant for us?"

"Some of it isn't," said the rabbi. "We no longer bring sacrifices. As to the details, there is a saying, in German. *Gott lieght im detahl.* God is found in details."

"What? In washing hands? Lighting candles? Saying the same prayers over and over?" Mitch had a sudden vision of being on the Santa Monica Freeway, roaring toward the Pacific Coast Highway in Ari's old convertible, with the radio on loud, singing and yelling, until they parked in their usual place beside the pier and raced into the surf.

He pulled his thoughts close. He did not want to speak. But Rabbi Nachum sat gazing at him, his eyes so bright that Mitch could not look away.

"You are perplexed," the rabbi said softly. "It comes with the territory."

Mitch squirmed in his chair. His face felt hot. "I don't mind the philosophy, Rabbi, and the debates, I love that part! It's the ritual that gets me down. It seems so—"

"Stupid? Archaic?" Rabbi Nachum turned the kaleidoscope back and forth in his hands; the shifting beads made a whispering sound. "I know what you mean. But we humans seem to need rituals. If we don't have rituals, we create them."

Mitch shook his head. "I don't think so," he said.

"Really? Some people refuse to go to synagogue or church, saying they hate ritual. But they'll stamp and yell out silly cheers at a ball game—that's a ritual. Like showing the colors, parades, salutes. We need ritual."

"But why does it matter," Mitch exclaimed, "what I eat or what time certain prayers are said?" He tried to push down the words, but they emerged, anyhow, and suddenly he was glad of it, needing to be free of them.

"It's a matter of order," said Rabbi Nachum. "The opposite of order is chaos."

"But if it's just for order," Mitch argued heatedly, "we could be doing anything at all."

"It's not *just* for order. No. The purpose is to reach closer. To God. He showed us how to reach Him, despite our limitations. Prayer. Ritual. Acts of kindness."

Mitch twisted in his chair. "I'm sorry if I offended you. Maybe I don't belong here after all. . . ."

"Maybe you don't. But I'm not offended. This is strictly between you and God."

"Why would God care if I eat a pork chop?" Mitch exclaimed. "We've got health regulations now. Trichinosis isn't a problem anymore."

"I don't know why God doesn't want us to eat pork. I figure, He has His own reasons. Why should I complain? If He made me, doesn't He know best how to keep this body healthy?"

"What about Christians? They can eat pork."

"They're not Jews. They have different rules. Who am I to argue?" The rabbi raised his hands, smiling. "No, certain things I don't get mixed up in. Pork and all that . . . I can't tell you reasons. Maybe it's just for the discipline of it. For me, the hardest to give up was shellfish. Prawns with red sauce."

"You?" Mitch lifted his head, astonished. "I thought you were always . . ."

"Always observant? No." Rabbi Nachum chuckled and

pulled at his beard. "I was nearly forty when I was ordained. Until ten years before that, I didn't even know the *Shema*. You see, you were way ahead of me. I think I understand your problem," he said. "You believe in a creator who did a great job making the universe, but who doesn't really want to get involved with us anymore."

"Well, if He wanted to get involved, why would all these terrible things happen to people? Innocent people?"

Rabbi Nachum nodded and pressed his fingers to his beard. "Yes, like the bus bombing yesterday. How do such things happen? Does God know? Can He stop bad things from happening? If He did, would we still have free will?"

"You said we have to use our intellect. I've been thinking about this for months now. . . ."

Rabbi Nachum smiled slightly. "Good, good."

"If God cares what we eat and all those details, why doesn't He care about the important things?"

"Who says He doesn't care? Caring doesn't always mean intervention, does it?"

"Sure it does!" Mitch cried. "Look, if I see someone getting hurt, someone I care about, you'd better believe I'd try to help them."

The pounding in Mitch's chest increased, and though he tried to hold it back, gasping for breath, the one thought he had held buried for so long now burst out. "If God loves us so much and cares about us, why does a little kid become an orphan all in a matter of a few minutes?"

Mitch's breath came in spasms. "Why did her parents get killed in a car crash? Who decides things like that?" Tears gathered in his eyes and pressed on his chest, and though he struggled against them, they gushed down his face. "She never cried. We never saw her. But—but in the night . . . I heard her. Oh, God, it was awful."

Finally Mitch was done. His grief lay between them like a tangible thing, a burden now set down.

At last Rabbi Nachum spoke. "I don't know why," he said.

Mitch looked up at him, saw the pain in Rabbi Nachum's eyes.

"I'm sorry," Mitch said.

"Don't be. It's better to let feelings come out. I finally had to learn that when my wife . . ."

Mitch had heard rumors, now he waited to hear the story.

"My wife died at the age of thirty-five," said Rabbi Nachum. "Massive stroke. Some months before her death, she was completely paralyzed."

"And after that you became religious?" Mitch asked.

"No. That was the blessing. I had found my faith before I needed it. After her death I came here, to Jerusalem. I began this work."

Later, Mitch lay awake, probing, questioning. He thought of films and articles he had seen, of primitive tribes using their kinds of magic to invoke spirits for their own benefit.

Is that what we're doing here? Magic? Superstition?

Mitch sat up and turned on the light. For a moment it blinded him, sickened him like a punch in the gut.

David pulled the blanket over his head. Josh was sound asleep, snoring on his back, openmouthed. Guy grunted, then called out, "What's wrong, Mitch? Are you okay?"

"I'm okay. Just restless."

"This happens at the beginning," Guy said, stretching, groaning. "It still happens to me sometimes."

"What?"

"The heebie-jeebies. Doubts. Like, am I being an idiot?"

"How do you deal with it?" Mitch asked.

Guy raised himself up, head propped on his elbow. "Well, it's like angels."

"How's that?" Mitch sat at the edge of the bed, bent low toward his friend.

"You can either believe in angels or not," Guy said. "It's a matter of choice. So you ask yourself what's better: a world with angels in it, or a world without?"

"But what's the truth?"

"Will you ever really know?" Guy countered.

Mitch nodded and sighed. "I see what you mean."

He lay back again in the darkness. Something had been opened up today, something long repressed. That whole business with Carlie, the shock, the sorrow, the confusion of feelings.

He had been shocked that his parents brought her home without even any questions. They certainly had never asked *him*. One day they were a family of three, the next day there was a girl in the house, a strange, moody girl who didn't talk much at first, and who later, somehow, got his parents' attention whenever she spoke, as if she were an authority. He could never understand how swiftly his parents labeled them both: "Oh, Carlie is so sensible. Carlie has a good head on her shoulders." What was he, then? "Mitch is all boy; he's a little unfocused, you know."

He remembered the strain, not knowing how to act in front of Carlie. Was he supposed to be like a brother? A pal? Did he dare object when she left her tennis racket in the hall to trip him, and borrowed his magazines without asking, and took his dog out without him even knowing? He was afraid of offending her, of making her cry. He was afraid of watching her too closely, of making her angry, so he learned how to make her laugh. Finally, he had learned how to make her laugh, and then everything was okay.

He realized now, it was a long time since he'd had one of those laughing sprees with Carlie, and he missed it.

CHAPTER 5

MEALTIMES WERE THE hardest. There used to be this constant banter, Mitch sitting opposite Carlie at the table, the two of them competing for time and attention, Mitch popping off jokes. Carlie would laugh or try to top Mitch; sometimes they argued until Vivian and Harry became exasperated, but at least there was life and excitement.

Now the three of them sat over their food with studied concentration. There didn't seem to be much to talk about. Occasionally one of them would make the effort: Uncle Harry looked up and declared, "An interesting man came into the store today—just built himself an eighteen-thousand-square-foot home. Only four people in the family, can you imagine eighteen thousand square feet? They'll get lost in all that space. Can you guess how many window treatments he needs?"

They talked about it, almost bleeding the topic to death, Carlie thought. Eighteen thousand square feet! My, my, how many windows, did you say? Oh, wow!

Aunt Vivian had a new decorating project: the front

office for a dental group out in the west valley. She brought her wallpaper swatches to the table and laid them out, commenting, "This one looks a little too sweet, don't you think, Carlie? For a dentist?"

"Right. Dentists and sweets don't exactly go together."

Their laughter was too prolonged, their effort too obvious. Carlie felt the tension, almost like something solid. Her eyes slid past Mitch's empty chair. Carlie tried hard not to talk about him. Still, everything seemed to lead to Mitch.

"Ari called today," Carlie said.

Aunt Vivian looked up expectantly, as if Ari were a certain link to her son. "What's new with Ari?" She kept her voice low and carefully modulated, but Carlie saw the worry and sorrow in her eyes.

"He's fine. Loves college. He wanted to know whether we'd heard—um—anything."

Uncle Harry bent over his food, eating industriously.

"I told him Mitch has just about decided to stay there the whole semester." Carlie waited for the words to drop into place, like bullets into a chamber. Nobody had really acknowledged this before. "Maybe he'll be back for the winter quarter. Maybe he can even make up the units next summer and graduate on time."

Uncle Harry pushed his plate away. His eyes skipped erratically around the room as he asked gruffly, "Any dessert, Vivian?"

"Sure, sure." Vivian hurried to the kitchen and returned with a platter of grapes.

Harry gazed at the fruit. "Seedless?"

"No. They didn't have any. . . ."

"Forget it." He strode away.

Carlie gathered up the dishes. "I thought I'd go over to

the club and work out on the ball machine."

Aunt Vivian followed her into the kitchen, bringing back the grapes. "No homework?"

"I finished this afternoon."

"You going alone?"

Carlie paused, restraining a smile. She felt the flush coming over her face. "Well, Kip said he might be there."

"I see." Aunt Vivian smiled. "Has he asked you to the club dance?"

"I'm not sure he's going."

"Of course he'll go. He always does. I think he'll ask you."

"I don't," Carlie said, turning away. "There's about a dozen girls that would give anything to go with him, and they're all older and . . ."

"Look, Carlie, go for it," her aunt stated firmly, hands on her hips. "Don't sell yourself short. You're a beautiful girl, bright, you've got a great sense of humor . . ."

"Kip's in college."

"He's only two years older than you. Anyhow, most boys like to go out with younger girls. Look at Harry and me. A ten-year difference in our ages. He wasn't even thinking of marriage. I had to propose to him, tell him how economical it would be!"

Carlie rinsed the dishes, hurriedly loading them into the dishwasher. "You want me to marry Kip Warner?" Her tone was muffled beneath the sound of running water.

"Of course not. You're much too young to get married. I just meant . . ."

Of course they'd want her to get married, Carlie thought, slamming the silverware into the little basket.

Maybe, if they were lucky, she'd get married at nineteen, like Aunt Vivian. Just three more years of looking after their niece, then they'd be free.

Aunt Vivian took her arm. "Don't bother with that," she said. "I'll finish up here. You go ahead."

Carlie turned. "Are you sure?"

"Yes. Go on!"

Carlie jogged the six blocks to the tennis club, past the pretty ranch-style houses and neat two-story colonials, all with their trim lawns and individual gardens. Here and there little kids were riding their tricycles, tooting and hollering. Two little girls sat on a stoop playing a game. A mother came out in her jeans, yelling for her kids to come in to dinner; four kids came running from all directions, and Carlie smiled to herself at the same time as that ache, the lion leaped into her throat. And she chided herself for the sudden loneliness; after all, she had a family, a wonderful aunt and uncle, a cousin, and an adopted grandmother, too.

This afternoon she'd gone to Grandma Rose's house to bring her the medication Aunt Vivian had bought for her. "Do you mind?" Aunt Vivian had asked. "You can take the Jeep."

"You'll let me drive it all alone?" Carlie felt the thrill, the flash of fear.

"Of course. You've got to start sometime."

She'd had her license for three weeks, but she had always driven with someone else in the car. If Mitch were here, she wondered, would Aunt Vivian still have given her the keys to the Jeep?

"Go!" Aunt Vivian gave her a little push. "Here are the pills. Give Grandma my love."

"Should I take the freeway? Or Ventura?"

"Whatever you want," said Aunt Vivian.

She decided on Ventura Boulevard, mile after mile of shops and eating places, an endless boulevard crammed with cars and pedestrians, almost vibrating with activity. Mitch's grandma lived on one of the side streets in a cottage Uncle Harry was renting for her. "No point in buying it for her," he said flatly. "She probably won't be around that long."

"What a dreadful thing to say, Harry!" Vivian had scolded.

Harry retorted, "Look, people have to face reality. There's no point in living in a dreamworld!"

Carlie had wanted to confront him with the truth: It's dreams that keep people going. But she'd said nothing. She wondered whether Harry ever had dreams at all. Maybe men don't, she thought. She didn't know about her father, had never asked him, and now it was too late.

Grandma Rose was outside waiting for her. Obviously Vivian had called ahead. Rose ran to open the car door, beaming, hands outstretched to touch Carlie's face, the way she always did, moving her fingers caressingly. "Carlie! What a sweet girl you are to come all this way. And you drove alone. Good for you!"

Carlie got out, smiling. She gave Grandma Rose a hug, taking in the warm, motherly scent of Grandma's hair and clothes, and something else, a faint lavender perfume. "Hi. How are you? How's the house? Are you settled?"

"Come in. You'll see. I've made half the kitchen into a workshop. It's wonderful! I'm using one whole cabinet for my sculpture, and also the spice shelves—it's perfect."

Indeed, Carlie could smell the floury heat from the oven, where cookie sheets of roses and little mannequins would be baking.

Excitedly, Grandma Rose said, "One of my new neighbors, a lovely woman, Hedda Morales, saw my roses and wants twenty-four of them for a luncheon at her church. She's using them on place cards. I'm in business again!" She picked up her pot holders and bent to pull her creations from the oven, dropped the pans onto the tile counter, and exclaimed, "Perfect! Sit down, sit down. Do you want to help me paint?"

Carlie laughed. "You know I'm a slob. My fingers don't work well with little things."

Grandma Rose sat down with her jars of watercolors—pink, yellow, red, pale green. "Your fingers are strong. You have healing hands. I should know. Now, what about Mitch? Will he make it back in time for my birthday party?"

"I don't know, Grandma," said Carlie. There was a chance Mitch might come back for the party, Grandma's eighty-fifth. "I hope so."

Grandma dipped her brush into the pink paint, nodding slowly, tongue pressed between her teeth as she painted. She finished the rose, then looked up. "Do you miss him?"

"Yes," Carlie said, grateful for Grandma Rose's nod and for her lack of platitudes. Grandma Rose rationed her words and listened beyond politeness. And she was the only person who seemed to take Carlie simply for herself, not as a victim of tragedy, someone whose past was the most important aspect of her being.

"It must feel a little empty in the house," Grandma Rose said.

Carlie said, "I used to complain about that damn bike of his blocking the driveway, or his ugly gym shorts on the floor. I'm glad all that's gone. But I do miss him."

"Vivian said you two used to scream and fight."

"Oh, just about silly things. He hated every boy I ever went out with, always found something wrong with them. Mitch wrecked it every time."

"Because when he said it—if the boy was stupid or silly or had bad manners—then you would see it, too."

Carlie nodded, chuckling. "That's true. I was meeting an awful lot of jerks."

"Now you have a boyfriend?"

"Not really. There's a guy at the tennis club. All the girls think he's gorgeous. And he is, besides being really sweet and a great tennis player. . . . I'm going up there tonight and maybe play a set with him." Carlie realized that she was only chattering, putting up a false front. She said, "Did you ever think Mitch would get himself involved like this? I mean, with those people?"

"Orthodox," said Grandma Rose. "Ultrareligious." She sighed. "I never thought about it. Of course, I always knew his good heart. He was always a sensitive child. His father thought that just because he was big and a boy, he was rough. Mitch was never rough."

"I wish I knew what he was looking for," Carlie said. She gazed around the small, warm kitchen with its homey appliances and checked curtains. Was it her age that made Grandma Rose so complacent? Without struggle?

"He is looking for what we all want," Grandma Rose said. She put her paintbrush into the water jar and looked up at Carlie. "He wants peace. And love. And a chance to do something special."

"Like, do you think he wants to be a rabbi?"

Grandma Rose frowned. "A rabbi? I don't know. Maybe

he just wants to find out if God will talk to him. Maybe for everybody there is such a time, when they wonder."

"Did you, too? I mean, want to talk to God?"

"Of course. But that was a long, long time ago. I gave up. Now, I only talk once in a while, before I go to bed, just a few words. I say the *Shema*, because I learned it as a baby. And I say, 'God, if you are there, keep me alive one more day!' And it has always worked, so far."

Carlie laughed silently. "Why did you give up, Grandma?"

"Oh, it's a long story. I think, really, I gave up on people, not so much on God. The way people behave, the things they do to you in the name of God. Terrible things."

"You mean the Holocaust?"

"What? No—yes, not only that. You know what I mean. Some people force other people to do things, and they say it is what God wants, but how do they know? Who is the expert? Mitch is looking around, trying to be his own expert. And I say, good for him!"

Now, as Carlie jogged faster and faster, the words joined in the rhythm of her run: Good for him! Good for him!

She got to the tennis club breathless, relieved. She ran into the women's locker room and bathed her face with cold water, patting down her hair. Her own reflection smiled back at her, as if she were utterly free of any cares. Good for you! she told the girl in the mirror, and she ran out to the pro shop, fingers crossed, hoping he'd be there.

Kip called out, "Hey, Carlie, how's it going?" He looked up from restringing a small racket. Carlie felt a flash of pleasure. She watched as Kip knotted the last string and held it out to the little girl who stood waiting, her hands clasped behind her back. "Here you are, Linnie. Good as new."

"Thanks, Kip. Are we having the workout now?"

"Two minutes. Tell the other kids to meet us on court seven."

Kip slipped a headband over his forehead, pushing back his hair. "Want to help me with their workout?" Kip asked.

"Sure."

Kip picked up his Prince racket, his muscles rippling under the white tennis shirt. There was an easy air about him. It was his smile, Carlie thought, a great smile, a gentleness, also a sense of assurance. She liked that.

"So, we'll give 'em a dozen forehand drives, a dozen backhands, set of cross-courts, then some net shots, finishing with lobs. Then we'll mix it up, just to keep them on their toes."

"Sure." Carlie grabbed a stack of paper cups for the kids. She could feel Kip watching her out of the corner of his eye as they walked together toward the courts.

"Have you heard from Mitch?" Kip asked.

"We talked to him about a week ago."

"I guess you heard the news."

"What news?"

Kip bit his lip. "This afternoon on TV, CNN."

"What? What happened?"

"A bus bombing. In Tel Aviv. A bunch of people were killed. Nineteen people, I think they said."

Carlie's heart lurched. Then she remembered, feeling suddenly weak with relief. "Mitch is in Jerusalem, not Tel Aviv." It felt cruel to be thinking only of Mitch, and not of the others.

"Oh, well, that's good. He's okay."

"Yes. He's okay." Nineteen people, but not Mitch. Thank God, not Mitch.

"It brings it kind of close," said Kip. "When you know someone. Like, my parents still have relatives in Ireland. They always worry when there's an uprising. You know?"

"Yes."

"And I guess Mitch doesn't get out that much, anyhow. Melanie told me he's with sort of a cult over there, like those guys on the street that hand out leaflets, you know. . . ."

Carlie stopped short. "It's not a cult!" she cried. "He's studying with a group of—of religious people. Jews. They're just studying religion."

"Sorry, sorry!" Kip raised his hand and backed away. "I didn't know you'd be so sensitive."

"Of course I'm sensitive when people gossip about us! I don't know what's wrong with Melanie. She goes around telling people that Mitch is into something weird, like the Moonies. . . ." Carlie's face burned with anger, and also with remorse. She ought to be more loyal to her friend. "I'm sorry, Kip," she relented, "but the word 'cult' really gets me going. Everybody's calling our house asking about Mitch and giving advice. One woman from the temple called and told Aunt Vivian we ought to go over there and kidnap him back. She said we should get a deprogrammer, as if Mitch were just totally out of control and taken in by those guys, as if he doesn't have any brains or will of his own. . . ."

"Melanie didn't actually say that, Carlie. I'm sorry. Look, let's forget it. The kids are waiting—they're acting nuts. Hey, guys! Ready for the workout?" Kip yelled. "Get in line. Murray, Ted, Linnie, you can pick up the balls and be first in line."

Carlie ran around the other side of the net and began forming the children into two lines. Resentment lingered. Even now, Mitch was giving her a hard time, making her defend him. He had explained nothing, really, in all those conversations and in his letters. What was it like for him there? Did he ever have time to goof off? To go to the movies or listen to music? Did he even care? Or was he like some monk now, sober and distant? Did he ever think of her?

Kip called across the net. "Wake up, Carlie! Let's go!"

She snapped into the appropriate stance and gave Kip's swift serve a whack that sent Kip running backward, calling, "Ho! Good one!"

They tossed balls for the children, ran, corrected, praised.

"You're good," Kip said after forty-five minutes of workout.

"Thanks," Carlie said. The sun was setting into a red glow on the horizon. She felt good now, tired yet invigorated.

"How about a quick set?"

"Now? Do we have time?"

"We can use the lights—or play fast," Kip said with a grin.

Her face and body were steaming, but Carlie felt a surge of energy in her arms and back and legs. She tossed the ball up high, watched it descend, and smacked it with her swift topspin serve. It swirled past Kip's feet, and he called out, laughing, "Great serve!"

She was elated at the final score: Carlie—6, Kip—4. She had never won a set from him before.

"Are you going out for the high school team?" he asked.

"I've been on it for the past year," she said.

"You know, with some coaching," Kip said, "you could get really good. I mean, competitive."

"You mean it?"

"You're fast, you've got a good eye, and you keep your concentration. You could do with a bit of work on your backhand. . . ."

"Want to play another set?" she teased.

He gave her a slight swat with his towel, grinning. "No way. Just because I can call 'em doesn't mean I can beat 'em!"

They walked back to the clubhouse slowly. The sky was turning lavender-blue; the trees stood like dark silhouettes, sentinels, along the carefully trimmed paths. Carlie breathed deeply, relaxed and happy. She felt Kip's hand on her shoulder, moving down to her back. She thought of the heat of her body, the sweat; he didn't seem to mind, nor did she mind the warmth of his hand, not at all.

Kip said softly, "This is my last week here. I'm absolutely overprogrammed."

Carlie took in a deep breath. She looked down at her feet moving in rhythm with Kip. It figures, she thought.

"Of course, I can still hang out here," Kip said quickly. "In fact, I'd have time to play."

She turned to smile at him. "That's great." She felt his eyes upon her; she felt a radiance.

"I was thinking," Kip began. He stopped walking. "My brother and sister-in-law just bought this boat. They take it over to Catalina Island. I was wondering, would you like to go with us some time?"

"Catalina! I'd love it!"

"You've been there, I guess," he said with a grin.

"Once," Carlie said. "When I was nine, my folks took me. We did the whole tour, went in the glass-bottom boat. I loved it. They said we'd go back sometime, but . . ." She sighed.

"Well, I'll see when we can go," Kip said. "By the way, when I leave here they'll need someone to do afternoon workouts with the little kids. I was talking to Ms. Ross about you. Would you like to do it?"

"I—do you think I could?" Carlie's face felt warm; her stomach seemed to do a flip.

"I think you'd be great. You're terrific with the kids, and they're crazy about you."

"No, it's you," Carlie objected, but she couldn't help smiling.

"It's up to Ms. Ross," Kip reminded her.

"I know. But thanks, Kip. I'd love to do it." Thoughts rang through her mind—suddenly her life was crammed full. She had places to go, friends, even Kip Warner wanting to spend time with her. For years it was always Mitch rushing off to some meeting or event. It was Mitch's ball game, Mitch's debate, Mitch's prom committee—on and on.

Kip walked her out to the back gate. He stood there with his hand on the railing, his foot on the step, as if he were reluctant to let her leave.

"I wanted to ask you to the club dance," he said, "but I'm just a hired hand. I'm supposed to be a host slash busboy, janitor and, by the way, see to it that none of the little kids fall into the pool." Kip put his hand out, grazing her arm. He stepped closer. Carlie could see the blue of his eyes, the flecks of brown, and the fullness of his lips.

"But if you're going," he said softly, his face very near hers, "maybe we can sneak in a dance or two. That is, if you aren't going with anyone."

"Just the folks," Carlie whispered.

"Good." One more step, and his lips touched hers, ever

so gently, and for a moment stayed, and she tasted him, sweet and soft and wonderful.

She tasted that kiss all night, and she woke to the memory of it the next morning.

For some reason Carlie could not fathom, she didn't tell Melanie about Kip; she didn't tell her about the kiss. Maybe she was a little mad at Melanie about that Moonie thing—maybe she just wanted to keep it to herself, something to savor.

They ate lunch together at school, as always, gossiping and laughing, and they rode home together on the bus.

"Want to come and study at my house?" Melanie asked.

"No thanks. I've got to get home and start dinner. Aunt Vivian has a new job and she'll be home late, she said."

"Is something wrong?" Melanie gave her a sidelong glance.

"Nope. Nothing's wrong."

"I guess you're just still bummed about Mitch," Melanie said. "You're going to have to get over it, Carlie. He might not be back. Look at it this way: Maybe you can drive his car."

"Will you shut up, please?" Carlie shouted.

Melanie retreated, pale. "What's wrong with you?" she cried. "I was only kidding! I was only trying to get you to lighten up!"

"Maybe I don't want to lighten up. Maybe I'm really worried. What if he is in a cult? What if it is like the Moonies, and he never gets back? How do we tell?"

"I'm sorry, Carlie," Melanie said, crestfallen. "Really. Don't be mad."

"I'm not mad."

"Promise?"

"Promise. Look, I've really got to get home."

"Okay. Call me later?"

"Sure. Bye."

At home, Carlie reached into the mailbox on the curb. Her hand, her entire being, seemed to know ahead of time that among the bills and brochures there would be this slim, pale blue envelope with the three Israeli stamps on it and Mitch's printing, small, dark letters.

She walked up the path to the front door, punched in the alarm code, and stepped inside. The living room was like a cool cave. The hallways still smelled slightly of new paint and carpet; Aunt Vivian had redecorated after the earthquake.

Carlie went into the kitchen, with its gleaming counters and huge refrigerator, which hummed gently in the stillness. She turned on the lights, laid her things on the built-in desk, and began preparations for dinner—meatloaf and roasted potatoes, a green salad, leftover berry cake. She liked to cook. She liked to keep busy. Her mom had never cooked, except on the weekends, when she made fancy casseroles that sometimes tasted really weird. Nobody ever said so, because her mom was so proud of her creations.

It was always like this. Whenever she was alone, memories crowded into the void, like real people just waiting in the wings to catch her alone. She remembered hearing her mother and Aunt Vivian arguing in their kitchen in San Gabriel. Carlie was very young, maybe four or five, but she remembered the angry voices.

"You want your child to be raised by a nanny while you traipse all over the world? A person who doesn't even speak English?"

"Consuela speaks English. She's a wonderful woman, and she loves Carlie."

"Well, excuse me, but I happen to think that a mother's love and concern can't be duplicated by a maid! I should think you'd want Carlie to have a normal upbringing."

"Vivian, what's wrong? Why are you so angry?"

That was all Carlie remembered. Something about Aunt Vivian's fury seemed the same now, a frustration and anger that stayed with her, just underneath the surface.

The front door slammed. "Hello! Carlie, are you home?"

"In the kitchen."

Her aunt came rushing in, bringing the heat and the tempo from outside in with her. Her look was anxious, harried. "Any mail?"

"There's a letter from Mitch. It's on the table. I didn't open it."

Vivian rushed over, her purse still hanging from her arm. She tore open the envelope and stood braced against the counter, reading. Carlie glanced at her aunt, her mother's sister. Sometimes, like now, she was overcome by the resemblance.

"What's he say?"

Vivian held out the letter. "Here. Read it for yourself."

Carlie took the letter. A smudge of meatloaf clung to the edge of the pale blue paper. She brushed it away, but a greasy little spot remained.

Carlie read the words once, then again to be sure.

" . . . new dimensions are opening . . . will stay here for at least a year or two . . . to get in touch with my real purpose . . . I need the money from my trust. Please wire me five thousand dollars immediately."

Carlie sat down in the breakfast nook. She set the letter on the table, where it fluttered momentarily, as if it were alive.

"What are you going to do?" Carlie asked.

"Nothing. He's not getting that money," said her aunt.

"Isn't it his money?"

Aunt Vivian raised her hands to her head; she tugged at her hair. "This is what they do," she said fiercely. "These people move in on kids with money. They try to get them to sign everything over!"

"How would they know Mitch had that trust?" Carlie asked, bewildered.

"They have ways," Aunt Vivian said. "They're just after his money. I knew it all along. But let me tell you something, they're not going to get away with it!"

CHAPTER 6

HE WAS ON a journey. Richard spoke of it with passion, and Mitch, listening, felt a slow sense of clarity, then elation, like a bird in a cage suddenly set free. He was on a journey, and he was not alone. The journey was known as *teshuvah,* "return," and the one who travels this road is called a *ba'al teshuvah*.

Mitch knew now that he had begun this journey a long time ago, before he met Tal or Rabbi Nachum. He remembered certain moments, even when he was very young, looking up at the night sky and asking himself, "Who put the moon up there? How do the stars stay put?" He remembered wanting to reach out and touch "something," uncertain about what that "something" was. In his mind he had traced a path in the darkness, imagining stairs, then a ramp made entirely of stars, moving onward, upward, to light. Silly ideas, he had pushed them away. His father would laugh. His mom would look worried if he told her. Now, it seemed not only natural, but right. Now he was a *ba'al teshuvah,* a traveler on this road.

Day by day Mitch began to feel the differences. He felt it in his walk—lighter and more assured. He looked back on himself with his California friends, hanging out at the beach, that rolling, bragging kind of walk, eyes roving, always looking for something or someone who glittered. Now, the glow was inside, his steps were sure and filled with a different purpose. Walk humbly, walk proudly: Twin dictates surrounded him in almost every area of life. The ideal was to strike the right balance.

Carlie, it seemed, had always known this. They used to talk about far-out things, like whether there were really aliens from other planets, and what they'd do if they were abducted. Carlie said, "I'd watch everything very carefully, and if they asked me what was the most important thing in our world, I'd say, 'eagles.'"

Mitch laughed. "Why would you say that?"

"Because then they'd go catch some eagles and let me go!"

Practical Carlie. But she could also dream. Once when they were hiking in the hills above Hollywood they saw three deer standing together, staring at them with large, lustrous eyes. Carlie had said, "When I see a hawk or a deer or even a coyote, I always think it is a special sign."

"A sign of what?"

"I—well, I've never really put it into words. But it's like, I feel a kind of love. I'm being trusted to see this perfect creature. . . ."

"You think animals are perfect?"

"Of course. Don't you?"

And they had talked about animals, whether they have language, whether they have souls, whether they go to heaven when they die, whether there *is* a heaven, and Mitch had asked Carlie the same question Josh had asked him, and she had answered without hesitation, "Of course."

"What do you think it's like?"

"Oh, we never know that until we die. But I know it's got to be good. It's got to be—someplace that I can't even imagine. We're not built to understand things like that."

"And you don't mind not knowing?"

"Of course not. I am what I am."

In class they talked about souls and "the world to come" not as possibilities, but as certainties. Mitch longed to tell Carlie, but it certainly wasn't the kind of thing you could discuss long-distance, especially at the *yeshiva,* where guys were always waiting in line for the phone.

Instead, he talked to the other students or with Richard, who lived near the *yeshiva* and often stayed late. Once they sat up until two in the morning talking about creation. How could God have created the world in just six days? Well, what was a "day" in God's time? They argued, debated, took books down from the shelves and spread them all over the table, reading aloud to each other. And in the midst of it Mitch suddenly realized there was no place in the world he'd rather be, no other moment he'd rather experience.

He stayed awake most of the night, with phrases clattering in his mind, and he dozed in a chair until the dawn. Then Mitch got up and he took Bernie's *tallit katan* from his bureau drawer. The fabric felt smooth and fragile in his hands, just a wisp of cloth, plain as a shroud, with fringes hanging down from its four corners.

Carefully he fitted it over his head and smoothed it down over his chest and back, then he replaced his shirt, letting the fringes show at his waist.

He moved slowly around the room, aware of the garment as it caressed him in its newness and its significance. " . . . so that you remember all my commandments . . ."

He waited that day for comments from his friends. There were none, only a certain look, a lift of the brows, a flicker of understanding.

Richard called Mitch aside one day. "Halle and I want you to come to lunch with Tal for *Shabes*."

"Of course," Mitch said. "I'd love to." The invitation to meet Tal's sister was like a sign that he had arrived.

Mitch and Tal walked along the tree-lined streets thickly populated with homes, all ancient, all built of stone. Tal stopped at an open black iron gate leading to a downward path strewn with pebbles and weeds. "This is it," he said.

Mitch walked carefully along the uneven path. A thick rope hung from a tree limb. A little tricycle lay in the path. A note tacked to the door explained that the bell didn't work: KNOCK HARD!

They were met at the door by six-year-old Dov, who shrieked with delight. "Uncle Tal! Uncle Tal! And you've brought your friend."

"Hey, Dov! This is Mitch."

The little boy pulled Mitch's arm, leading them through the living room to the kitchen, where Tal's sister, Halle, was slicing melons, alternately feeding the baby in his high chair and sending four-year-old Daliah to fetch things from the pantry.

"Come in! *Baruch ha-ba,*" she called. "Welcome."

Richard emerged from the back porch carrying a bucket of ice. "Tal! Mitch!" he called out, beaming. "Good to see you. I've got some new books to show you. . . ."

"Later, Richard," Halle said, half scolding. "They just walked in the door." Her smile was radiant, her face glowing with perspiration. She wore no makeup at all, but her dark eyes sparkled. "Excuse the mess, Mitch. The children leave toys everywhere. Daliah! Come collect your books." She strode across the large kitchen, her long skirt billowing around her ankles. "Sit down here on the sofa, Mitch, not on that chair; it's a monster. Besides, the baby wet on it yesterday. I've been wanting to meet you, Richard's star pupil, I hear."

Halle sat down on the "monster" chair, while Tal stood at the sink, washing his hands. "Richard says you're interested in Abraham Joshua Heschel—he's my favorite. Did you know he also wrote poetry?"

"Papa! Papa!" cried Dov, pulling at his father's arm. "Yosi said I should come to his house this afternoon."

"No," Richard said firmly. "You stay here. No more talk about it."

Halle said, "I already told Dov he has to stay here with us." She gave her husband a swift glance, so tender, it might have been a kiss.

To Mitch and Tal she said, "Richard is frantic since that last bombing. Do we let the children go out like normal human beings? Or do we keep them in, protected? Well, it's a constant tension, isn't it?" She turned to Mitch as if they were already old friends. "So, what's going on in the States? Still looting and shooting there?"

Mitch frowned. "It gets so you hate to watch the news."

"Here, too," said Halle. "But what can you do? People can't seem to get along. Even in families, there's fighting."

"I know."

"You have brothers and sisters."

"No, I just fight with my dad." He tried to pass it off as a joke, but Halle seemed to know better.

"My dad used to give me a very hard time about"—she pointed to her kerchief—"my hair. When I became observant, that seemed to bother him more than anything else."

Mitch glanced at the fringes near his pockets. "Why are people so freaked out by a piece of cloth?"

"Come on," Richard called. "Come to the table."

"Not yet, Richard!" Halle leaned toward him, whispering. "Don't you remember?"

"Sorry," Richard said with a faint smile.

Halle took the baby from his high chair and put him into a playpen. "Actually, we're expecting some other people," she said. "I hope you won't mind. My friend Orli and her husband, with their baby. And Orli's sister, Miriam."

"Why would I mind?"

The little girl, Daliah, stood in front of Mitch with a book in her hand. "Will you tell me a story?" she asked.

"Sure. Let's see the book."

"You have to make it up," Halle murmured. "She doesn't like the actual words."

"Of course," said Mitch. "I know that." He took the book and began. "See, this bird has gone looking for cake. He's having a party, you know. It's his birthday. Oh, look—who's coming to the party?"

"A frog!" The child burst into laughter.

"You've just made yourself a friend," Halle said.

"Several friends, I hope," Mitch replied.

That afternoon passed as if in a dream. Was he dreaming? Or was the food really the best he'd ever eaten, the soda pop in plain bottles more sparkling and satisfying than any he had ever drunk?

Miriam sat opposite him, talking to Halle and to her sister, Orli, talking around Mitch, talking to him with her eyes, her gestures. He loved to hear the way she spoke English, giving a lilt to the words, then smiling slightly, as if she had erred.

"You come to Israel alone?" she asked him, eyes slightly downcast. "I think it is—ah—brave. I never travel alone. Oh, to Ein Geddi with my friends. It is so wonderful there, you must go for sure to the caves. Yes? And see Timna, the"—she turned to Halle for help, then back to Mitch, smiling—"formations. Yes, big rocks higher than a house or a factory—beautiful, beautiful, one looks like a—a castle."

Mitch tried to keep focused on her words, but he was constantly distracted by her face, especially her eyes. Miriam was the most beautiful girl he had ever seen, with shining dark hair cut short, and the most gorgeous almond-shaped eyes, a dazzling shade of blue-green, all the more stunning because of her deep complexion. She walked like a queen, he thought. Watching her, Mitch felt almost paralyzed, but then suddenly he was inspired and he knew exactly what to say to make her laugh. He could be fascinating and witty. She made him feel brilliant—and he was.

"Thanks, thanks for inviting me," he told Halle and Richard later. He felt almost dizzy with happiness.

"Pretty girl, isn't she?" Richard said. And he and Halle glanced at each other and began to laugh, and Richard murmured, "She told Halle she likes you, too."

In the next few weeks he saw Miriam several times. She came by the *yeshiva* with Halle one afternoon. Mitch looked up from the study table and Richard summoned him, beckoning and whispering, "Someone outside you might want to see."

And there she was with Halle, smiling at him, waiting on the porch. Halle said something about an errand inside, and then Mitch and Miriam were alone, and they started to talk. They talked about music and discovered their shared favorites; she still loved the old Simon and Garfunkel albums, and so did he. "Classics," he said, and they talked about what makes a classic, and she told him about liking poetry, looking embarrassed at first, then elaborating about the Israeli poets. "When you learn more Hebrew, I will read them to you—you will love them."

A promise, then, of a future. He took her to the corner and bought fruit ices; they stood watching the cars go by while pigeons pecked at specks in the sidewalk, and the neighborhood seemed marvelous, full of colors and shapes that Mitch had not noticed before. A whole hour passed before he knew it.

"I have to go home now," Miriam had told him, "and do my schoolwork."

"Where's Halle?" he asked.

"Inside. I'll go tell her I'm ready."

Only then did it dawn on Mitch that Miriam had come specifically to see him.

Another time he and Tal were in the Old City, picking up some books from the bindery, and Miriam was there, sitting on a stone wall, looking like a Moroccan princess in her dark print skirt and white blouse. Her hair shone in the sunlight. When she saw him, Miriam leaped up and went to him, and he wondered what sort of coincidence this was—or whether it was a gift. She introduced him to her younger brother and sister. "We are here for my grandfather. My father is bringing him to the clinic," she said.

"Is he sick?" Mitch asked.

"Heartsick," she said seriously. "He will live in our house now, I think. Before, he was with his sister, but she passed out."

"Passed on," Mitch corrected gently.

"You can teach me English," Miriam said with a smile. "Maybe I can teach you some things, too."

"I'm sure you can," Mitch had said warmly.

A few nights later he bought a book of modern Israeli poems, a slim volume with beautiful woodcuts. He kept it by his bed, reading word for word until he could feel the meanings. They were all poems of love. Someday, he thought, he would read them with Miriam.

"Letter for you, Mitch."

Tal tossed down the envelope. Mitch took the letter and held it in his hands for a long moment, as if to gauge the contents.

"It's from my folks," he said. "Now they're sending photographs." He grimaced.

"Aren't you going to open it?" Tal asked.

"After I finish reading this commentary," Mitch said.

"Such discipline!"

"Don't I wish." Mitch smiled and stretched his neck and back. He had been sitting at this thick, battered wooden table for hours, surrounded by books. At the end of the long, narrow study hall three other students had drawn their chairs together and were debating a Talmud passage about harvesting fruit. Now and then he heard phrases. "It's purposely left vague . . . you're supposed to be generous . . . leave the fallen and the leftover fruit for the poor. My grandfather always said that if you drop a coin, you must leave it lie . . . someone who needs it will come along . . ."

Their voices made a pleasant rumbling background to Mitch's own studies.

Tal turned to leave. "Wait," Mitch said.

"I thought you'd want to read your letter in private," Tal said.

"I don't even need to read it to know what it says," Mitch replied. "They want me to come home. They implore me. I can feel my mother's tears through the writing."

"Are you being overly dramatic?" Tal asked.

"I asked them to send me the money from my trust," Mitch said.

"Mitch, I told you we could probably get your funding extended."

"I'm tired of freeloading!" Mitch exclaimed, and the three students whirled around, registering his outburst.

Swiftly Mitch tore open the envelope. First came the photographs, in color. There was Carlie, kneeling on the front lawn, with his dog, Arnie. The dog was panting, grinning. Mitch could almost feel the satin-sleek fur under his hands. Carlie was dressed in a white V-neck polo shirt. Her hair was loose, and she wore her turquoise and silver earrings. The second picture showed Carlie and his mother standing in front of the store, both of them eating Frosties. His dad had obviously taken the picture carefully, to include the sign WINDOWS OF THE WORLD.

Wordlessly, Mitch passed the photographs to Tal. His throat felt tight. He had not expected this sudden surge of longing.

"She's very beautiful," Tal said. "Your cousin? Carlie?"

"Yes," Mitch said. "And my dog—an Irish setter. Arnie is his name. Oh, she is so devious!" Quickly he scanned the letter. It was short, to the point:

"At least come home for Grandma Rose's birthday party. It's a once-in-a-lifetime event. Grandma calls every day, wanting to know whether you are coming. She loves you, Mitch. She's an old woman. Who knows how many more years . . . ?"

"Who is devious?" Tal asked.

"Read it," Mitch said, giving the letter to his friend. In the small, crowded study room the walls and books suddenly seemed to be closing in on him.

"Let's go outside," Mitch said.

They walked along the dim corridor, past cork-covered walls filled with notices about lectures, courses, desert treks, and archaeological digs.

Outside, Mitch leaned against the wall of the building. It was made of Jerusalem stone, grayish-white by day, turning to a mysterious golden haze at sunset. Broken stones and bits of wire, iron pipe, and trash lay in small piles in the gutter. Across the street a large crane stood idle, amid rubble: Jerusalem. Jerusalem was continually wearing down, rising up, being rebuilt, he thought. An Arab walked past quickly, his *Kaffiyeh* swinging at his back. He kept his eyes straight ahead, in the manner of one who either knows no fear or needs to hide it.

Mitch said, "My mother didn't send pictures just to be

nice. She wants me to feel—the way I feel now."

"How do you feel?"

"Like I've been socked in the gut."

"What's this about your grandmother's birthday? Should you go?"

"That's the problem," Mitch said. "If I go, how can I ever come back here? They'll pressure me. They'll make it impossible."

"How can they stop you?"

"I don't know, but they'll find ways," Mitch said. "First of all, my grandmother will cry. 'How can you do this to your parents?' she'll say. 'After all your father went through to come to America, you throw it away. He built this business for you, and you spit on it.' "

Tal seemed amused. "She sounds feisty."

"She is," Mitch said. "She's the one who thought up the name for our business. She can't read or write, but she makes these marvelous little sculptures."

"Ah, that's where you get your talent." Tal pointed to the photograph. "Is that your father's store?"

Mitch nodded. "Yes. Windows of the World. My dad built it up out of nothing. He started out washing windows for office buildings. Now we've got three big outlets, window blinds and shades."

"I thought blinds and shades are the same thing," Tal said.

"Oh, no. Not at all. Blinds come in hundreds of materials, plastics, metals, all sizes, and they . . ." Mitch smiled ruefully. "You see, I've been well trained. I started working at my dad's store when I was thirteen. He plans for me to be his partner."

Tal said, "Well, you can still study Torah and sell window blinds or do anything you want."

"You don't know my dad." He pointed to the letter and read over Tal's shoulder.

"We're not sending you the money from your trust because we think it would be a mistake. Later on, when you change your mind about your present lifestyle, you would regret it. I know that five thousand doesn't seem like so much now, but if you ever wanted to start a business of your own, or buy a house, it would come in very handy."

There was a scribbled note at the bottom. "Mitch, someday you will thank us for this."

"It's my money," Mitch said angrily. "They have no right to keep it! My mother's father left twenty-five thousand dollars in trust to each of his grandchildren, Carlie and me."

"It's in trust, though," said Tal. "When does it vest?"

"You mean, when do I get it?"

"Yeah."

"When I'm twenty-one, I think. Unless it's an emergency or if I need it for . . ."

Someone ran out, calling, "Mitch! Phone for you. Hurry! We've been looking all over for you."

"Who is it?"

"Do I know?"

Mitch grinned. "Always answer a question with a question," he said. It was one of their in-jokes, imitating the rabbis of old who always followed one question with another.

Mitch hurried inside to the telephone, mounted on the wall in a dark alcove. The letter and the photographs were still in his hand. Carlie. Maybe it was Carlie. Maybe she'd talk to him about something besides coming home, something to make him feel less an outcast, a bad son.

To his delight, it *was* Carlie, shrill and excited.

"Are you all right, Mitch? We heard about that bombing in Tel Aviv. Yes, I saw the news on CNN. I know you're in Jerusalem, but . . ."

"I'm fine, Carlie. Terrific. It's so exciting here!"

"Yes, we know," Carlie said dryly. "Mitch, when are you coming home? Are you coming for Grandma's birthday? She really wants you. And I . . . please come, Mitch."

"I—I have to think about it, Carlie."

"Your dad wants to talk to you."

He could imagine his father pulling the telephone away from Carlie, his body braced and tense, like a ferocious dog ready to bite. "Mitch!" It was a shout, and he knew his father's stance, holding the receiver as if it were hot and dangerous. "What do you want me to do with your car, Mitch?"

"What? What about my car?"

"Well, it's just sitting in the garage taking up space. A car needs to be kept up, tuned and serviced."

"I don't care, Dad. Let Carlie drive it. She told me she got her license."

"What about insurance, Mitch? Who's supposed to pay the insurance?"

Mitch sighed deeply. From the parlor he could hear the voices of several students, one of them he recognized: Josh. "Even if it's your enemy's mule," Josh said excitedly, "and it's in pain, you have to help. You can't just walk away . . ."

Mitch felt the agony like blows to his stomach. He was walking away from his father. The car thing was just a sham. He knew it. Still, he said, "I got myself a little workshop here, Dad. It's in the back of a jewelry store, and the owners really like my stuff. Also, I'm doing some repairs for them. So I'll be able to send you some money soon to pay for car insurance. Okay?"

"Okay. Listen, your mom was very upset about that bombing. She's very worried about you."

"I'm sorry, Dad, but I'm fine. Really. Take care."

"Take care."

Mitch stood in the hall, his back to the wall. Nothing seemed to work right. Each step on the path led to still more choices, more conflicts.

The telephone rang. Mitch answered.

"Hello?"

"Mitch Green, please."

"This is Mitch." He knew her voice, knew immediately.

"This is Miriam Sarodi. How are you?"

He stood there perplexed. Why would she call? "I'm fine," he said. "And you?"

"Fine, thank you." There was a pause. "My family—my parents and I," Miriam said, "want to invite you for *Shabes* dinner a week from this Friday."

Mitch's heart pounded, as if he'd been running. *Shabes* dinner was special. Why were they inviting him? Maybe she felt sorry for him, here alone without family. His mind raced over possibilities. It was considered a *mitzvah,* a kindness, to show hospitality to strangers. Maybe her parents suggested it. Or maybe—maybe it was Miriam's idea.

Now he stood in the alcove, his heart thumping against his chest as Miriam continued. "Next Friday, you come to us. *Shabes Va-yetze,*" she said.

Mitch felt a certain pride in knowing what she meant: Religious Jews often called the week by the name of the particular Torah portion being read. He glanced at his pocket calendar, one Halle had given him. It contained both the Jewish and the secular dates.

"November twelfth?" he pondered, biting his lip. Clearly, it was meant to be. As Tal said, "*bashert,*" predestined.

"Okay?" She loved to use American slang. "Is it okay?"

"Yes, it's okay," he said.

"My parents will be glad," Miriam said. "Also, my little brother and sisters. They love to have more company."

"Thank you, Miriam. And thank your parents, too."

Mitch hung up. He stood in the hallway, inhaling deeply, amazed at how easy it had been for him to decide. November twelfth was the weekend of Grandma Rose's party.

Now he saw the choice clearly: Grandma Rose, his family, his entire past life stood poised against a single evening with Miriam, an eighteen-year-old Israeli girl he hardly knew. He had decided instantaneously.

His father's voice seemed to echo from the past. "You have a responsibility to others. To the family. To your cousin Carlie."

Mitch hadn't known his cousin Carlie all that well, even though they lived only an hour away. They seldom got together. Aunt Joanne, a big wheel at some foreign bank, was always traveling.

Mitch remembered the call before six one Sunday morning, from the highway patrol. They'd all been asleep, of course. Mitch's mom came to his room, pale, looking shrunken. "There's been a terrible accident. My sister Joanne. We have to go. Come on, don't bother with socks—we have to go."

Mitch's father said nothing the whole way, but hunched over the steering wheel like a race car driver, as if their speedy arrival could possibly make a difference.

Carlie was with a neighbor, lying on the sofa, curled up

like a little child. The neighbor shooed her own three children outside with a shrill, "Go out and play now, kids! Go on!"

Mitch sat down on the sofa beside Carlie. His parents went next door to gather some of Carlie's things. It was one of those days that was frozen forever in his memory, the starkness of it, the feelings.

Within a few hours, their family had expanded; everything changed. The den became Carlie's room. The table was set with four places. Carlie's laundry, her tennis racket, her magazines, and most of all, her unrelenting sorrow made the house suddenly seem small, made Mitch feel awkward, too large and too loud.

"You have a responsibility," his parents had said, "to your cousin Carlie. You can make her life better. You have a choice."

That was the big word, the capital letter word, "choice." Now he'd been given a choice between family and an acquaintance, someone he hardly knew.

At the *yeshiva* they talked constantly about choices, too, entities that buzzed into people's ears. One was the *yetzer hatov,* the good inclination, and the other was its opposite, the evil urge.

He wondered now which had prevailed.

CHAPTER 7

AUNT VIVIAN WANTED Carlie to invite a date to Grandma Rose's birthday party. "You might enjoy the party more," Aunt Vivian said. "Arlene's bringing a date."

"Thanks, Aunt Vivian," Carlie said. "I don't think so." She felt funny about having Kip at a family party. But then Kip phoned to invite her out.

"How about coming to Catalina with us next Saturday?"

"Sure! I'd love it. Oh—nuts. I can't. It's Grandma Rose's birthday party here at the house."

"Oh, your grandmother . . ."

"Well, she's adopted me. She's Mitch's grandma." Carlie's thoughts raced. She said, "I was going to call you, Kip, to invite you. Aunt Vivian said I could invite a guest." Carlie held her breath. What if he said no? What if he said yes?

"Well, sure. I'd love to come," Kip said. "We can go to Catalina some other time."

"Twelve noon," Carlie told him. "It's for lunch."

Friday afternoon and Saturday morning passed in a blur of preparations. Carlie arranged flowers on all the tables. She baked frosted brownies and helped set the table with the best linen and the good china.

Everyone arrived at once. The house seemed to rock with their energy.

"So! Long time! God, it's hot—have you got air conditioning?" Cousin Leonard unbuttoned his Hawaiian shirt.

"Hi, Aunt Vivian. Nice to see you. This is my boyfriend, Paul." Arlene, skinny and fretful, peered into the house. "Is the dog put away? Where's the dog?"

"Out in the yard, honey," said Uncle Harry. "Don't worry."

"Beautiful house," sighed Cousin Leonard's girlfriend, Tilda. Stuffed into a tight red dress, she looked like an overgrown Kewpie doll. "I like the colors," she said. "Vivian, you're a marvelous decorator."

Leonard called out, "Is this Carlie? You're a young lady! Hasn't she grown?"

"Where's Mitch?" asked Leonard's son, Blake, looking around. "Isn't Mitch here?"

Kip stood behind all of them, smiling, looking more handsome than ever in his loose-fitting slacks, white shirt, and tie.

Carlie pressed her way past the relatives and went to him. She felt suddenly shy. Maybe this was a mistake, she thought, but she was glad, so glad to see him. Kip held a large bouquet in his arms.

"For the birthday grandma," Kip said. From behind his back he drew a single long-stemmed red rose wrapped in cellophane. "This is for you."

"Oh, Kip, that's so sweet." Carlie flushed as she read the card: *Thanks for inviting me—I know it will be a wonderful day. Kip.*

Behind her, Carlie felt a presence, like sudden wind. She turned and saw Uncle Utz, tall and reed thin, with his worried, inward look. "Uncle Utz!" She spoke softly. Utz seemed too frail for enthusiasm. "This is my friend, Kip Warner."

"Pleasure," said Utz, nodding, stepping back stiffly. "Nice to see you. Happy occasion. Birthday party. Mitch didn't make it?"

"No. He's still in Israel."

Carlie introduced Kip all around.

"Warner—Warner," said cousin Leonard, squinting at Kip. "Any relation to the ranch interests in the north valley?"

"My uncle," said Kip with a nod and a handshake.

"Ah, yes." Cousin Leonard's squint implied that he was making a quick calculation. "Very *good*," he said. "Are you going into ranching, too? I know the Warners are also into farm machinery, big suppliers."

"I just started college, sir," said Kip. "I'm hoping to go to veterinary school."

Aunt Vivian ushered Grandma Rose to the center of the living room, where she greeted everyone. Carlie brought Kip to her. Grandma touched Carlie's cheek.

"Carlie, Carlie," she murmured. "Such a beautiful girl." To Kip she said, "Isn't she beautiful, our Carlie?"

"She sure is," Kip said. "Happy birthday, Grandma." He presented the bouquet.

Grandma Rose took the flowers, beaming. "What a nice boy!" She stepped closer to Kip. "Are you Jewish?" she asked.

Carlie stifled a gasp.

"No," Kip said, smiling, looking amused. "I'm Irish."

"Well, I used to love that program, *Abie's Irish Rose,*" said Grandma Rose. "It was on the radio. I always say, you don't have to be Jewish to be a good person."

"Excuse us, Grandma," Carlie murmured, pulling Kip away. To Kip, she whispered, "I'm sorry."

"What for? She's wonderful. Reminds me of my grandmother. Irish, you know. She thinks everyone is, or ought to be."

The guests swiftly found the buffet table, laden with Grandma Rose's favorite salads and cold cuts.

Kip handed Carlie a plate and moved aside as Tilda pushed in front of him. "I'm starving," she gasped.

"Be my guest," Kip said.

Arlene and Paul, standing in line, gazed at each other with undisguised lust. Carlie tried not to notice.

Kip took a plate. He hesitated. "What's that?" he whispered.

"Smoked cod," Carlie said. "You don't have to eat it."

"I like to try new things," Kip said. He took some cod, and a large spoonful of chopped liver. "Bagels," he said, spearing one. "I like bagels."

"Paul hates this stuff," Arlene said. "It's so *ethnic.*"

Aunt Vivian, dishing up coleslaw, pretended not to hear, but Carlie saw her smile stiffen.

"So, I hear Mitch is into some weird cult in Israel," said Arlene.

Carlie pushed back her hair, her gaze steady upon Arlene. "No," she said. "He's studying at a *yeshiva.*"

"What's a *yeshiva*?" asked Arlene.

"It's a school, dummy," said her brother Blake. He reached for a brownie and ate half of it in one bite. Carlie saw how his hands trembled. He seemed even more tense than usual.

She gave him a smile. "How've you been, Blake? This is my friend, Kip," Carlie said.

"Hey, how's it goin'?" Blake nodded, his head lowered, eyes skimming around the room. "Anyone else coming? Where's Mitch?"

"Haven't you been listening, dummy?" his sister retorted. "He's in Israel."

"Well, he might have come back for the party."

"You know what the airfare is?" Leonard leaped into the conversation, forceful and loud. "You kids think money grows on trees."

"How could we?" Arlene snapped. "We hardly ever get any."

"Bingo," said Blake. He took a cigarette from behind his ear, glanced at Tilda, replaced it again.

Cousin Leonard heaped his plate high and sat down at the head of the table. Uncle Utz took half a bagel and a thin slice of lox.

"Utz! You never eat!" scolded Aunt Vivian. "Have some potato salad, for God's sake!"

"Utz," murmured Grandma Rose. "I haven't seen you for so long. Are you all right?"

"I'm fine," said Uncle Utz with his morose little smile.

Everyone settled down.

"So, Mitch didn't come home yet," said cousin Leonard.

Aunt Vivian cut her pickle into several slices. "That's right," she said. "Mitch is studying in Israel."

"I went to Israel once," said Tilda. "Right after the Six-Day War. I saw camels in the streets. You should go, Leonard."

"Camels I can see at the zoo," said Leonard. "You've been to Israel, Harry?" Leonard asked.

"No. All that nasty business with the Arabs. Of course, now with the *intifada* over, we thought it was okay for Mitch."

Cousin Leonard said, "I have no desire, myself, to see it."

Kip sat up very straight, listening, eating coleslaw.

From the living room came an occasional lyric, a sentimental oldie. Aunt Vivian had found CDs of Tony Martin and Bobby Vinton, Grandma's favorites.

"Well it's good we have a place," Tilda said stoutly. "If we'd ever need a homeland—I mean, after the Holocaust . . ."

"Please," said cousin Leonard. "This is a happy occasion." He poured cream into his coffee until it turned white.

"So, Mitch is going to be one of those guys with the black coat and the beard, *peyos*, even?" Cousin Leonard said.

"What's *peyos*?" Carlie asked. She was aware of Kip beside her, his movements, his warmth.

"Ha! You don't know what *peyos* is?" Leonard slapped the table. A cup jiggled.

"I know," said Blake. "It's long sideburns. Curls. They won't cut them off. Some religious reason."

"I've seen these guys," Leonard said, "the way they dress. Like something out of the Dark Ages."

"Mitch wears blue jeans," said Harry.

"Only kidding," said Leonard. "I didn't mean Mitch."

Blake leaned toward Carlie. "What happened with Mitch?" he said softly. "He was always so cool, so regular."

She shook her head. "I—he'll be okay," she said.

"Remember that Seder we all had at Grandma Rose's? When was that?"

"Four years ago," Carlie said. She remembered; it was the year her parents died.

"Mitch fell asleep at the table. I think he was drunk!"

"We all had too much wine," said Carlie. She looked at Kip. He was grinning.

"Like an Irish wake," Kip said. "Except we have whiskey."

"I remember that Seder," Blake went on, giving Carlie a wink. "Arlene was playing footsie with this awful guy she was dating—his name was Hunt or Fox. What was his name, Arlene?"

"Shut up, Blake," said Arlene.

"Mitch is just taking a little time off," said Aunt Vivian. She smiled brightly. "Actually, we encouraged him to go. Travel is broadening."

"So, he'll come back a little fatter," said Leonard, laughing. He lit a cigarette, waved the smoke aside, and called across the table, "Carlie, are you still dancing? Ballet?"

"No," she replied. "Not for over a year. It got too time-consuming." Scenes flipped through her mind—the feel of ballet shoes, gliding on the smooth, wooden floor to the music of Tchaikovsky. Maybe she'd been wrong to quit. Everybody had something they were passionate about—Blake and his business, Kip's dream of being a vet, Melanie's singing. Now Mitch had a dream, too. He had told her a certain name for it, but she couldn't remember the words, something about a journey. Everyone was on the road to somewhere, except for her.

"I took ballet when I was a little kid," said Arlene. "Now I'm into tai chi."

Kip and Paul were talking about baseball now; they were laughing, having a good time. Uncle Utz had fallen asleep, his head lolling to one side.

Kip took a spoonful of chopped liver. "Put it on some

bread," Carlie said, but it was too late. The struggle showed on Kip's face. He reached for water, drank deeply.

"What was that?" He grimaced.

"Chopped liver."

"Raw?"

"No. I guess"—Carlie stifled a laugh—"you have to acquire a taste for it."

Uncle Utz awakened with a grunt.

"So, this is your boyfriend, Carlie?" Tilda burst out.

Carlie wanted to laugh, to cry, to leave.

Cousin Leonard intervened. "Blake's got girls all over him," he said loudly. "That's why he moved out. Had to have his own phone lines. Only kidding."

Blake tapped his foot nervously; it made the table shake. "Would you excuse me? I've got to make some calls." He whipped a cell phone out of his pocket, punching in numbers as he strode out to the kitchen. Occasionally his voice echoed back. "You promised shipment last Tuesday . . . I'm tired of this bullshit . . ."

"You know what that boy grossed last year?" cousin Leonard said. "Harry, take a guess."

"Fifty thou," said Harry.

"Over a hundred and fifty thousand bucks!" cousin Leonard exclaimed. "This winter he's going into a line of sports clothing. Sells 'em by computer."

Kip's hand moved along Carlie's arm under the table. She clasped his hand and gave it a quick squeeze. From outside came a furious barking, a series of high-pitched yips.

"Carlie—would you go check on the dog?" asked Vivian.

Gratefully Carlie got up, taking Kip's arm. "Come with me," she said, and they went quickly out through the kitchen where Blake sat sprawled out in the breakfast nook, talking into his cell phone.

Outside, Arnie was ecstatic. Kip bent down and let the dog lick his face. "Great dog," Kip said.

"He's getting his ball," Carlie said. Arnie trotted back with a well-chewed tennis ball and dropped it at Kip's feet.

"Arnie loves parties," Carlie said. "I wish Arlene wasn't so uptight about dogs. Arnie wouldn't even bother her."

"No, if she's afraid of dogs, he'd know it. He'd be on her case in a minute."

Kip tossed the ball, and Arnie retrieved it, tail wagging. Soon the dog had enough, seeking relief under the tall ferns. Carlie looked around at the garden; it seemed so different now that she and Kip were here together. The bougainvillea hedges were in full bloom. Crimson and fuschia blossoms covered the fence and climbed up the pale gray side of the house. Carlie kicked off her sandals, luxuriating in the cool grass under her feet.

"Shouldn't we go back in?" Kip said, but he was looking at her as if he didn't want to move.

"We could sit down for a minute," Carlie said. Her heart was racing. "Arnie's so lonesome." She sat down on the grass in the shade. Kip sat down beside her.

Carlie sighed. "Why are families so strange?"

"Aren't they all?" Kip agreed.

"Here they are, come to celebrate Grandma Rose's birthday, but they hardly even talk to her."

"In my family half the people aren't talking to each other half the time," Kip said. "Last family picnic we had there were fifty-three people; ten of them were in a feud."

"I'd love a big family," Carlie said.

"It's fun sometimes. But Aunt Jenny was mad at cousin Patty because Patty thought it was great that Jenny's daughter went into the convent, but Jenny was still trying to talk her out of it." Kip threw up his hands. "They're all sort of crazy."

"Why? Wouldn't they like having a nun or a priest in the family?"

"No. One uncle's a priest already. Everyone figures that's enough. You know, like the old-time Catholics used to give one son to the king, the other to the church."

Carlie nodded, as if she understood. "I guess," she ventured, "it's sort of like Mitch going off to be—religious."

"I don't know about the Jewish religion," Kip said. "But for us, it's like losing someone. Like, when they go into the convent or the priesthood, they're marrying Jesus and leaving their family behind."

Carlie turned and saw Kip's eyes, and in them a look of concern. Why? she wondered. It was as if he knew her feelings, her sorrow and her longing. She felt suddenly tender, achingly tender. She breathed the fragrance of his hair, a faint sweetness; she saw the flecks of brown in his eyes. And as he drew closer she moved into his embrace with a sudden yearning so powerful that she never wanted this moment to stop, and she clung to him, kissing him back.

At last they drew apart, and Kip's eyes were wide and wondering as he said, "Carlie. Oh, Carlie—I—never knew you'd be so . . . I thought . . ."

"What?" She smiled at him. "What did you think about me?" she said teasingly. "That I wouldn't want to kiss you? Or that I didn't know how?"

"Well, I guess I thought you and Mitch . . ."

"Me and Mitch? What about us?" She felt stunned and confused—why would he be thinking about Mitch?

Kip seemed sorry, almost embarrassed. He looked away, saying, "It's nothing, just . . ."

"What? What are you saying?"

"I guess I thought you guys were sort of the dynamic duo, hanging out together, and sometimes I'd see you looking at him like—like he hung the moon!"

She felt numb, almost as if she had stepped into a void, and the words came out in an odd, distorted tone. "You thought that Mitch and I were—that we were . . ." Carlie pulled herself up and hurried toward the house. Images whirled in her mind, words and thoughts that were ugly and forbidden.

Kip came after her. "Carlie! Look, I'm sorry if I hurt your feelings. I didn't mean . . . I like you a lot, Carlie. I just never thought I had a chance. Are you mad?"

"No," she said. "I'm not mad. We'd better go in, Kip." The thoughts and the words continued—what people were saying, what they were thinking, that she and Mitch—what? Carlie pushed open the door and hurried past Blake, who was still on his cell phone.

The party had moved into the living room, and it seemed to be dying. Leonard and Harry sat in front of the TV watching pictures without sound. Arlene and Paul sat on the floor, holding hands. Utz was looking at a book. Vivian, Tilda, and Grandma Rose were arguing about vitamin E, arthritis, and cancer.

"Oh, here they are!" Vivian called as Carlie and Kip entered. "It's time for presents! Everyone—let's open presents!"

As Grandma Rose opened the presents, Aunt Vivian read each card out loud.

Carlie could feel Kip watching her. She felt his hand slip into hers, and she clasped it tight, as if he were an anchor to something she now desperately needed.

Grandma held up Carlie's gift, a white wicker basket filled with sachet and bath salts and pink glycerin soaps. She kissed the soap, blew Carlie a kiss, and mouthed, "I love you!"

Mitch's gift, delivered by Federal Express that morning, brought tears to Grandma Rose's eyes. It was a silver bracelet with a highly polished jasper stone, mottled pink and green. The bracelet was made of four intersecting slim bands of silver; the stone was mounted to one side, adorned with three silver leaves.

Vivian read the note aloud:

"Dear Grandma, my thoughts and my spirit are with you on your birthday. May you live to be 120! I made this bracelet for you myself. There is a fine silversmith shop where I have been able to get a small worktable. The jasper stone reminded me of you, the rose color for your name, and because it is both strong and beautiful. I love you. Mitch."

Everyone left soon afterward. Carlie walked Kip to his car. He had parked a block away, and she was glad, for he kissed her lightly on the lips and held her hands. "I had a great time."

"They're a little—much," she said.

Kip said. "They're great. And so are you."

They stood together for several minutes. Carlie didn't want him to leave. He touched her hair gently. "You know," he said, "I've joined a fraternity. We're having a Christmas formal. I know it's early to ask you, but—would you go with me?"

"I'd love to!" Carlie exclaimed.

"It's a date, then. December seventeenth. Saturday night."

She ran in, feeling elated, confused, excited all at once. Too much had happened, it seemed! He liked her! That thing about Mitch—how odd. How could he have thought that she and Mitch . . . ?

In the kitchen Vivian and Harry were stacking up the dishes. "Nice party, Vi," Harry said. "It would have been even nicer if our son had made the effort to get here."

"He sent a beautiful gift," Aunt Vivian said. "Grandma loved it."

"I thought he was staying there to study. Now he's fooling around with jewelry. He was doing that three years ago. I thought he'd gotten past that."

"Harry, you talk as if making jewelry is a criminal offense!"

"It's not my idea of a man's work, that's all."

Carlie, watching, bit her lip. Why did there have to be these scenes all the time? She wondered how it was at Kip's house, with his family.

"Male chauvinist," Aunt Vivian muttered as Harry retreated.

Carlie began to wrap the leftovers.

"What'd you say?" Uncle Harry snapped. "If you have something to say, tell me directly, don't mutter."

"All right." Aunt Vivian turned from the sink. She wiped her hands on a towel. "I think this thing has gone far enough."

"What thing?" Uncle Harry looked offended.

"Mitch."

"So, what are you going to do about it?"

"I didn't want to show you this letter, to spoil the party. It came this morning, along with Grandma's present." She reached for the pale blue envelope stuck into a brass holder on the desk.

"Mitch wrote?" Uncle Harry exclaimed. "Why would you hide his letter?"

"I told you. I didn't want a big discussion. Especially, I didn't want a family forum about this. Mitch wants money from his trust."

"We already know that," said Harry. "He's not getting it."

"Listen to me, Harry! Grandpa's will stipulated that the kids could invade the trust for educational purposes. Legally, Mitch can get that money, and he knows it. He's not stupid!"

"Damn!"

"There's more."

Carlie moved back into the shadows.

"Carlie, don't leave," said Aunt Vivian. "You're our—you're part of this."

Carlie moved to the breakfast nook. Thoughts drummed in her mind, awful thoughts. If Kip thought that she and Mitch were—in love, did her aunt think so, too? Was that why she wanted Mitch to go on the trip, to get away from Carlie? She remembered Vivian's words: "Carlie hangs on him too much."

Vivian was still holding Mitch's letter; her hand shook with her vehemence. "He can take his entire trust fund out and there isn't a thing we can do about it. But beyond that, he's met a girl."

Carlie felt her heart thumping. She was on a roller coaster suddenly, unable to make it stop so she could think. A girl? What girl?

"She's an eighteen-year-old Israeli girl. Apparently one of the rabbis arranged it."

"Arranged what?" Harry cried.

Aunt Vivian waved him aside. "I've been reading about all these sects. I haven't been just sitting around! These people try to get the kids married young. They don't want them to start fooling around."

"Vivian . . ."

"It's true!" she cried. "Eighteen is not unusual. Sometimes the girls are even younger."

"Are you saying that Mitch wants to get married?"

"I don't know what Mitch wants. I think he's being influenced." She gave him the letter. "Read it for yourself, Harry. He writes about this girl, this Miriam, as if she were a goddess."

Carlie watched as Harry scanned the letter. She wanted desperately to read it, but she only stood there, feeling betrayed, but not knowing how or why.

As Uncle Harry read the letter, his eyes widened. "You mean . . . he might get . . . married over there?"

Carlie cried out, "Why would Mitch get married? He's only eighteen." Her voice rose, and she trembled, her thoughts and feelings veering out of control. "Everyone's gone off the deep end suddenly—why is this such a big deal? Why shouldn't he be dating? What's the problem?"

"This is not just dating!" Vivian cried. "Haven't you listened to what I was saying? They don't just date! You know what I mean. You're not a child. And if he gets married, they've got him. For keeps!"

"So, what can we do?" asked Harry. He seemed stunned and meek.

"I'm going to find out what's going on."

"How?"

"The only sensible way. I'll ask Mitch. In person."

"You're going there?" Carlie said. "To Israel?"

"I thought we'd go next month," Vivian said, "over Christmas vacation."

"Vi, you know I can't leave the store during Christmas. It's our busiest season!"

"Actually, Harry," said Aunt Vivian, "I didn't mean you. I meant me and Carlie. We'll both go. We'll talk to Mitch. I think when he sees us—realizes what he has left behind here . . ."

Uncle Harry looked dumbfounded.

Carlie stared at her aunt. No need to ask whether she meant it; Carlie had seen that look on her aunt's face before, the day she came to their house in San Gabriel after the accident. She had told Carlie, "You're coming to live with us. I will love you and take care of you like my own. My sister would do the same for a child of mine."

Now Carlie shivered. She wanted to see Mitch. She wanted to go. But what was Aunt Vivian thinking? What did she mean, "When he sees us . . . "?

"Can you get tickets? Last minute, like this?" asked Uncle Harry.

"I've already talked to the travel agency. We'll get them."

"Well," said Uncle Harry. "You've been busy." He seemed stunned.

Aunt Vivian went to him. "Don't worry, darling. We'll be back by New Year's Eve. We'll go to the club party, like always."

"Sure, sure," said Harry.

"And we'll have Mitch with us, I promise." She turned to Carlie. "We'll go shopping, maybe we'll get you that red turtleneck sweater we saw at the mall. How about it?"

"Great," Carlie breathed. Something was wrong. *She's using me,* Carlie thought, *to get her son back. I'm the bait.*

CHAPTER 8

IT WAS ONLY three in the afternoon, but already the streets of Jerusalem were alive with the tension that always preceded the Sabbath. Pedestrians raced across boulevards, carrying bags of food, bunches of flowers, long loaves of bread. Drivers blasted their horns, careened around double-parked cars, calling out, "*Nu?* Are you crazy? Get out of the road!"

Mitch waited impatiently for the florist to finish up with the last customer, an elderly woman, her face a mass of smiles and wrinkles. "I always buy myself *Shabes* flowers," she chirped. "*Shabbat shalom!*"

"*Shabbat shalom,*" Mitch said.

The shopkeeper hurried to pull in the last of his buckets. "Yes?"

"I'd like a mixed bouquet and . . . ," Mitch hesitated, glancing around at all the flowers. "One rose. Separately."

"For a young lady." The man smiled broadly, selecting the rose with a flourish.

Mitch was glad to see that the rose was tucked into its

own small glass container, filled with water. It looked so elegant. He also had bought a handkerchief for Miriam, wrapped in blue tissue paper. He could imagine the white lace against her skin.

The man pulled a mixed bouquet out of the bucket and held it out for Mitch to see. Mitch nodded soberly, as if he had been buying flowers every Friday afternoon of his life.

The shopkeeper walked Mitch to the gate. He pulled it shut, saying, "*Yofi!* Have a nice day."

"Thanks, I will," said Mitch, laughing at the blend of Hebrew and American slang. He hurried along the boulevard, dodging cars and baby strollers, leaping over a low barricade. He wanted to whirl and dance. Instead, he only quickened his steps, calculating all that he must still do. He and Tal had discussed the options at length. He had to avoid driving after sundown, or even being driven.

"Usually you'd be invited to spend the night," Tal said, "but it might be awkward."

"Yes," Mitch agreed.

"So this is what we'll do," Tal proposed. "We'll take the bus to my house. From there you can walk to Miriam's, and after dinner you'll come back and spend the night with us."

"I don't want to impose," Mitch said.

"What? My folks are always asking about you. Tomorrow Halle and Richard and the kids are coming for lunch. They'll want to see you. You can't get out of it. You're with us."

Now the lilt spread through Mitch's body. He quickly undressed, turned on the shower full force, and bellowed out one of the Hebrew songs he had learned:

"How good it is and how pleasant,
Sitting together with brothers . . ."

Mitch hurried to dry himself. Others were waiting for the shower. He patted some lotion onto his face, feeling the soft hairs that covered his cheeks and upper lip and chin. The beard was still new, not entirely filled in yet, and it still surprised him every morning when he looked in the mirror. It made his face look fuller, more serious. But the biggest surprise was the reddish cast that appeared more plainly every day. How could one have brown hair and a reddish beard?

Richard was impressed and told him, "Red hair is supposed to be the mark of a *tsadik*. You should be proud and pleased."

Mitch had laughed. "Me, a *tsadik*? Ignoramus, more likely."

"Some wisdom is innate," Richard said. "You're on the path, Mitch."

The path. His new friends and teachers spoke about being on the path, as if all his life he had stumbled, straying from the center, and had just now found his way. Now, preparing himself for *Shabes* at Miriam's house, Mitch felt more whole and more centered than he could ever remember.

They made Mitch feel like a king. From the moment he arrived, everyone greeted him, offered him the best, listened to his words.

Miriam's two younger sisters and her little brother stood at the window, watching for him. "Miriam, Miriam, he's here!"

Miriam hurried out to greet him. Her movements were graceful; she wore a pale blue dress. "Hello. We are all glad to see you."

"Thanks. I'm glad, too." He gave her the rose and the tissue-wrapped package. She took them from him, carefully pressing her fingernail under the tape to save the tissue paper. She drew out the handkerchief, smiling. "Thank you, Mitch," she said softly. "This is so beautiful. Real—what do you call this?"

"Lace," Mitch said. He could not remember having said that word before. It had an exotic, romantic sound. "Lace," he repeated. He gave her the rose. "This is for you."

She took it from him, inhaling its fragrance. "How beautiful." She smiled her dazzling smile; he had never seen eyes like hers, large and lustrous.

He stood watching her, until she reached for the bouquet and said teasingly, "Are these for us, too?"

Mitch laughed. "Yes, of course. For you and your mother."

Miriam carefully arranged his flowers in a large vase and placed them on the coffee table. Then she went out, smiling back at him. She walked like a queen, elegant and composed.

"She is like a flower," Mr. Sarodi said, watching his daughter.

Miriam's little brother offered a tray full of roasted nuts and dried fruits. The little boy and his sisters ran back and forth, playing. Then they settled down on the floor with a game. Mr. Sarodi led Mitch to a large easy chair, obviously the best chair, and sat down beside him. "So, how is school? How is your family? Your parents are well? Do they call you on the phone?"

"Oh, yes. We talk every couple of weeks, at least," Mitch said.

"Strange to realize," said Mr. Sarodi, "that in America it is still morning. Your mother works?"

"She is a decorator, part time. She works on her own."

"So you get your artistic talent from her," Mr. Sarodi said. "Miriam tells me you do beautiful work. Silver. It is good to have work like this. Good for the pocketbook and also"—he patted his heart—"here."

Mitch could see into the dining room, to the long table set with a white cloth, beautiful dishes, and heavy silver candlesticks. Miriam and her mother moved back and forth with trays of food; their soft talk and murmurings to the children made a pleasant sound. Mr. Sarodi raised his hands in mock alarm. "The women always cook too much, but what can we do? We must eat, eat, or they are insulted." He laughed. "In California, people are thin, yes?"

"Not all of them," Mitch said. "My folks play a lot of golf and tennis."

"Ah. Yes, tennis. Here, we walk from sofa to table, yes? It is our best exercise." He nodded, glanced at Mitch. "Your parents, they don't mind you are so far away?"

"My father would like me to be home," Mitch said. "He wants me in his business someday."

"Of course." Mr. Sarodi nodded. The weight of unspoken complications lay between them; Mr. Sarodi sighed. "My father wanted me to be a tailor. Instead, I decided to mend books for a living. Here, there are plenty of books to repair, believe me."

Mitch could imagine his mother asking, in that quick, anxious way of hers, "What does the girl's father do? He binds books? How can he make a living?" Mitch would try to explain about the lifestyle here: the small houses, rooms stuffed with ancient furniture, floors creaking and bricks crumbling but somehow lasting for centuries. His mother would be appalled at the single tiny bathroom with its cracked tile and leaking faucets.

"They live differently in Israel," Mitch would say, but his parents would never understand. "They are happy," he would say. His mother would nod and try to smile. Happy was a concept tied up with other words, like "success" and "million bucks." He thought of his cousin Blake, suddenly, and he shuddered.

"You are cold?" asked Mr. Sarodi.

"No, I'm fine," said Mitch.

"You have brothers and sisters?" Mr. Sarodi asked, his tone casual.

"No. Only—my cousin lives with us. Her parents were killed in a car accident. She is two years younger than I." Carlie. He had not seen her in four months. Had she changed?

He remembered how she had changed before his eyes as the years slid away—twelve, thirteen, fourteen. Her legs grew long and firm, flashing when she ran, and her hair bounced, flowing and sassy. He remembered her misery when she first came, how she had shut everyone out, until he learned how to make her laugh. And suddenly she was no longer that miserable little girl, but almost a woman.

"Your parents are very good people to take in your cousin," said Mr. Sarodi, sizing it all up. "Your parents are from America? Originally?"

"My mom is," said Mitch. "My father came from Holland. During the—Holocaust." It was not a word he used often or with any degree of familiarity.

"Ah! He must have many stories."

"We don't talk about it much," Mitch said.

Mr. Sarodi jumped up as an old man approached the doorway. "*Aba!* Here, take my chair. Aba, this is our guest, Mitch Green, a friend of Halle and Richard. Mitch is from California. This is Miriam's grandfather, Amos," Mr. Sarodi explained. "Mother's father. We are glad he is home from the hospital now."

The old man extended a gnarled hand to Mitch, nodding slowly. His hair was still salt-and-pepper dark, but his brows were snow-white over eyes the color of dark water. His stance was cautious. He must be ninety, Mitch mused, older than Grandma Rose, but completely in control. He spoke to his son-in-law in a firm, almost commanding, tone.

Mr. Sarodi rushed out and returned with a frosted liquor bottle and three small glasses on a tray. He poured out a clear liquid.

"My father-in-law says we must begin with a special *L'chaim*. We drink *L'chaim!*—to life."

Mitch raised the glass to his lips. "*L'chaim!*" His voice blended with theirs. The liquor was sweet and strong, the taste of licorice.

"Arack," said the grandfather, licking his lips. "We make it here in Israel."

"It's time! They're here!" A frenzy of excitement erupted as Miriam's older sister, Orli, came in, followed by her husband with the baby. Orli gave Mitch a wide smile. "Glad to see you again! I know you from Halle's house, remember?"

"Of course," Mitch said. She was more outspoken than Miriam, not as beautiful, but then nobody was, he thought.

Everyone hugged and kissed; the children squealed. "Where do they live?" Mitch asked Miriam.

"Only four blocks away," Miriam replied. "They are with

us almost every *Shabes*. Come, we eat now."

Miriam showed Mitch to the place of honor beside the father. Everyone watched intently while Mr. Sarodi filled his goblet with wine. The father gave the blessing, his voice rising from a low chant almost into song. He poured a little wine into each glass. Everyone drank. They went to the small sink at the end of the dining room; a silver cup with two handles was used for the ritual washing of hands. Orli took the baby's hands and gently poured the water, murmuring the prayer in slow, quiet syllables. Silently then they returned around the table. The father lifted the cloth from the two loaves of fresh *challah*. Mitch joined with the others in the blessing. Mr. Sarodi sliced the bread, his gestures grand, and passed a piece to everyone. Then the talk burst out.

Miriam and Orli were animated by each other's presence. They drew Mitch in, along with Shuka, Orli's husband, discussing everything from the latest films to a protest at the parliament, the prime minister, subjects changing and flying, all accompanied by kisses to the baby. They passed him around, took turns admiring him, and the young father was flushed with that look of success that Mitch had seen only in football players or rock stars. Mitch felt the glow, the aliveness in himself.

Shuka leaned toward him, asking, "What do you think, your president will come to Israel? Is he good for the Jews?"

"I don't know," Mitch said. "I never thought about it that way."

It was a joke, they thought; everyone laughed. Not to have thought about politics, or the Jews? Impossible!

Miriam's mother spoke no English at all, but she seemed to keep everything going. One of the children started a song;

everyone joined in. The grandfather kept time on the tabletop, using the flat of his hand. Mitch knew the words, and he sang along. He thought of the barbecue kettle in the backyard at home, his father forking up huge steaks, yelling for mom to bring out the salad and baked potatoes—Carlie would be rushing in for cold drinks, yelling at Mitch to get off his duff and help—they would laugh and talk and kid around, but nobody ever sang. When they finished eating, the parents would go upstairs to their bedroom to watch TV, the kids might go cruising on the boulevard or run to the phone to call their pals. Food was food; dinner was quickly over. Here, everyone lingered.

An aunt and uncle and their three children came for dessert. Again, excitement prevailed; even the grandfather rose to embrace the newcomers, kissing, patting, leading them in.

Miriam told Mitch, "We are always together—this aunt and uncle and cousins. The children play. I hear in America people live far apart from their relatives. Is it true?"

"Well, yes. It's true."

"Isn't it lonely?"

"Yes," Mitch said.

"I would like to see America," she said. "But I don't think I could live there."

The minutes flew by; Mitch was aware only of Miriam's voice as they stood close together talking.

Back at the table, everyone was ready for dessert. The men argued about the stock market, hastily adding, "Not to speak of it on *Shabes*!" They criticized cabinet ministers, they complained about taxes, shouting and gesturing, until the aunt called out, "Politics! Politics! Is this talk for the *Shabes* table?"

Everyone laughed and settled down, but soon they started again, this time about the bombing of the Diezengoff Street bus.

There was a dark silence. The mothers sighed. "Of course, the schoolchildren are always under guard," said the aunt. "How is it in America? Also dangerous for children, isn't it?"

Mitch frowned deeply. "We worry about gangs and guns and drugs. A boy I knew at school," he said, "died of an overdose." The words slipped out so readily, unplanned. He had not realized he was thinking about Joel.

The adults made sounds of sympathy. "Yes. We have troublemakers here, too. We have drugs."

"The biggest problem," said Miriam, "is the terrorists, shooting over the border. My friend in the army is stationed at a school in the north. At night, often the children have to sleep in the bunkers, the rockets are coming over, and all the teachers run out with their rifles."

Mitch asked, "When will you go into the army, Miriam?"

Aunt and uncle looked down at their plates. Miriam's older sister glanced at her husband.

"Religious women do not go into the army," said the grandfather. He gestured with his fork. "Miriam does not want to go into the army."

Miriam murmured to Mitch, "Some of my friends have gone into the army. They work in offices or schools."

"Grandfather says it is not modest," said Orli. "I didn't go."

"You got married," Miriam said.

The grandfather said loudly, "What could be better than to have babies, like this beautiful little one here!"

Suddenly all eyes were upon Mitch.

Miriam's mother rushed to the sideboard and passed the cakes again. "Eat!" she said in English. "Eat."

It was late when he got to Tal's house. Tal sat outside on the porch hammock, waiting. "So, how was it at Miriam's?" he called out.

"It was wonderful," Mitch said.

"When are you seeing her again?"

Mitch leaned against the porch railing. "Wednesday," he said. He inhaled deeply; a sweetness filled his senses. "What's that smell?"

Tal laughed. "Some would say it's *Shabes* fragrance. Or it could be that hedge over there. What will you do on Wednesday?"

"Well, I'm not sure, but Orli said we could all take the children to the museum."

"Perfect, perfect!" Tal said.

"What's so great about that?" Mitch said. "Miriam didn't ask me. Her sister did."

"Well, of course, she put her sister up to it," Tal said. "Miriam likes you, Mitch, it's obvious."

"But when do I get to see her alone?" Mitch strode across the small porch. "When can we really talk?"

"For heaven's sake, use your imagination!" Tal said. "While Orli and the children are in the museum, you and Miriam can sit in the café and talk. Then, when you walk back to the house, you can talk again. Orli will go ahead with the children. She'll give you some space."

"What about at night?" Mitch said. He felt agitated, constrained. "I want to take her someplace nice. I want to spend time with her, real time."

"This isn't real?" Tal rose. "Look, I know it's hard to get used to. But religious girls don't go alone with a man, except to a public place. You can take her to a restaurant, but . . . you know. Nothing physical."

Mitch stood at the railing, looking up into the night sky. A hazy band of lavender lay at the horizon. Above, the stars were thick and bright. Suddenly he felt drained. Tal touched his shoulder. "Look, this is why I don't even go out," Tal said. "It can get frustrating. But you—I know you like to go out. You're used to the company of girls."

Mitch nodded, thinking of Carlie and all his friends back home. "It's true. But why wouldn't you even want to date?"

Tal shrugged. "Next year I'll be finished with school. I'll start working with my father in his insurance business. Then, when I have some money saved, I'll find a wife."

"Simple as that, is it?" Mitch smiled ruefully.

"It usually works out," Tal said. "I figured I'll be married by the time I'm twenty-three, then start a family . . ."

"A family," Mitch repeated.

"Well, that's the point, isn't it?"

"I don't think the grandfather likes me," Mitch said. "He asked whether my parents are religious."

"What did you tell him?"

"Miriam told him I'm a *ba'al teshuvah*."

"Ah, that's fine. What could be better? Look, you come to Torah learning by your own decision, not like someone born to it, without choice. The grandfather knows the saying 'Where a *ba'al teshuvah* stands, even the perfectly righteous cannot stand.'"

Tal led him to a small room with a narrow cot against one wall. The rest of the space was crowded with furniture and boxes of books and clothing. "I'm sorry it's so cluttered," Tal said.

"It's fine. Where will you sleep?"

"Oh, I'm sleeping on the sofa," Tal said. "No problem."

As he lay on the small cot in the darkness, Mitch recalled the entire evening. When the others had left, Miriam and her mother cleared the table, and Mr. Sarodi and Mitch and the grandfather sat together talking. The grandfather's family had come to Israel from Russia. "But back then, it was called Palestine," the old man said, nodding. "Seven generations of our family have lived here in Jerusalem."

"Seven!" Mitch exclaimed. "How did they get here?"

"Walked. From the Ukraine. It took five months. Thirteen people started. Eleven made it. One child died, and a woman, giving birth."

Miriam came in and sat on a low stool beside her grandfather. "Grandfather's family has many famous Torah scholars," she said proudly. Then Miriam told her grandfather, "Mitch is a *ba'al teshuvah.*"

The grandfather did not respond, but he began to chant, patting the sides of his chair. The three youngest children came and climbed on his lap, joining in.

At last Miriam took the two little girls by the hands. "Excuse me, Mitch," she said. "I take my sisters to bed now. Please wait, and I can say good night to you."

"Sure," Mitch said, rising to his feet. "*Lila tov,*" he told the little girls. The grandfather, too, excused himself, and Mitch and Mr. Sarodi were left alone.

"She is lovely, my Miriam, isn't she?" said the father. "Pardon me, I see how you look at her. I was the same when

I first met her mother. From the first moment, I knew I would never marry another woman."

Mitch sat up on the edge of the bed. His mind raced. He felt caught in a whirlwind. How could they talk of marriage? Miriam wanted to go to school, into the army, despite what her grandfather said. Marriage was years away. Obviously, Miriam's father wasn't thinking marriage; he had to know Mitch couldn't support a wife. The very idea was preposterous.

He thought of Tal's comments, no contact, nothing physical. How many times could he possibly sit at their *Shabes* table, talking to Miriam, watching her move, and then walk away without even touching her? It was too much to expect.

He remembered Diane, the girl he'd gone with a year ago, her round, happy face and frizzy dark hair. Diane laughed all the time, teasing and flirting. She had driven him nearly crazy with her tight T-shirts and gestures, and when things got really heavy, she had pushed him away.

"Are you safe?" she had asked, leaning away from him in the car, her face suddenly closed off, her eyes angry.

"I—I don't know," he had gasped, fighting the urgent pounding of his heart, the sensations within him erasing every other thought.

"Well, have you been tested?" Diane asked sharply, tucking in her T-shirt, her hand on the car door.

"No, I mean, I've never . . ." He couldn't tell her the truth, that this was the first time he'd even come close. She would have shrieked with laughter, maybe, told everyone that Mitch, the basketball ace, was just a kid, a virgin.

"Wise up," she'd said harshly. She got out of the car.

"Let me take you home!" Mitch had pleaded. "At least let me walk with you."

"It's okay. I can find my way. Don't bother."

Two weeks later Diane was making it with Chuck Frazier. Everyone knew. Chuck Frazier just about drew pictures for all the guys on the team.

Mitch lay down again, his spine stiff and aching from the metal bedsprings and from his own tension. Home, California, the San Fernando Valley, all seemed so far away, another world, another life. He wondered whether, if he went home now, things would look familiar. Or had he gone too far away ever to return?

CHAPTER 9

CARLIE TRIED TO phone Mitch. The line was busy, or there was no answer. Finally someone responded, and after what seemed an interminable bout of questions and answers, Carlie was told, "Green? Mitch Green is gone. To the Negev. For retreat."

"Wait!" Carlie shouted into the receiver. "When will he be back?"

"Ten days."

She called again into the receiver, "What's the Negev?" but it was too late; the speaker had hung up.

The next afternoon Carlie went to the library to look it up. She found it in a book about the deserts of the world. And there it was, on glossy pages before her: rock mountains, vast sky, and bleak descriptions: "Barren, desolate, dry."

She imagined Mitch there, wandering endlessly in the wilderness. And as Carlie sat with the book, she felt bereft. Mitch was far beyond her reach. For the past four years they had been a twosome, us against them, like brother and sister only better, because they hadn't been babies together and were still learning what it was like to have someone else around all the time, someone nearly the same age.

"Did you like being an only child?" Carlie had once asked Mitch.

"I never thought much about it," Mitch answered. "My mom always thought it was terrible that I didn't have brothers and sisters. So they got me Arnie. Much better than a brother, don't you think?"

Carlie and her parents had kept a tight schedule, with wedges of "quality time" carefully arranged, dutiful times that had to be honored, no matter what. Then there was "adult time," another sequence that, as her mom explained, "is private time for me and Daddy."

With Mitch, things could unfold: They'd sit on the floor in the den watching TV together; they'd take Arnie for a run or hit tennis balls back and forth for hours, not even keeping score, just playing. That was the great thing about being with Mitch—he didn't have to define things all the time or keep score or make plans in advance. It was just easy and fun, and sometimes he amazed her with his ideas. He was smart, though you wouldn't really know it; he didn't study enough to get mostly A's, as she did. He had other things going on in his head, things he wouldn't talk about. Then he'd retreat into his room or out to that workshop in the garage. She'd go after him, wanting company.

"Leave me alone," he'd yell. "I'm busy."

Mitch would remain silent behind his closed bedroom door. She supposed he was working on something—an intricate design, a mobile or a bit of jewelry contrived from a piece of bone, a polished stone and a leather thong. Later he would emerge, and she would admire his creation.

Now, as Carlie beheld the picture on the page, it seemed as if Mitch had vanished into it. Behind that pillar, surely, he was hiding. Or just around the curve of that hill, in the cleft of a rock, beside that trickle of a stream, where it had meandered off the page—surely there Mitch was waiting.

She sat with the open book, feeling a growing sense of confusion and embarrassment. Times when they'd wrestled on the floor, or Mitch caught her by the shoulders and thrust her, hard, against the wall—times when he'd rushed into the bathroom, having forgotten to knock first, and she stood there in her underwear. What had she felt, then? What did she feel about Mitch now? She didn't know.

"Try Mitch again," Aunt Vivian said.

Carlie stood with her back against the kitchen counter, feeling rigid, angry. "Why don't *you* call him? You're his mother." She heard the reproach in her voice; she wasn't going to soften it.

Aunt Vivian's frown was deep and sorrowful. "He always argues with me, Carlie. With you, he's mellow. He doesn't feel threatened. Please call him," she said. "Don't you want to?"

Carlie relented. "Sure. I'll call." Aunt Vivian, standing beside her, seemed smaller, somehow. Or maybe Carlie had grown. She wished her aunt and uncle wouldn't depend on her, as if she were the last and only hope. What if she failed?

Uncle Harry waited in the breakfast nook with the newspaper held up like a shield, but Carlie knew he would be listening to every word. Aunt Vivian stood beside Carlie, hands clasped and coaching. "Tell him we won't interfere with his studies," she whispered. "Tell him we won't stay too long."

Carlie tensed as the phone rang and rang. At last someone answered. "*Shalom!*"

"I'd like to talk to Mitch Green. Is he there?"

There were shuffling sounds, loud talk, then Mitch was on the line. "Hello?"

"Mitch, it's Carlie."

"Hey, Carlie! They told me someone phoned. A beautiful American girl, they said." He laughed.

"I've been calling all week. Where were you? What were you doing?"

"I went on a retreat, a hike. It was fabulous, Carlie! We went into the Sinai. Part of the way we took camels. Oh, I can't even describe it but, hey, I've got a workshop now, a small room in back of a store that sells artifacts and jewelry. I've got so many ideas. I'm making a huge collage. It was inspiring, those shapes and textures in the desert. I'm thinking of combining copper with cloth—burlap, you know?"

"It sounds wonderful," Carlie said. "Maybe you should show me," Carlie said. Her heart raced. Mitch sounded so happy; like that summer he'd worked in the garage, he'd come in glowing and excited. She felt a twinge of envy.

Mitch said, "How was Grandma's party? Did she get my present?"

"She loved it, Mitch. It was the best. Mitch, I guess you didn't get my drift," Carlie said. "Do you want to show me the Negev? Would you like to take me around Jerusalem?"

There was silence for a long moment. "What are you saying?"

"Your mom said she'll bring me. We can see the country. We could come over Christmas vacation. You wouldn't have to break up your studies. We'd take a tour bus . . ."

"No way."

"What?"

"No tour. We *walk* Jerusalem, from one end to the other." He sounded jubilant. Carlie felt the excitement rushing through her body, down to her fingertips. "Carlie, do you mean it? Are you really coming?"

"You want us to?"

"What do you think?"

"Why do you keep asking questions?"

Mitch laughed. "Sorry. It's the style here. Of course I want you to come! What do you think I am, crazy? When are you coming? Where will you stay? Tell Mom . . ."

"I'll put her on, Mitch."

Carlie handed the receiver to her aunt, nodding, mouthing the words, "Yes. It's okay."

Aunt Vivian stood with the phone pressed tightly to her ear, scarcely breathing. "Yes. Yes. Yes. Of course. We will. December fourteenth. We arrive the next day, at two in the afternoon. Oh, Mitch, I can't wait to see you!"

Aunt Vivian put down the receiver.

Uncle Harry appeared. "So you're going," he said.

"Yes. Everything's settled." She gave Carlie a strange look. "What's the matter, Carlie? You look as if . . . are you sick?"

"Kip Warner," Carlie said slowly, "asked me to go to his fraternity dance with him on December seventeenth. It's formal, a Christmas dance. I accepted."

There was a gap, then the outburst. "What?" Vivian cried. "You accepted without checking with me first? Why would you do such a thing?"

"I'm sorry. I didn't know the dates, Aunt Vivian. Can't we change the tickets?"

"No, we can't change the tickets, are you nuts? You don't know what I had to go through to get those tickets. Why did you accept without asking me?"

"I thought it was okay." She held back her anger. "You always want me to—to mingle more."

"But you knew we were leaving for Israel, Carlie! It was all planned. Did you forget? How could you forget such a thing?"

It took all Carlie's resolve not to shout. She gritted her teeth. "I told you, I didn't know the dates. We hadn't even reached Mitch yet. I thought we were going the week after school was out. You never want us to miss school."

"Well, you'll have to miss a couple of days. It was the only reservation I could get," Vivian said. "You'd better call Kip and tell him."

"What'll I tell him? I feel so dumb."

"You were dumb," Vivian shouted. "You didn't think."

Harry intervened. "She isn't dumb, Vivian, what's wrong with you? She just made a mistake, that's all. Pull yourself together."

"Don't tell me to pull myself together!" Aunt Vivian cried. "I have been under so much stress! I'm not doing this for my pleasure. I'm going to bring back our son. I thought Carlie cared about him, I thought she . . ."

"I do care about Mitch!" Carlie cried out.

Harry looked abashed. "Look, you made her cry. Don't cry, honey, please."

"I'm not crying!" Carlie exclaimed. She ran to her room and closed the door, sat down on the bed, her hands covering her face.

She wanted to flee, both from them and from her own thoughts. What does it mean to care for someone? Really care? Does it have to be everybody's business? What if you think about someone and miss them and are angry and jealous all at the same time—does that mean love? And if it's love, does that mean you also want to be—physical?

Last night she'd had that dream again, of herself swimming in the ocean, swimming until she was exhausted. Just ahead of her in the waves was Mitch, his shoulders glistening from sun and water. No matter how hard she swam, he was always still far away. Nor did she call his name, because crowds of people stood on the shore, watching and wondering what she would do. And she knew that once she called to him, nothing would ever be the same again.

She heard a soft knock at her door. "Carlie, why don't you phone Kip and explain. I'm sure he'll understand," said her aunt. "Do you have his number?"

"Yes." She wanted to say "go away," but she didn't.

"I had an idea, Carlie. You could invite him to the New Year's party at the club. It's formal, too. We'll get you a beautiful dress. You could wear your mom's rhinestones. How about it?"

Carlie opened the door. She stood with the half-open door between them. "I was thinking about Mom's rhinestones, too," Carlie said, her voice muffled.

"Maybe it's time," Vivian said, "for you to take all her things now. You're nearly grown up. I mean, if you want to."

"No!" Carlie exclaimed. "No, I don't want them now, Aunt Vivian. It's okay. I'll just get the rhinestones when I need them. I'll call Kip now."

Her aunt reached out, then withdrew. "All right, Carlie."

Carlie sat down at her desk. Her room had once been the den. Uncle Harry had ripped out half the bookcases to make space for her bureau. He had put an extra rod into the closet, and bought a hanging bag with separate little compartments for her shoes. Carlie remembered the day he had come home with the things for her closet—two packages of white plastic hangers, a large garment bag, and that bag for the shoes. He had held it out to her, trying to smile through his frown, trying to make it all right.

Now she picked up the phone and dialed Melanie's number. She was glad for the comfort of Melanie's voice, and she let herself go. "You won't believe this," she said heavily. "I can't go to the dance. We're leaving for Israel for two days before. Isn't that a bummer?"

"Well, but you get to travel," said Melanie. "You get to see Mitch."

"Yeah. I always wanted to travel. But I'm supposed to make Mitch come home. What if he won't come? My aunt will be so upset. She thinks I can talk him into it."

"Maybe he's ready, anyhow," Melanie said. "He's probably tired of all those classes. Maybe we should all write him notes, you know? All his friends—tell him we miss him and want him to come home. Think so?"

"Yeah, great idea," Carlie said, but without enthusiasm. "I'd better call Kip."

She called Kip's house. He happened to be there, sounding surprised and pleased. "Hey! I was thinking about you," he said. "I'm renting a new tux, and I want to figure out the color. What color dress will you be wearing to the dance?"

"Oh, Kip, I hate to tell you this."

"What's wrong?"

"I've got some bad news, Kip. I can't go."

"What? Why not?" He sounded stunned.

"My aunt is taking me to Israel. We're leaving on the fourteenth, and we can't change it. All the airlines are sold out—it's Christmas season."

"Yes, I heard," Kip said dryly.

"Kip, I'm really sorry."

There was a silence that lasted too long. "I wish you'd told me before," Kip said. "Now it's going to be impossible to get a date."

"I'm sorry, Kip! There's been so much going on here."

"Seems like it would be hard to forget something like that."

"I know it sounds stupid. . . ."

"Carlie, why do you have to go? I'm sorry—of course you'd want to go. I—I'm just kind of surprised. I have to think. Listen, I'm driving back to campus with a friend. I'll call you later."

"I'm really sorry, Kip," Carlie repeated. He won't call, she thought.

"Have a good time in Israel," he said.

Sometimes I dream that I'm in our old house, and Mom is in the kitchen, putting away all this food she just bought at the supermarket. She's got everything organized, and she looks beautiful in her good suit and gold earrings and her bangle bracelets. I go to her and I put my arms around her, tight, and I just cry and cry, and she asks, "What's the matter, Carlie Baby?" And I say, "You're okay. You didn't die—it was a mistake."

And I feel so happy. Then I wake up and realize it was a dream. Sometimes I hear something in the news about the 210 Freeway, and I just cringe. I know it was in the newspapers, but I didn't read the articles. I couldn't. Aunt Vivian kept the newspaper clippings in a box, along with a lot of other stuff, mostly Mom's personal things, what she called her junk, that old costume jewelry, and all these cookbooks. Daddy always brought takeout during the week, ever since I can remember, or he grilled hamburgers or hot dogs. On weekends Mom made fancy casseroles and sometimes cookies. The cookbooks are all in a box saved for me, in case I want them someday. I don't want them.

Carlie put her journal on top of her red sweater and plaid slacks and turtleneck top. Her aunt had advised her to pack lightly. "We may have to carry our luggage," she said. Still, every day she reminded Carlie of more necessities. "Don't forget your hair dryer and that special converter. Bring your vitamins. Let's take some soap—I hate hotel soap. Let's bring something for Mitch, something from home."

"How about Arnie?"

"Very funny. I know, we'll bring him some tapes. You pick out what he likes, Carlie."

To everything Carlie nodded and said yes. She felt anxious, cut off already, a little afraid. She had never been so far from home before. The journal would be like a friend.

Carlie suddenly didn't want to go. What if they were hijacked? What if they crashed? What would become of Harry and Mitch? Arnie, lying on the rug beside Carlie's bed while she packed, let out a loud groan.

A clatter came from downstairs, then Aunt Vivian called, "Carlie! Melanie's here."

Carlie leaped from the bed. "Hi! I'm glad to see you. I

was just suffering from separation anxiety."

Melanie smiled. "Maybe this will help." She held out a small package. "Something for your trip," she added.

"Melanie, how sweet!" Carlie took the gift, smiling. "I'm only going for two weeks. But I love presents." She tore off the wrappings and took out a silk scarf in shades of blue and green. "It's beautiful, Mel. Thank you."

"Actually," Melanie said, "my mom bought this at a Hanukkah boutique. We thought you'd like it for Israel. When you go to a church or a synagogue, you know, they want you to have your head covered."

"That's really nice of your mom. Thanks. Sit down. Don't mind the mess," Carlie said.

"I really can't stay long," Melanie said, still standing. "I just came to bring you the scarf and . . ." Melanie's eyes were fixed on Arnie. She bent to pat his head. "I wanted to check something out with you," she said. "Like, well . . . are you in love with Kip?"

Carlie faced her friend, shaking her head, smiling self-consciously. "I don't know, Mel. He's great and gorgeous and . . . how do you know when you're really in love?"

"You'd know," Melanie said, her eyes narrowed, expression vague. "You just think about him all the time. You dream about him."

"I like him a lot," Carlie said.

"But you're not actually *in love*, are you?"

Something in Melanie's tone caught Carlie by surprise. "What's wrong, Melanie? Did something . . ."

"Kip called me last night."

Carlie felt an odd sensation, as if a gap had opened in the atmosphere. Kip? Called Melanie?

Melanie's eyes scanned the room. Her words were swift. "He invited me to that fraternity dance. I told him I'd have to think about it. I mean, I thought I'd ask you and—if it would upset you, I'd just . . ."

"Upset me?" Carlie's hands began to shake.

"I figured, it isn't as if the two of you are actually *going* together, so, I figured you wouldn't actually mind."

Carlie braced herself, arms crossed over her chest. "I said I wasn't in love with him. That doesn't mean I want you to start dating him. Give me a break, Melanie!"

"Forget it." Melanie threw up her hands. "I really didn't think you'd mind. I've never been to a formal before. My mom even said it's okay to go, as long as you and Kip aren't actually *going* together."

Carlie turned, about to back away, then she stood firm. "Well, I do mind, Melanie. I finally find someone I like, and now just because I'm going on a trip, you think you have the right to move in on him." She clenched her hands, felt the amethyst ring digging into her fingers.

"Good grief." Melanie groaned. "You don't own Kip Warner. What do you expect me to do?"

"I guess I expect you to act like a friend."

"He's the one who called me, Carlie! Okay? Can I help it if he wants to take me? Why should I stay home? You're going to be away, having a great time. You're going to be with Mitch."

"So what? What's Mitch got to do with it?"

"You just want all the guys. You always did!"

"Liar!" Carlie shouted, furious. "It's entirely different," Carlie cried. "Mitch is my *cousin*."

"So what?" Melanie looked strangely jubilant. "I always thought you had a thing for Mitch."

"Shut up, Melanie. This is disgusting."

"Why? Actually, in some states, cousins can get married. It doesn't mean your children turn out crazy or deformed, you know. That's an old wive's tale."

"Shut up!" Carlie cried.

"If it isn't true, why are you so mad?" Melanie moved in closer. Her eyes were narrowed, her breathing rapid, like an animal that has cornered its prey. "From day one you were always butting in whenever I'd talk to Mitch even for a minute. If I even looked at him when I came over, you'd get on my case. Don't you realize it? Mitch is all you ever talk about. You're in love with him. . . ."

"You're crazy, Melanie."

"Who's crazy? You can't even get in touch with your feelings."

"Get out!" Carlie yelled. "I don't need this. I'm trying to pack."

"Do your packing. Good riddance."

"Take your scarf!"

"I will not!" Melanie rushed out, letting the door slam.

Carlie ran after her. She threw the scarf down the stairs. It billowed in the air like some fragile flower before it floated slowly down. The front door slammed shut. Vivian came to the stairway. "What's going on? What's all that shouting about!"

"Nothing!" Carlie yelled.

She hardly slept that night.

If twenty people say something is true, does that make it

so? What about ten people? Or five? Or three?

In the morning her throat was sore, and her back ached. "I can't go," she imagined telling her aunt. "I'm sick. I think I'm coming down with the flu."

But Carlie put on the new red sweater and smiled brightly as they waved good-bye to poor Harry, who stood in the doorway, feigning a hearty smile. She could see through his mask anytime.

CHAPTER 10

MITCH STOOD WITH Haim, the proprietor of the small jewelry shop, leaning into the waist-high window. "Here. We put these in the safe," Haim said. "The rest can stay for the night, for the tourists to see."

Mitch sprayed the glass and wiped it with a rag, then he took the jewelry tray from Haim and watched him arrange the small oil lamps and wooden figures in the window. The figures, about two inches high, reminded Mitch of Grandma Rose's little men, except that these were fertility goddesses, idols with rays around their heads, pointed breasts, and wide hips. People used to pray to these, Mitch thought wonderingly.

"You want to lock up when you're finished?" Haim asked.

"Yes," Mitch said. "I'd like to stay and work awhile longer."

"Okay. Listen, this woman from Connecticut gave me a credit card, but I can give you the cash now if you need it."

"Actually, I could use it," Mitch said. "My mom and my

cousin are coming to visit. I can take them out."

Haim reached into his pocket and drew out a stack of bills. He peeled off several, counting. "One hundred eighty dollars. Okay? I take ten percent commission."

"That's fine, Haim. Thanks." Mitch felt the flush on his face, that feeling of elation. His collage would be hanging on the wall in some house by the beach in Connecticut! It was one of his "Negev" themes, wide swathes of color and texture, mountainous regions dipping down into deep valleys, blending into a broad sky that seemed to change as one stood nearer or farther away.

"It is a small masterpiece," said Renate, Haim's wife. "Really. You are good."

Miriam thought so, too. Everyone—Tal and the other students, Rabbi Nachum and Halle and Richard—all thought his art was something to be proud of. Here, nobody said anything about "man's work" or putting bread on the table.

Late November, Mitch and Miriam were walking along King George Street, eating crisp bits of falafel from small waxed paper bags. Tantalizing smells of food came from the many shops and sidewalk stands: pizza and falafel, pita pockets stuffed with humus and vegetables, and the spicy, paper-thin sliced beef called *schwarma*. They passed the shop of a local artisan.

"Your work is as good as this," Miriam said, pointing to an intricate silver necklace in the window. "No—it is better." She smiled up at him.

"Thank you," he said. "I am making you a present for Hanukkah."

"What is it?"

"I won't tell. It's a surprise." He had been working on the pendant for weeks. "Today, back home," he said, taking a bite of falafel, "it's Thanksgiving." His thoughts were bombarded by pictures of home, like still shots in the midst of a movie—Arnie begging at the table; Carlie laughing and eating sweet potato pie, her favorite; his mother bringing in a huge roasted turkey on a platter; his dad saying, "Now we'll be eating turkey for a week!" but there was gladness in his voice. His dad loved Thanksgiving.

"What's Thanksgiving?" Miriam asked.

He was astonished. "You're kidding me. Don't you know?"

"No."

"Well, it's a day for being thankful."

"I am thankful every day," Miriam said. "Aren't you?"

"Of course. But Thanksgiving is—well, it's a holiday. To celebrate the harvest. There's more to it, but everyone eats a lot. It's one big party."

"Oh. I see. Like Sukkot."

"Well, yes. Exactly." He wanted to hug her. If they had been in America, he would have kissed her right here, on the street. And he wondered, if he brought Miriam to America, would she change? Would he want her to? Or might she simply wither, like a wildflower ripped from its field?

He said, "My mother and my cousin are coming to visit in a couple of weeks."

She stopped walking and stood looking pensively into a shop window. "They will take you back," she said.

"Nobody takes me where I don't want to go," Mitch replied. He wanted to put his arm around her shoulder; he resisted.

"How long are they staying?"

"Until the thirtieth. They want to be home for New Year's."

"Only two weeks?" Miriam scoffed. "You can't see Israel in such a short time."

"Well, they can see me. And you."

Miriam shook her head. "They don't come here to see me. They must see the land! Take them to the Negev, and they must see the Golan and a *kibbutz* and Kinneret . . . they will want to walk through the Old City."

"Will you come with us?" Mitch asked. "You could show them everything and explain."

"I don't know enough."

"But you love it so!"

"Yes. I love every blade of grass."

He stood for a moment, looking at her reflection in the shop window. "Have you thought about visiting the United States?" he asked.

"Maybe." She gave him a swift glance. "Some friends of ours moved to California. He was getting a good job there. They come back every two years, and the wife cries. She wants to raise her child here. It is a terrible thing. I would never leave Israel. I would rather die."

Mitch felt her passion, mixture of love and longing, and he wondered how it would feel if Miriam loved him the same way, and if he and she were together here, in Israel. Would she come back to California with him, ever? Would she change her mind?

Miriam glanced at him, then looked away. "Tell me about your mother."

"Oh, you'd like her," Mitch said. "She's easy to talk to.

She loves to entertain. Like your parents," he said quickly, thinking of the *Shabes* dinner, although his mother's parties weren't anything like that. "She's artistic."

"Oh, she is an artist, like you!"

"No, she's a decorator."

"What does she decorate?"

"Homes, mostly. She's also done some doctors' offices."

"She gets paid for this?"

"Of course. It's her career."

Miriam sighed. "She will say I am a stupid schoolgirl."

"No, she won't!"

"I have no career," Miriam said. "Only some sketches in my sketchbook."

"Nobody expects you to have a career," Mitch said. "You're only eighteen."

"I want to go to University," Miriam said, her color deepening now, her eyes bright with passion. "My family is always talking about me, saying yes or no. Don't all girls in America go to University?"

"If they can afford it," Mitch said. "And if they have good grades."

"I'm perfect in school!" Miriam exclaimed. "Almost every paper, one hundred percent."

"Then you should study, if that's what you want," Mitch said earnestly.

Miriam gave him a look of wonder, almost of pity. "You really do not know how it is," she said. "You would never understand it."

"Try me!"

She shook her head. "It is too hard to explain. Maybe another time."

That night Miriam telephoned Mitch and invited him and his mother and Carlie for *Shabes* dinner the day after their arrival. "They will have time to rest," Miriam said. "Is it all right?"

"Yes. We'd love to come," Mitch said, his mind rushing over the arrangements. His stomach felt queasy. He had not felt like this since the day he had first met Tal at the Wall. He tried to imagine his mom talking to Mrs. Sarodi, Miriam and Carlie side by side—it was too strange. What would they say? How would they know what to do?

Things always seemed to happen too fast, control veering away from his grasp.

Tal's father lent him his old VW. It was rusty in places where the paint had worn off. One side of the front bumper hung down. The upholstery was cracked; dirty cotton stuffing showed through. The car smelled stale from too many miles and hot days.

Mitch left himself two hours to get to the airport, to park the car, and rush to the terminal, a huge building swarming with people. Travelers streamed out in all directions, pushing luggage carts, dragging their bags, herding their children, rushing to embrace relatives. They looked around with wonder; some ducked down and kissed the ground.

Mitch parked the car and hurried to the building. "May I see your ticket?" said a guard. He was young, armed with an *Uzi*.

"I'm meeting people from the U.S."

"Only travelers allowed inside," a soldier said, with the typical tough frown that Mitch had come to expect in such cases. Too often the Jews had been accused of being meek, too agreeable, going silently to the slaughter. The young Israelis were eager to change that image. "You wait outside for your people," the soldier grumbled. "Here, behind the ropes."

On the sidewalk an Arab woman, with her full retinue of relatives, bent over an open suitcase, distributing gifts.

The soldier strode over to her. His strong gestures and loud voice left no doubt as to his message: Get out of here. Pack up and go home.

Mitch felt the tension. Bombs were always a threat. On the city streets, lost in one's own affairs, things seemed almost normal. Here at the airport the danger was apparent from the watchful, mistrusting glances and curt orders. "Step back! Step away from the building," spoken in English, repeated in Hebrew, grumbling and sharp.

Mitch waited, searching among the travelers who came out, all walking with that peculiar traveler's gait—tiredness and concern.

He saw her first, struggling with her bags and looking bewildered, and he marveled at the strangeness that a few months' absence can bring. She seemed like a parody of herself, not the mother he had always known, and yet he could not pinpoint the changes, not at all.

"Mom!" he called. "Over here. I had to wait out here."

"Mitch! Mitch!"

He hurried toward her, and she threw down her bags, waving her arms in the air. "Mitch!" Her voice seemed too shrill, too American. People turned to look. A man smiled knowingly.

"My God, Mitch, is it you? Is it really you? I've been searching all over—we've been here for half an hour already, our flight was early. Let me look at you! My God!"

She pulled him toward her. The scent of her was both strange and familiar. She felt small in his arms, and stiff.

"Mom." He drew back to see her face, tears and smiles together. The lines on her forehead looked deep. Her hair was freshly colored, he could tell, but the artificial blondness struck him now as being coarse.

"Look at you!" she exclaimed. "I wouldn't have recognized you. Mitch, you've actually got a beard! When did you grow a beard? Doesn't it itch?"

"No, it doesn't itch," he said, laughing. "Where's Carlie?" He felt a jolt of disappointment. "Didn't she come with you?"

"Ladies' room. It's one of the few Hebrew words we learned on the way—you know, that little book of phrases—*sherutim*," she said proudly. Her eyes narrowed as she plucked at his jacket. "Mitch, you're so thin! Darling, you look so drawn, so thin."

"Not really. It's this coat."

"Where on earth did you find it?"

"One of the guys took me to a shop—what's wrong, Mom?"

She hung on his arm, crying, wiping the tears with her scarf. Bluish eye makeup smeared onto her cheek.

"Here, let's get your luggage out of the way," Mitch said, making his tone brisk. And then he saw Carlie running toward them and he forgot the luggage and his mother and he ran, too, and caught her around the waist, holding her off a little to look at her, but she flung herself at him like a child, wrapping her arms around him so tightly that it took his breath away.

"Mitch! You look great," she exclaimed. "Distinguished with that beard, I must say. Where did you get that jacket? It's so cool! I saw a guy at Tower Records in Hollywood wearing a coat like that. I think he was a rock star. I brought you the newest tape, just out, Nirvana. You don't have it yet, do you?"

Mitch shook his head, laughing, watching the way she moved when she spoke, seeing how long her hair had grown, how it gleamed. The years tumbled back over him, and feelings he had forgotten, all the feelings that Carlie's presence provoked—wonder and doubt, glee and confusion. She was a presence; she made things happen, shining things. How could he have forgotten?

"Thanks," he said, taking the tape. "I don't have it yet. How did you know what I wanted? It's great to see you. How was the trip?"

"Great," said Carlie.

"Terrible," said his mother. "I was never so cramped in my life. Couldn't sleep more than three hours. People were constantly talking, roaming up and down the aisles."

"They never stopped feeding us," Carlie said. "I'm still stuffed. Mitch, I'm so excited to see you! I can't wait to see everything. Will you show us everything?"

"Of course. We'll start now—this is the airport, ladies and gentlemen, bilingual announcements, taxi cabs—oh, one cardinal rule of transportation in Israel," he said, feeling giddy and excited. "No taxi is allowed to drive away until there has been a good, loud argument. It's the law."

He loved the way Carlie was laughing, pointing at the two cabbies fighting over a parking space.

"Come on, you kids," his mother said irritably. "Let's get out of here. Let's get a cab."

"I brought a car," said Mitch. He picked up two suitcases; Carlie and his mother each carried another. "What have you guys got in here? Stones? You won't need them. Israel is full of stones. Why so many? They say that for every traveler who comes to Israel, a stone falls from his heart." He stopped, seeing the look on his mother's face. He had meant to say it lightly.

The car seemed farther away than he had thought; twice he was utterly lost. At last he spotted the old heap, swung open the trunk, and unlocked the doors. He hadn't noticed it was only a two-seater. His mother looked exasperated. Carlie squeezed into the small space in back.

"Carlie, are you all right?" his mother asked anxiously. She tucked her jacket around her as if for insulation. "Can you sit like that? How far is it, Mitch? Where in the world did you get this car?"

"It belongs to Tal's father," Mitch said. A heaviness began to settle over him, almost an ache. "It was nice of him to lend it to me. He had to take the bus to work."

Mitch drove out of the airport, concentrating on traffic; the last thing he wanted now was an accident or some problem. His mother and Carlie stared out the windows and commented.

"The weather is just like in L.A., isn't it?"

"Look at those Arabs."

"Everything's so old here!"

The car hit a bump in the road. "My God!" his mother cried. "This car doesn't have any springs!"

"Sorry, Mom."

"Look out! Look out! You nearly hit that person—does everyone jaywalk here?"

They settled down and took turns telling him things—regards from everyone, Dad sends his love, Grandma Rose sent him something. Could he guess what it was? Yes, Mitch guessed. It was one of Grandma's small figures, a tiny gnome with painted-on clothes. Carlie passed it to Mitch. He slipped it into his pocket. Suddenly he had so many questions, but none of them seemed to take shape, exactly. He was like two different people leading two different lives; now the two worlds came together, here in this rusted old car. It was hard to hold on to reality.

"Grandma missed you at her party," his mother said. "It was a wonderful party, all her favorite foods." Then she went on. Cousin Leonard sent his regards. Blake was co-sponsoring a golf tournament in Palm Springs, planning to gross half a million dollars on it. Blake's business was doing phenomenally well. "He is only twenty-one years old," Mitch's mother said, tapping her fingernails against her purse.

"How nice for him," said Mitch. "Does he ever sit still these days?"

"You never liked Blake," said his mother.

"He's a jerk," said Carlie.

"Don't you start."

"Well, he kept walking out on Grandma's party, making phone calls. I think he's on something. He's so incredibly jumpy. He could be on cocaine. I've seen people like that. . . ."

"How can you say such things, Carlie? Cocaine!"

"Don't you think he's on something, Mitch?" Carlie asked.

"He always was pretty tense."

"You kids are just jealous," said his mother. "Blake's a wonderful boy. His father's so proud of him."

At last the preliminaries were over, and they drove in silence. Mitch gazed about at the landscape, aware of the rubble, the old tanks left to rust on the roadside, reminders of the conflict and the sacrifices—people had died on this very road. That was history. Did they care? He glanced at his mom. Her mouth was pursed tight, her eyes glassy.

He saw Carlie in the rearview mirror, watching the passing scene, her face close to the window. The hills and trees and shrubs were like those in California—but different, somehow. Ancient and cherished. He imagined her inhaling the atmosphere, already loving it, as he did.

His mother called out, "What's that? Those stone buildings? Looks like some—caves. Or pueblos."

"Jerusalem," Mitch said. "The outskirts of the city—those are town houses, a living wall, you might say." To himself he added, "Protection for the heart, the city." Always, as he approached Jerusalem, he felt this lifting sensation, pride and longing. He had thought it was something all Jews shared, inbred, a collective memory of past glory.

His mother's voice was sharp. "Are we going to the hotel? I need to get some sleep."

"Sure, Mom. Listen, I've got an important lecture tonight," he suddenly said. "Maybe I should get you two settled and we can see each other tomorrow."

"Yes, yes, I think that's wise," his mother said. "There's no point in trying to talk tonight—we've been traveling for twenty hours. Carlie wasn't feeling all that well, either."

"I'm fine, really," Carlie spoke up.

"Tomorrow is better," said his mother. "Besides, you heard Mitch. He's busy tonight. We don't want to intrude. We didn't come here to disrupt him."

Mitch glanced at Carlie in the rearview mirror and saw the swift look of disappointment on her face, then her steady gaze. She nodded slightly, as if in warning: Don't answer. Don't talk.

Throughout the years he had always pushed his point, while Carlie remained silent and controlled. "You'd catch more flies with a little honey," she used to tell him.

"Who wants flies?" he'd retort.

Now, for the first time that he could ever remember, Mitch held his peace. It was not until he left Carlie and his mother off in front of the hotel that Mitch told them about the invitation.

"*Shabes* dinner? That's sweet, dear," said his mother. "Very sweet of them. What did you say their name was?"

"Miriam," Carlie said. "Her name is Miriam."

Mitch glanced at Carlie, seeing that same little girl of years ago, chin high in a sassy look. She always said something sassy about his girlfriends. He started to say something about Miriam, that he hoped they would like each other. But it sounded hollow, even in his mind. "I'll call you in the morning," he said with a quick kiss for his mother and a wave to Carlie. He had forgotten how these encounters were like walking a tightrope, trying to balance his own thoughts with his mother's demands, and Carlie standing there watching.

He shuddered as he thought of presenting his mother to the Sarodis. What would they possibly talk about? How would his mother understand anything that was going on? The Sarodis would be hospitable, but they would see her as any other American woman, too flashy, too materialistic.

Maybe he shouldn't have accepted. And yet, what choice did he have? To refuse the invitation would have been rude.

Besides, meeting them, seeing how they lived, might take the sting out of his being here; his mother would see that these were good people, and he was perfectly safe.

He only hoped she wouldn't talk so loud or pat him or pluck at his clothes. He tried to imagine Carlie and Miriam together, and for a moment he imagined that they might actually like each other. Maybe they'd even become friends.

Anything's possible, Mitch told himself, trying to be optimistic in spite of his fears.

CHAPTER 11

ON THE PLANE to Israel, Carlie had struggled, her thoughts crowded and confused. The airplane interior was a miniature world; in it all her problems swirled around her like the clouds outside. Past events flashed through her mind. Names echoed: Kip. Melanie. Mitch.

She glanced at her aunt, who was sipping a drink, looking distant, submerged in her own thoughts. She wanted to ask her questions—how do you know when you're in love? How did *you* know? Melanie's answer had seemed like something out of a magazine's questionnaires. Melanie was always taking those tests, coming out on top—"YOU'RE IN LOVE!"

Now—it was so clear.

Melanie, accusing *her* of being in love with Mitch, when all along she was the one. From the very beginning, Melanie had always looked for Mitch and asked what he was doing. The summer Mitch was a lifeguard it was Melanie who had always found ways to hang around at the beach. Maybe that was the basis of this entire friendship: Melanie's desire to get close to Mitch.

That very first time they met, Melanie came to the door with her mother, smiling shyly, glancing inside. Carlie remembered. Melanie, at twelve, already looked like a teenager in a black sweater and tight jeans, with fabulous boots in Western style, and a row of silver bangle bracelets. She looked great. She wore a bra, Carlie could tell. And that first day Melanie made a point of telling Carlie she'd already been getting her period for over a year, and Carlie felt like a jerk in her little white shorts and middy T-shirt, flat chested, with stringy, dull hair, no grace, not even a dimple.

"I wanted to meet you," Melanie had said. "My mom and your aunt have been friends forever. My mom told me what happened to your parents. It's horrible. I'm really sorry. Anyhow, we live pretty close, and we'll be going to the same school—hey, do you like horses?"

"Sure."

"Well, we can go riding over at Chester's; it's not very far. My mom will take us. I'm always pestering her about going riding—maybe your aunt will take us sometimes, too."

"Sure."

"I really prefer to ride English, but all they have at Chester's is Western; I like to canter. Trotting doesn't feel too good—do you want to go out next weekend?"

"Sure."

For several weeks, Melanie had done most of the talking. Those were the weeks when words were locked tightly inside Carlie, the weeks before Mitch came into her room one afternoon and stood there, hanging on to the doorway, looking at her.

"I got this neat new Rhythm skateboard," he said. "Want to watch me?"

She shrugged.

He pulled the board into view; it was wide and solid, wildly painted in shades of magenta and green. She reached out to touch the smooth surface. She adored skateboarding. Since the accident, she hadn't even thought about it.

"Come on," Mitch said. "Let's go try it on the driveway."

It was late afternoon. The clouds formed a rosy canopy, a gorgeous display. And Carlie remembered her dad once saying, "Every day the sky is different, like a new painting. Isn't it wonderful?"

Carlie felt that flash of grief all over again, more than pain, shock mingled with denial.

Mitch gave her a glance, said nothing, only thrust the skateboard at her. "Want to try it?"

"I'll watch you first," Carlie said.

Poised like a circus performer, clowning a little, Mitch set the board in motion, jumped on, executed a long glide up the driveway, then a spin, and he came down, knees bent, catching the board in his arms as he jumped off.

"Want to try it?" he asked.

"Guess so." Carlie took the board under her arm, feeling its weight, its possibilities. She took it along the sidewalk, slowly at first, feeling its balance under her foot. The glide, the ease, the centeredness brought her in close to herself; she was in charge. At the end of the street was a steep hill. It beckoned. Carlie's gaze was focused on a single tree, bushy and green and thick with pods. She didn't know the name of it, but it was perfectly shaped, and fragrant. She could smell it from afar.

Carlie set her goal. She kept her eyes on the tree, her

body loose, knees slightly bent and back limber. As she made her way up the hill she felt herself gaining speed, felt the sidewalk spinning away beneath her, felt the breeze against her cheeks, felt free. To the top she sped, then turned, flipped the board up and over, so that it somersaulted beneath her. She leaped high into the air and, as the board slammed down again, she met it squarely, careening down the hill fast enough to make the sparks fly, then rolling, rolling with the descent, her arms wide, and wondering—how could things still be so good?

As she approached Mitch, feet still balanced on the skateboard, she saw his openmouthed look. He cocked his head, then broke into a grin. "Beginner's luck," he said. "Perfect kick-flip."

"Yeah," she said, laughing.

He caught her in the arm, gave it a squeeze. "Come on. Let's go over to the park. I've got an old board I can use—you take this one."

"Okay. Cool."

It was the beginning.

On the plane, Carlie eventually slept, cradled by memories—she and Mitch in the backyard, building a campfire, sleeping out, pretending to be on the Oregon Trail.

"Like brother and sister," Aunt Vivian told people. "They have their moments—but they're good pals, too."

The fights. He stole her hairbrush. She took his razor. "You've got your dumb hair in my razor!"

"You've got nothing to shave, anyhow."

"Look who's talking? You look like a boy on top."

"Who's looking?"

Was that love? Was it brother-sister stuff, or something

else? Maybe she'd know when she saw Mitch again, after this absence. But maybe she didn't want to know.

Vivian turned to Carlie. "What was all that yelling about last night, you and Melanie?"

"Nothing," Carlie said. "Nothing important."

"Sounded like World War Three." Aunt Vivian laughed to herself.

"She's going to the formal with Kip."

"*Your* Kip?" Aunt Vivian bristled.

Carlie smiled. "Well, he's not actually mine, is he, if he invited Melanie."

"She's boy crazy, that one," said Aunt Vivian. "Her mother better watch her—she's been that way since she was ten." She patted Carlie's hand. "You're much prettier," she whispered.

"Thanks."

"You look so pretty in that sweater," Vivian said. In the next moment she had withdrawn, pulling the blanket tightly around her shoulders, her head down.

"What's wrong, Aunt Vivian?" Carlie asked. She looked so worried, Carlie wanted to touch her, give her a hug the way she did with Grandma Rose, but Vivian was not a hugging sort of woman.

"They might not let him go," she said. "They have ways of holding people."

"What ways?" Her fear was catching; Carlie felt it, too.

"I don't know. The trouble with fanatics is, they want everyone to believe the way they do. When it comes to what's good for your soul, they think they have the answer, and it's no holds barred. Anything goes."

"Why? Why do they care about other people's souls so much?"

Vivian shrugged. "Beats me."

The next time they opened their eyes it was bright outside. Several men made their way up the aisle, their shoulders draped in long white fringed shawls. Thin leather straps were wound around their heads and arms, with small boxes attached. They clustered together near the door of the plane, facing the windows, and they began to sway in silent prayer.

"Morning prayers," said a traveler across the aisle. "They face east—Jerusalem."

"*Meshugah,*" said the other. "Nuts."

The men looked so solemn, so engrossed. And Carlie wondered, was this how Mitch looked now too?

Aunt Vivian stood at the counter, negotiating for a different room. She spoke loudly, pointing her finger. "I said a quiet room. Not near the elevator. No, not on the street side. Don't you have something overlooking the garden? I don't care. I'll pay more."

Carlie moved to the wide picture window, looking to the boulevard below, the constant bustle of traffic, people walking by, busy and assured. Two young women talked eagerly as they walked, each pushing a baby carriage. They wore long skirts and long-sleeved blouses, and their heads were covered with kerchiefs. Orthodox, Carlie thought, gazing down at them. She had seen women dressed that way before, on Pico Boulevard, when they had driven by the butcher shops and markets with huge signs in the windows, GLATT KOSHER. She was never really sure what "glatt kosher" meant. The women's faces glowed; perhaps it was lack of makeup, a clean look.

In a corner of the lobby stood three men all dressed alike

in long black coats and black felt hats. Their eyes and lips showed bright in their bearded faces. Their voices made erratic, rumbling sounds. What were they saying? Carlie wished she could understand. They talked with their hands and bent bodies and bobbing heads.

"Carlie! Come on." Aunt Vivian's impatient voice pulled Carlie out of her reverie; she could have stayed here in the lobby for hours, just looking.

"I'm coming."

Two women stepped into the elevator. One of them smiled sourly at Carlie, showing bad teeth. "First time in Jerusalem?" she asked.

"Yes."

"We're visiting my son," said Aunt Vivian. "He's studying here. Temporarily."

"We're here for a wedding." The woman nodded toward her companion.

The second woman moaned. "My daughter. Marrying an Israeli—they don't even speak English. Yemenite people. Wedding parties will go on for a week."

"Sounds like fun," Carlie said.

"They don't even speak English!" wailed the woman.

Her friend took her arm. "Come on, Roberta, this is our floor. Good-bye. Nice to meet you." The elevator door slid shut behind them.

"They didn't look very happy about it," Carlie said.

"Obviously, they're not," said Aunt Vivian. She hoisted her bag over her shoulder, grunting.

"Where are our other bags?"

"Being brought to our room."

"Can we go out?"

"Out? Where?"

"I thought we could go to the Wall," Carlie said. "I was reading about it. Most people go there first."

"I suppose we could," Aunt Vivian said dubiously. "Aren't you tired?"

"We could go while it's still light and then take a nap before dinner," Carlie said. "I think it's in walking distance."

"Oh, I wouldn't walk," said Aunt Vivian. "We'll take a taxi."

Carlie felt a kind of pressure in her chest. A bird in a cage must feel this way, she thought. In the room she tried to smile and to sound lighthearted. It was a small room with drab bedspreads and curtains, a small window.

She said, "I think Mitch looked good, don't you?" She had never seen him with a beard before. He looked older and a little worried, but his smile was the same, bright and wonderful. In those first moments she had tried to assess her feelings, but it was impossible. She was just glad to see him, to know he was not that different after all.

"He looked all right," Aunt Vivian said. "Except for that coat. And that beard. Carlie, I wish you wouldn't admire . . . never mind. I don't want to tell you what to say, but . . . really, the point is that we want him to come home."

Carlie looked out at the distant hills, and the buildings all of chiseled rock. Even as she watched, the sun began to strike the stones, forming a faint golden sheen that seemed to emerge from within, not without. It was strange.

"Don't we, Carlie?" her aunt persisted.

"What?"

"We want Mitch home, don't we?" Her aunt's voice rose.

"Yes. Of course. I was just thinking . . . maybe we should plan something, like a trip. A family trip."

"You mean, give Mitch something to look forward to?"

Carlie nodded. "Maybe he doesn't want to go to college, Aunt Vivian. Maybe he just wants to be an artist."

"You think so?"

"Maybe he could go to a good art school, study religion on the side. He could have it all. He has to know it's okay with you."

"Anything is okay!" Aunt Vivian exclaimed. "As long as he comes home."

"Okay. We'll work on it," Carlie said.

"Come on, then," said her aunt, "if you want to get to that wall before dark. I don't relish the thought of being out there in the dark."

Afterward, Carlie lay on the bed, trying to nap before dinner. Her body felt drained, her hands and feet almost without sensation, and though she wanted to sleep, visions kept moving before her eyes, mostly the faces of women.

The astonishing gathering of women at the Wall had overwhelmed her. Their clothes looked as if they had been gathered from all the four corners of the earth. From the far end of the courtyard Carlie heard murmurs, strange tongues. Then, as she entered their midst, only the sound of footsteps, slow movements, quiet faces. One after the other the women stepped forward to touch the Wall.

All of them prayed for something, or someone. What did they ask for? For money, a better career, for healing, for love. Certainly, everyone knew exactly what to petition for. Some people had little slips of paper already prepared, and they wedged these in between the stones so that their prayers became part of the wall. And if an angel were to appear at this moment to ask Carlie her wish, what would she say?

She stood watching the others, wishing she knew. But there was something hypnotic about this place and in the slow, deliberate movements of the women as they drew closer and closer to the Wall. Carlie found herself moving with them. She reached out and laid the palms of her hands flat against the stones. They were cool and moist, warm and throbbing.

And Carlie wept. It was a different weeping than she had ever known, deeper, wrenching, and at last cleansing, as if she had swum for hours in the ocean and emerged fresh.

Suddenly her aunt spoke out in the darkness. The sound astonished Carlie; she had thought Vivian was asleep.

"Why were you crying at the Wall?" Vivian asked. Her voice sounded distant, hollow.

Carlie did not answer for a long moment. "I don't know," she said. "Did you? Cry?"

Again, the pause was long. "No. What's there to cry about?"

"They all seem to," Carlie said, feeling defensive and very tired. And she remembered standing there, as if it were a moment singled out in time. If she were to grow very old, looking back on her life, certain events would stand out. This moment at the Wall would be one of them. She would live it again and again, the wracking tears, the feeling that she did not come here alone, but at the end of a long, long line of men and women, all part of her, reaching back to a thousand years—all Jews. The weight of their sufferings and their desires lay upon her, too. And if she did not come alone, then it meant that, even without mother or father, she was not an orphan, because she belonged to a family so large and so unquenchable in spirit that it would never die. Her tears flowed from longing and relief and love—all the things she could not now articulate.

"Like a mass hypnosis or hysteria," said Vivian.

"Yes," Carlie said with a sigh. "I guess that's it."

"Well, I can't sleep," said Aunt Vivian briskly, snapping on the light. "Let's go get a bite to eat. I saw a coffee shop downstairs."

But the coffee shop served only dairy, the host said, bobbing apologetically. "You like blintzes?" he asked, smiling broadly. "We have cheese, blueberry, cherry blintzes with sour cream."

Aunt Vivian shuddered. "No, thank you. Isn't there anything else?"

"We have our gourmet dining, but, alas, I believe it is full until ten o'clock. This season . . . people have reservations."

Aunt Vivian took Carlie's arm and pulled her aside. "Let's go," she said.

"Where?"

"I didn't come all the way to Israel to eat lousy cheese blintzes. Never liked them, anyhow. Say, I saw a little Arab restaurant—something Abdullah, I'm not kidding, only two blocks away. Looked sort of—interesting. What do you think?" she asked, her tone airy. "Want to try something different? I think as long as we're here, we should try to experience—um—different things."

"Sure." Carlie glanced at her aunt, the brisk steps and bright plaid jacket. Obviously, Vivian was making an effort. She would gather experiences like souvenirs, just to have a story to bring back home. "It sounds like fun."

They walked among the many tourists, stopping at the small door which was ajar, with golden light and food fragrances wafting out.

"This is it," Vivian said. They went in and were led immediately through the center of the restaurant and its throng of diners sitting back in luxuriant style, and waiters holding huge trays aloft over their heads.

The smells, the smoke, the steamy room, and the plinking music surrounding them, all made an envelope of time and space that kept them sealed in for nearly three hours.

Food appeared. Sweet liquid in small glasses—it burned and brimmed in the chest, but they quickly asked for more. A dozen small bowls filled with spicy things—red lentils, beans, grain, pickled currants and radishes and vegetables one could not even imagine. They ate. They drank. Water was brought in a large green bottle, and Aunt Vivian protested, "Too much! Too much!" But then she ordered still another bottle, to wash down the liquor and the spices and the tastes that lingered. For dessert there was a sticky honey mass, surrounded by a creamy pudding, and a rose-colored tea poured out of a long-spouted silver teapot. They emerged, stuffed and singing, bracing themselves against the night air.

"I think we're drunk," said Aunt Vivian. "They didn't even ask your age." She flung her arm around Carlie's shoulder.

"It tasted like licorice. Liquid licorice." Carlie began to giggle. "I love it."

"Me, too. Don't tell Uncle Harry. He'll say I'm decomposing you—no, what's the word? Deteriorating?"

Carlie laughed. "I think it's 'debauchery.' "

"Hey! That's good. Actually Shakespearean. Did you read Shakespeare?"

"A rose by any other name . . . ," Carlie said, giggling. "I think the word you seek is actually 'corrupting.' Uncle Harry will say you corrupted me."

"Not to mention the bill. A corrupt bill." She laughed and laughed, pulling Carlie close.

"It was great. I'll never forget it."

"Neither will I."

In the night Carlie was awakened by groans, flushing, moaning.

"What's wrong?"

Reeling in from the bathroom, Aunt Vivian groaned. There were dark blotches in her pale, wracked face. "I feel as if I've been poisoned."

Carlie sat up, frowning. "If the food was poisoned, wouldn't I be sick, too?"

"Oh, God, don't be logical, Carlie, I think I'm dying!"

"Want me to call the front desk? Want me to get a doctor?"

"No—I have to go back to . . ." She ran into the bathroom and slammed the door shut.

When Carlie woke up in the morning, Aunt Vivian lay in bed, looking ghostly. She raised herself up, still groaning, peering at Carlie. "You feel okay?"

"I'm fine. A little hungry."

"Oh, God. Don't mention food! You're like your mother," she said accusingly. "Joanne always had a cast-iron stomach. I was—more fragile. Oh, God, why'd you let me eat all those spices?"

"I didn't . . . ," Carlie began, then fell silent. "Want me to send for some tea, Aunt Vivian?"

"No, no. Just leave me alone, Carlie. My head's splitting, and my stomach is on fire. Just go and—call Mitch. He'll show you around. Just let me—don't make me talk. Put out the Do Not Disturb sign. Turn out the light. It hurts my eyes. Oh, God, how am I going to make it tonight?"

CHAPTER 12

CARLIE PHONED THE *yeshiva*. "Your mom is sick."

"What's wrong?" Mitch was alarmed.

"Upset stomach. We pigged out last night."

"Where did you eat?"

"Some Arab café—it was fantastic. We were both drunk."

"My God, I should have warned you. I'll be right over."

He went to the hotel, up to the small room where his mother lay on the bed, dressed in an old sweat suit, looking drained and pale. He could see the puffiness underneath her eyes.

Carlie sat on the small sofa, watching Israeli cartoons on TV with the sound turned off. She smiled as he entered and then she drew back, pulling her legs up under her.

"Hi, Carlie."

"Hi," she said softly.

He went to his mother's side. "What happened, Mom?" Mitch sat down on the bed beside her.

"Arab food," she said. "Some kind of revenge, I guess. Don't shake the bed. My stomach can't take it."

"What are you going to do?"

"Lie here. Drink tea. You and Carlie," she said, closing her eyes, "go on and see the city. I'll be better by tonight. I want to meet your friends. Now, I feel terrible."

"I'm sorry," Mitch said. "Should I call the hotel doctor?"

"Carlie already phoned. We're waiting for a call back."

His mother stared at him. Mitch felt his face grow flushed; he felt self-conscious about his beard, his clothes. His chin itched; he resisted scratching.

"I hate to spoil your plans," she said. "What about tomorrow? Were you going to take us around?"

"Well, tomorrow is *Shabes*," Mitch said. "I go to services."

"But after services you can come here and we'll have lunch and go out somewhere."

"Mom, it would be hard for me to get here. It's too far to walk from the *yeshiva*."

"Then take a bus or a cab."

"Mom," he said uneasily, "I can't do that, either."

"Can't? Why not?"

"It's hard to explain," he began. "The thing is, on *Shabes* we can't drive, nor can we let someone else drive us, because . . ." He sighed. "It's—well, it's a day of rest. We refrain from work."

"And taking a cab is work?" his mother exclaimed.

"Look, Mom, it has to do with exchanging money and lighting fires. A car engine is like a fire, with all those spark plugs."

Carlie had left the sofa and stood behind him, listening. He glanced up at her face in the mirror. He took a deep breath and patiently he slowed his speech. "Mom, there are certain rules about Sabbath observance. I can't violate them."

"Oh. Since when are you ever bound by rules?"

"Please, Mom." He rose, went to the window, then stood by the wall, looking at the two of them. "The Sabbath is the cornerstone of Judaism. It's more important than any of the festivals, more important than Yom Kippur. . . ."

"That's ridiculous," his mother snapped. "Everyone knows that Yom Kippur is the holiest day. If Jews go to temple no other day in the entire year, they go on Yom Kippur."

Mitch sighed and turned away. He did not want to confront his mother; he wanted to honor her, but his pulse beat hard with annoyance and it was all he could do to keep silent.

"Look, I'm not a complete idiot," his mother called out from the bed, lifting herself up against the cushions. "I know that orthodox Jews don't work on the Sabbath. But this—don't you see that this is extreme?"

"Work, Mother, is defined differently—there are certain clear rules. Work is defined as anything that—"

"Will you stop with your definitions!" she exclaimed, eyes blazing. "All I know is that we have traveled thousands of miles to see you, and you won't change your routine for even one day."

"It's not just a routine, Mom. All these things are part of a whole fabric, a way of life. If you'd come to the *yeshiva*, they have a beginner's lecture on all these things; then you'd understand."

"You think I came here to be indoctrinated?" She swung her feet out of the bed, clutched the covers around her shoulders. "I know about orthodoxy. Your grandma . . ."

"I'm not trying to indoctrinate you." His voice rose. "I'm

just telling you what I am doing, that certain things have priority."

"More than your family?"

"Yes!"

She stared at him, her face taut. "I don't get it, Mitch. How can you stand all these restrictions? I read somewhere that kids want structure. But this isn't structure. It's rigidity. Do you really want to live like this? Totally out of the mainstream?"

"What's the mainstream, Mom? Is it so terrific? Read the papers! Look at the TV news—the mainstream is pretty rotten. I want to find something better. Something spiritual."

"I understand that, son," said his mother. "Look, I do. As soon as we moved to the valley we joined a temple."

"But not for religious reasons."

"How do you know our motives? Who are you to judge? Are you the only Jew here, with that beard and those—those *things*?"

Mitch glanced down at the fringes. Of course, that's what would offend her, even more than the beard. Patiently he said, "I'm not judging you, Mom. Maybe it is structure that I want. That doesn't mean you failed. It just means that I'm growing. . . ."

"You never even used to make your bed! You wouldn't sit still for two hours in Sunday school. They had to expel you. Now you say you wanted structure all along? You hated rules, you argued constantly, wanted to be so damn free! Is this the freedom you wanted?"

"I chose it freely."

"I don't think so," she said harshly. "You never knew what you wanted."

"Well, I know now," Mitch said. "I'm sorry I was such an

awful kid." He felt a strange sense of detachment. How could they ever have been close? She used to defend him.

"For God's sake, Mitch, there's the mirror," his mom cried out. "Will you take a look at yourself?"

Mitch went to the mirror. His hair was a bit too long, and his beard not quite filled in yet. But he still liked what he saw, an earnestness.

"You don't even look like yourself," came his mother's voice, soft, from the bed.

"Yes, I do," Mitch said. He whirled around, walked to his mother again, his voice low but firm. "This is the real me." He clenched his teeth against other words that threatened to break loose.

The telephone by the bedside rang. His mother snatched up the receiver. "Yes?" She sat listening, then put the instrument down. "The doctor is coming up. Go now, I don't need you here."

"Maybe he'll give you a prescription," Carlie said. "Maybe we should wait and get it for you."

"Whatever it is, I'm sure I can handle it. Go." She waved her hands at them, then added, "Have fun."

Outside, Mitch stretched and groaned, reclaiming his own space. He turned to Carlie. "Has it been hard at home?"

"Not too bad." She gazed at him. "I keep trying to figure out," she said, "whether you've really changed, or whether it's just—" she waved her hands, uncertainly—". . . just the way you look."

"Everyone changes," he said. "Even you."

"We were talking about you," she said pointedly. "You know, we want you to come home. Your mom doesn't mean to be so hard. She's scared."

"I know. Let's not talk about it, please."

"Mitch, we have to talk about it. I told your mom they should let up on you, I told her . . ."

"Carlie the mediator." Mitch smiled slightly.

"Well, okay. I don't mind being the mediator. You could go to art school, Mitch, that school of design in Pasadena? You talked about it once. And if you're into spirituality, there's so much going on, lectures and groups. I saw an ad in the paper about Jewish meditation. You don't have to go halfway around the world to be spiritual, do you?"

Mitch laughed. "That's so true. And if I were more focused, sure, I could find it there. But I'm not. I like it here. It feels—like home. Carlie, let's not talk about it now. I want to show you Jerusalem."

"Okay," she said, relenting, but he knew this wasn't the end of it. "Come on," he said. "What do you want to see first?"

"The streets," she said. "The people. Let's just walk."

They walked past the same stores that Mitch had browsed in with Miriam, then to the Cardo, and Carlie ran her hands over the ancient Roman pillars. He showed her the churches and the Via Dolorosa, where the Christian pilgrims gathered. In the Jewish quarter they heard little boys chanting their lessons from the one-room basement school. Mothers took babies in strollers, and little kids played in the lanes. They passed the bindery where he had once met Miriam, and Mitch thought of her voice, the way she spoke English, putting words together in her own sweet way. He couldn't wait to see Miriam. He couldn't wait for this night, the peace of *Shabes* washing over him, that sense of complete rest and lightness.

His mother and Carlie would get a taste of it. The sweet

taste of *Shabes*. It would heal his mother's rancor. Carlie would be enchanted with the children, the family, their ways.

Carlie talked about home, the tennis club, Kip Warner, about Ari, who had started at UCLA and loved it, and Jonathan, happy at USC, taking prelaw. "Even the neighbors ask about you," she said.

"What do you tell them?"

"That you're in Israel studying."

"Not that I've gone bonkers?"

"Have you?"

He shook his head and gave her a grin. "Let's go to the museum now. I'm tired of walking."

Half a dozen soldiers were hanging out by the museum. Of course, they noticed Carlie and signaled with their eyes and their mouths—nice.

"It's weird to see soldiers in the streets," Carlie said. "With those rifles. Are they loaded, do you think?"

"Of course."

"We read about the bus bombing in Tel Aviv," Carlie said. "How far is that from here?"

"About forty-five minutes by bus or car."

"So close! Can we go there?"

"We can go anywhere. Everywhere. It's a small country."

In the museum, Carlie touched the railings, running her hands over things. She moved like a dancer, was a person of touch, while Miriam was visual, always pointing, "Look at this—see this."

Carlie stopped in front of a large, stark display of rectangular clay containers, some decorated with strange symbols.

"What's that thing you wear?" she suddenly asked, pointing to his waist.

He smiled. "It's a fringed garment."

"Underwear, you mean? And it sticks out from your pants?"

"It's like a small shirt. You wear it next to your skin." He did not say more, did not tell her that it was a reminder to keep from lusting, " . . . so that you will not follow after your heart and after your eyes by which you go astray . . ."

They stood looking at the ossuaries, symbols of death and dying. It was hard, now, to think of anything but life and this moment. Tonight he would see Miriam! He thought of the play they'd been forced to read in eleventh-grade English, *Cyrano D'Bergerac,* how Cyrano, in love, rhapsodized, "Roxanne, Roxanne, your name is like a bell ringing in my heart." Now he understood.

And yet, Carlie standing beside him was like a fresh breeze. It was so easy to talk to her. He could read her expressions and her body language. They had their own history.

Carlie pointed to the exhibit. "What are those for?" she asked.

"Bones," Mitch told her. "When people died, after their flesh was gone, they'd put the bones in these boxes. It saves space."

Carlie shuddered. "It's awful to think of being packed inside such a small space," she said. And he knew she was thinking of that funeral with the twin coffins and the rich, almost sickening, smell of roses and lilies.

"What happens when you die?" Carlie suddenly asked. "Do they teach you that? Do the rabbis explain it?" Her look was challenging, almost defiant.

Heavily, Mitch replied, "They say there is life in the

world to come. We don't know exactly what it is, or how it will be, but only that it will be good. Like an everlasting Sabbath."

"And what about the people who never believed in it? What happens to them?"

"What do you think?" he countered.

"I don't think that God would be so petty as to keep out people just because they didn't light candles or say certain prayers." Carlie slid her hand along the sleek railing. "Let's just try not to die for a long time yet."

"Okay," said Mitch. "It's a deal."

She held out her hand. "Let's shake on it."

They clasped hands, the way they used to do. Only this time Carlie's touch felt entirely different. Maybe it was because he hadn't touched a woman for so long.

It was just like the first *Shabes* at Miriam's, only for Mitch it was like seeing everything through a prism or a kaleidoscope, the view splitting, breaking into pieces. Before, he was absorbed and involved in it. Now, he was judge and jury and spectator, trying to participate, but wary.

From the moment Miriam opened the door, Mitch felt the tension, like static. Miriam was wearing a pale blue sweater and the silver-and-turquoise pendant he had given her for Hanukkah. Mitch wanted to say something; he could only smile. It was like a secret between them, the pendant lying between her breasts.

Mrs. Sarodi, smiling, greeted her guests. She led them into the living room. On the wall above the bookcase hung the collage Mitch had given her for Hanukkah. Mrs. Sarodi touched the frame. "Mitch," she said. "He make. For me."

His mother looked. "You made this, Mitch?"

"I did."

"It's amazing."

"Thank you."

Carlie came to look. "What do you call it?" she asked.

"*Bamidbar,*" Mitch said. "It's not very original. It means 'In the Wilderness.' Also, it's the Hebrew name for the Book of Numbers."

He stood back assessing his work: layers of texture and color, subtle shadings and changes—like Torah study, he thought. This was what he'd tried to show, different layers of meaning.

"It is wonderful," said Miriam.

Mr. Sarodi, Miriam's little brother, and the grandfather came rushing in, apologizing. "We were at the synagogue," said Mr. Sarodi, nodding to his guests. "Excuse us."

Mrs. Sarodi led the way to the dining room. There was a lingering silence after the blessings were said; no spontaneous burst of talk. Then everyone started at once, feeling the urgency to make something happen.

Carlie talked too fast; Mitch could see the others straining to catch her words. Never did she lower her eyes, as Miriam did, or keep her hand down in her lap. When Carlie spoke, her entire body moved; her hands fluttered and waved, and her voice rang out over the room.

Mr. Sarodi and Miriam and the grandfather listened politely. They asked Carlie how she liked Jerusalem. How did it compare to Los Angeles? Carlie told them about seeing the film trailers on the streets in West Hollywood, stopping to watch a shoot, seeing the actors. Miriam wanted to know all about it—the crew, the lights, celebrities, the glamour.

Somehow a gulf was bridged. Mitch saw it happening, but he couldn't for the life of him figure out how. One minute the two girls were sitting stiffly side by side. The next minute they were whispering, laughing, focused on each other like old friends. Carlie admired Miriam's pendant. They were serious; they were intent. It was amazing. Like night and day, the two of them, yet they seemed to have found each other.

His mother, meanwhile, was listening to Mr. Sarodi's recommendations. "It is beautiful, Eliat, and the Negev. Our ancestors walked there. You must see the beaches."

Carlie talked about Venice Beach, where people roller-skate all day and grown men play volleyball on the sand and kids practice hackey sack on the boardwalk. Miriam seemed enchanted.

"Maybe you'll come to visit," Carlie told her.

Miriam smiled and nodded. "Maybe."

The grandfather took a sip of his arack and turned to Vivian. "Mrs. Green," he said, "how long did it take you to travel to Jerusalem?"

Everyone fell to a respectful silence, even the little children.

"Counting the time it took to drive to the airport," she replied with a steady gaze, "about twenty hours."

"My family," said the grandfather, his tone deliberate, heavy, "walked from Ukraine. It took five months. On the way, two died, a woman giving birth, and a child. It was a girl child. Her name was Leah Risha. We remember her still in our prayers."

"When was this?"

"I am the seventh generation born in Jerusalem," the grandfather said.

"Interesting," said Vivian.

The grandfather began to drum his fingers on the table, humming, then he started a *niggun*, a melody without words.

Miriam's little brother joined in, and so did the little girls. Carlie cocked her head, listening, trying to hum along. Mitch felt a flush flooding his face. Everything felt so skewed, his two worlds colliding. Separately, he could keep things under control. It wasn't right to compare Miriam and Carlie. But questions confronted him: Did he love Miriam? Did he love Carlie? Were they different kinds of love, demanding different things from him?

Mitch glanced at his mother, sitting up straight in her chair. Candlelight caught the golden sheen of her large earrings. She wore a modest beige suit and a dark blouse underneath, but there was no mistaking the gleam of her lipstick, a butternut brown shade, and the heavy makeup on her face. Beside Mrs. Sarodi, she looked painted, like a model in a magazine, a woman of the world, a distant world. Comparisons again. Was it right to compare?

"Do you know," the grandfather suddenly said, "that even Moses did not see Jerusalem? No. He died on the mountain, before his people crossed the Jordan."

"I didn't know that," said Vivian. She looked tense.

"Yes. Our greatest prophet could not enter this land. Today, we come and go. It is all so easy. Too easy, perhaps."

Mrs. Sarodi got up with a great show of cheerfulness, chattering in Hebrew about dessert, reaching for the platters of cake and fruit from the buffet.

Mitch asked, "Miriam, is your sister coming tonight?"

"No," she said. "Their child is sick with a fever."

"Oh, I'm sorry," Mitch said. He was sorrier than they

could know, for the room suddenly seemed too empty, the talk veering dangerously into Torah topics, the kind of debate from which Carlie and his mom would never be able to extricate themselves.

"What about your aunt?" he continued.

"They are visiting relatives in Netanya."

They had all been here for Hanukkah, the eighth night, when Mitch was invited. He imagined echoes, now, of the children laughing and playing *dreidel*, the little girls clinging to his arms, jumping up and down in excitement over the candy he had brought. There were a few presents, hair ribbons for the girls, a small wooden car for Miriam's little brother, nothing fancy. Back home most of his friends made a terrific haul at Hanukkah time. He and Carlie usually got nice clothes, "necessary luxuries," as his mom called them.

"Your husband," said Mr. Sarodi, nodding toward Vivian, "he is home? In Los Angeles?"

"Yes. He couldn't get away now. The Christmas season is his busiest time."

Everyone nodded and kept on nodding, echoing, "Busy time. Oh, yes."

Mitch felt hot. His stomach ached. Why did she have to say that word? Christmas, at home, was always a time for ambivalence. They didn't celebrate Christmas, exactly, but they didn't *not* celebrate it, either. His mom went out and bought a moderate-sized tree, called it a Hanukkah bush, saying it was for the children. "Why should we have to feel left out? It's just a pine tree." She spent hours decorating it, each year a different theme. Last year everything was mauve and purple. Christmas morning there was always something wonderful to open.

"Well, when *Meshiech* comes," said the grandfather, leaning forward in his chair, his gaze intent upon Vivian, "then everyone will come to Jerusalem."

"All the Jews in the world?" Carlie asked. "Would there be room for all of them?"

Miriam dropped her fork.

"The Messiah?" asked Vivian.

"Yes," Mitch said quickly. "The sages tell us that all the Jews will be gathered here."

"The dead will be revived," said Miriam.

Carlie opened her mouth to speak. She glanced at Mitch and closed it again.

"They say," Mitch began, making his tone light, "that a meal without Torah is like a meal without bread."

His comment was greeted with total silence.

His mother settled herself, head high. "Did Mitch ever tell you the story of *his* grandfather?" She put a slight stress on the word "his."

"No," said Mr. Sarodi.

Things seemed to shift, as if a spotlight suddenly shone upon his mother, and she took on a different look, too, almost strident. She said, "Mitch's father was born in Holland. Before that, his family had lived in Spain. At the time of the inquisition, 1492, they were expelled from Spain."

Mitch gasped. "I didn't know that," he blurted out.

She gave him a stern look. "Yes, they went first to Germany, where they lived until the First World War, then to Holland. It was in Germany that they took the name Greenberg."

"Greenberg," said Mr. Sarodi. "Green mountain," he murmured.

Vivian nodded. "They changed it later, in America, to Green. Shorter and easier."

Mitch felt things whirling away from his grasp. Greenberg? Green mountain? He had never heard this before. Green seemed like such a steady, forever kind of name. What else was there that he hadn't been told?

His mother continued. "Mitch's grandfather was a traveling salesman in Amsterdam. So he had a car. They got word on the radio that the Nazis were coming. The queen left, went to London, and all the Jews knew they were in terrible danger."

Everyone was listening, Mitch holding his breath. He had heard this story before, of course, but his father always cut it short. His mother's words were measured, heightening the tension.

His mother said, "Mitch's grandfather, Max, packed up what he could, took Harry, his son, and his wife and they left everything standing there and headed for the small village of Ymuiden by the sea. There was no way to get out by land. Their only hope was to find a boat. Max called some friends who also had cars, and they made a small convoy toward the shore. One man turned around and headed for the city to get his money from the bank. He was never heard from again."

The grandfather groaned loudly. Mr. Sarodi frowned. "Then what happened? How did they get out?"

"On the shore was this little red lighthouse and a café, packed with people. It was a chaotic scene. People were shouting, desperate. Max took charge. He jumped up onto a table and yelled for silence. 'Listen, we all have to stick together,' he shouted. 'I will find someone to take us across the channel. But we have to pay. Whoever will come with me, I want you to put all your money and your jewelry in this blanket. Everything. Hold nothing back!'

"He had brought a blanket, which he spread out on the floor. He took his wife's jewelry, even her wedding rings, his watch, all the money in his pockets, and he put it all into the center of the blanket."

Vivian paused. Everyone waited. She continued. "For a few moments nobody moved. Then one man came and tossed in his watch, his wife's diamonds, and others came, until there was a pile of money and jewelry. Max gathered it all up into a bundle. He took his son, Harry, Mitch's father, and he went to find a boat."

"How old was the son, your husband?" Mr. Sarodi asked.

"Six years old. Well, Max raced up and down the docks, stopping everyone. He asked, he pleaded. Several sailors turned him down. Too dangerous. The channel was rough; the Germans would come with machine guns and shoot them out of the water. They had already mined part of the harbor. Finally Mitch's grandfather found an old seaman with a boat, used to transport ore. The boat would hold fifty or sixty people, packed in. Max pleaded. The sailor hesitated. 'What will you give me if I take you?'"

Vivian paused again, gazing from one person to another. Mitch stared at his mother, amazed.

"'We'll give you everything we have,' Max said, and he opened up the blanket there on the dock. The sailor was astounded. They shook hands on it."

"Everything," repeated Mr. Sarodi. He translated softly for his wife. She puckered up her face, intent upon the story.

"He was right," said the grandfather, wiping his forehead. "He was absolutely right."

Miriam asked, "What happened then?"

"Max and little Harry went back to fetch the other people,"Vivian said. "Then Max remembered that his friend had gone over to the other side of the harbor, also looking for a way out. So he went to get his friend." She looked at Mitch, nodding.

"My grandfather was killed in a blast," Mitch said. "A grenade or a mine, we don't know."

He had heard that part of the story before, his father telling it briefly, face set like stone. "So, we came from Holland. The Nazis were chasing us. They killed my father." He did not want to dwell on the past. "What's the point?" he'd say. "I live for today. That's it."

The grandfather sighed. "Well. Praise God. The child and the mother were saved. They got out."

Mitch wanted to leave, to leave the story behind, the emotions behind. *Shabes* was supposed to be joyful. He felt like crying. Carlie, too, was subdued. "I never knew any of this," she whispered.

His mother's voice shook. "My husband worked very hard all his life," she said. "They call America the golden land. Well, not everyone in America is rich."

"Yes, yes," said Mr. Sarodi.

There was a strangeness now, a stiffness among them, as if someone were to blame. The little girls had fallen asleep on the floor. Miriam rose and began to clear the table. Her mother stood there, trying to smile.

Outside, a car horn sounded. "We have to go," said Mitch's mother. She nodded and smiled her good-byes. "Thank you. It was wonderful. Our taxi is waiting. The hotel arranged it for us." She extended her hand to the grandfather. He drew back.

Outside, Mitch started to explain that orthodox men do not shake hands with women. But he said nothing and, after Carlie and his mother got into the taxi, he walked all the way back to the *yeshiva*, steeped in wonderment. Why hadn't they ever told him the story before? Why hadn't he been given his grandfather's courage? Why had his father ignored their own family history?

He felt deprived, cut off. That, he thought, must be exactly how Carlie felt when her parents had suddenly died. He wished she were here now. They would talk.

CHAPTER 13

AUNT VIVIAN FLUNG down her shoes, slammed down the window, and paced through the room. "Mitch doesn't belong here," she said. "Why can't he see it?"

"They were nice to us," Carlie said tentatively. "The food was wonderful."

"Yes, the food was good, and they were very polite. Polite and smug, with their families and their heroes. Who do they think they are? They're the only ones who ever suffered? They think all Americans are rich. They think we have no values, only money on the brain. I know that they think."

"I liked them," Carlie said. "Didn't you?"

Vivian sniffed. "Like has nothing to do with it. Didn't you see how they patronized us? They feel so superior because they live in Israel. Like they are the only Jews, the only ones that count. I'm a Jew, too,damn it!"

"Aunt Vivian . . . I don't think they meant to insult us. They were just making conversation. They're proud of their family. That story about Mitch's grandfather—it was wonderful. I never heard it before."

"Neither did Mitch. Not all of it."

"How come? Uncle Harry should be proud."

"Harry doesn't like to talk about the past. Says it's irrelevant."

"But—Harry's father helped everyone escape. He made the plan that saved them."

"Harry never forgave his father."

"For getting killed?" Carlie exclaimed.

"For going back. For—yes, for getting killed and leaving him." Vivian threw up her hands, raking her fingers through her hair. "Besides, he wasn't such a hero at home."

"What do you mean, Aunt Vivian?"

"Forget it. The point is, everything Harry's got, every dime, he got by his own initiative and sweat. I've known Harry since I was eighteen years old. Even then, he was working two jobs. Hardly had time for anything else. He and Rose—they had a hard life. You know why she made those figures out of flour and water, don't you?"

Carlie shook her head.

"She had no money for art supplies. So she took what was at hand. She told me once, she used to make red paint out of beet juice, green out of dandelion leaves. They lived on bread and tomato paste, for months at a time. These kids that came out of the Holocaust," Vivian said, "all have scars."

"Uncle Harry seems fine," Carlie said.

"He never had a childhood," Vivian said. She dabbed at her eyes with a tissue. "Mitch doesn't know the half of it. He thinks his father's so uptight, preoccupied with money and the shop. It's all he has. Harry remembers those days. He just won't admit it. His mother worked sixteen hours a day cleaning houses, two jobs. He started selling newspapers when he was eleven. Before that they had him sweeping out the market on the corner. He had to bag all the trash."

"I didn't know any of this," Carlie said.

Vivian dabbed at her eyes. "God, I'm exhausted. I ate too much. I feel nauseous. Why does Mitch want to stay here? What's he trying to prove? Sometimes I think it's just to get even with his dad. For what? What did his father do to him?"

"Nothing! Uncle Harry's a great father. He's wonderful to me."

"He always wanted a daughter, too. I feel so bad. I'm so tired. Maybe you can talk some sense into Mitch."

"I'm trying," Carlie said. "I told him you'd let him go to art school."

They got into their beds. Carlie listened to Aunt Vivian's breathing, her turning and struggling with the blankets.

Softly her aunt said, "It's nice sharing a bedroom with you, Carlie. It reminds me of Joanne and me. We used to share a bedroom. She always kept her bed so neat. She'd get so mad at me for being a slob." She stopped. "I'm sorry. Forgive me. It makes you sad."

"No, no," said Carlie, though that wasn't true. It was like a sore that you rub, to feel the soreness. She wanted to hear about her mom, yet there was this involuntary flinching, fear of pain, of hearing something she would then be unable to forget.

Somehow, Carlie felt brave tonight, felt it like a roar inside her. "Tell me about her," she said. "How it was with the two of you in that bedroom. Did you lie awake and talk?"

"Oh, yes. Joanne, being three years older, always had a lot to tell me. I followed after her in school. The teachers expected me to get A's, like she did."

And Carlie remembered a certain look on her mother's

face when she used to talk about Vivian, a lift of her brow—oh, Vivian. Impulsive Vivian. Funny Vivian, never really held a job. While Joanne was becoming a manager, then a vice president of the bank, Vivian was still playing around with paint and wallpaper samples, trying to create illustrations for children's books, never quite making it.

"We used to talk about boys all the time," Vivian continued now, her voice distant in the darkness. "Joanne liked to go out with guys in business, guys who wore suits. Even while she was still in highschool. She had her whole life planned. She planned where she'd go to college, what she'd major in—business administration, minor in accounting, another minor in economics. Bright girl."

"You're bright, too," Carlie said. "You're artistic."

"Thanks, honey. That's sweet. I don't have any illusions. I was never as smart as Joanne. I always thought that, after she got established, you know, we'd be able to do things together, like go on vacation, take shopping trips, but then . . ."

Silence. Carlie lay very still, feeling the pain. "Me, too," she whispered at last. "I always thought that later . . ."

Vivian sat up and snapped on the light. Her eyes looked puffy and red. "I'm sorry," she said. "Please forgive me, Carlie. I'm so sorry. Of course you miss her more than I do."

"You miss her, too," Carlie said.

"I miss the things we never did together, the vacations, the parties with our kids . . ."

"She didn't like giving parties," Carlie said.

"Too messy. Joanne liked everything tidy."

"I know." And Carlie remembered all the times she'd asked her mom about having a little brother or sister, and her mom would grimace and throw up her hands and say, "Oh,

God, diapers? That mess again? No, thanks, honey, you're all I need."

Carlie pulled the blanket up around her shoulders. "Did you want more children, Aunt Vivian?"

Vivian looked startled. "Yes. Oh, yes, lots of them. When we got married, I told Harry I wanted four or five. It didn't work out," she said. "I remember when you were born. I was so jealous! I wanted a little girl so badly. I even told Joanne . . ." She fumbled with her blanket. "Let's go to sleep."

"What did you tell my mother? Tell me," Carlie said, for she had heard the anguish in her aunt's voice.

Vivian sighed. "I—I told Joanne I'd take care of you. I mean, she could have brought you to my house. Day care, you know. Or even overnight. Honey, you were so adorable!"

Carlie felt tears in her eyes, a tightness in her throat. "What did my mother say?" she asked, her voice low.

"Oh, you know. It would have been a lot of trouble. We lived so far apart. Still, we could have changed that. We could have moved closer."

"You would have moved?" Carlie exclaimed. "Just to take care of me?" She sat up, looking over at her aunt, at the disheveled hair and puffy cheeks. "You wanted me way back then," she whispered.

"Well, it never worked out," Vivian said. "Joanne had other . . . she'd already made plans. Oh, my stomach hurts. I'll turn over and try to sleep. Are you okay, honey?"

"Sure. I'm fine," Carlie said. She lay back, feeling enfolded by the bedclothes, warm and soft. All those times she'd ached to be with her mom, when her mom was rushing off somewhere, ready for the world. "Hey, back off, kiddo! You're wrecking my blouse!" She'd laugh, as if it were a joke, but

Carlie always knew, even when she was little, that her mother didn't want to get mussed. And Carlie had been holding herself back, assuming Vivian was the same way.

"Listen." Aunt Vivian's voice came from afar, as if she were bunched together now under the blankets. "You and Mitch, you two kids should spend time together. Alone, just the two of you."

"What about you, then? What would you do?"

"Don't worry about me. I'll go on some sight-seeing tour. I just rub Mitch the wrong way."

"No, you don't . . ."

"Yes. I do. If anyone can soften him up, Carlie, it's you. So tomorrow, and the next day or two, I'm going to lie low. I'm not feeling that great, anyhow. Besides, I want to sit on that wall and do some sketches. I haven't done anything like that in so long! I always thought . . . I want to draw that windmill and the hills, the dome on that mosque. I used to think I'd take up stone carving. I used to imagine doing something in alabaster."

"Why don't you do it, Aunt Vivian?"

"Maybe I will someday. Maybe I'll be a great artist. Ha! Wouldn't that be something? A late bloomer, like Grandma Moses." She laughed slightly, but Carlie heard the sadness in her voice.

"I've got to go to class in the morning, at least," Mitch told her. "Maybe you'd like to come by and see the *yeshiva*. Maybe you'd like to meet Halle and visit with her for a while, then we could all have lunch together."

"Sounds great," Carlie said.

The *yeshiva* was a run-down building with brown siding,

rusty railings, and sagging steps. Inside, the carpets were threadbare, the tables scarred. Shelves were stuffed with books.

Mitch showed Carlie the dining room, the stairway to the upper floor and the dim alcove with the telephone. "This is where I stand," he said, "when I call you on the phone. Right here."

"You like it here?"

"You know I do."

"How many people in your room?"

"Four of us." Mitch smiled. "I know, at home I have my own room, a closet full of clothes and sports equipment. So, call me crazy."

"Crazy." She grinned at him. "Come on, point me to Halle's house. This place feels like it's closing in on me—all those books and those sullen guys."

"They're not supposed to notice you. You're a distraction."

"Thanks."

They passed the rabbi's study. "Rabbi Nachum!" Mitch called. "This is my cousin, Carlie, from California."

Carlie expected him merely to nod, but the rabbi leaped to his feet, hurrying to the door to draw them in. "Welcome! Come in, sit a minute, you have time to talk?"

"I have a class, Rabbi," Mitch said. His tone was mild, respectful, and he nodded, with almost a slight bow. "Carlie's going to spend some time with Halle."

"Well, go on," said Rabbi Nachum with a wave of his hand. "I'll take care of your cousin. When we're finished talking, I'll walk her to Halle's house."

"But, Rabbi . . ." Mitch flushed.

"Enough. Can't I take half an hour off?" He laughed,

pointing to the only empty chair. "Sit down, Carlie, please."

Carlie sat, trying not to stare at the clutter, at the rabbi with his full, dark beard and gleaming dark eyes. His exuberance astonished her.

"So, how was your trip?" he asked, beaming at her.

"Fine. Thanks."

"How do you find Mitch? Much changed?"

Carlie hesitated, then decided not to hold back. "Well, he's never had a beard before. Back home he was, you know, kidding around a lot. Laughing. He was happy," she said pointedly.

"Ah, yes," said the rabbi, pressing his fingertips into his beard. "And you think now he is less happy? Too serious?"

"I think he's gotten into something very deep," Carlie said, twisting her ring around her finger. She felt odd, as if she were playing a part, being an adversary while, actually, she couldn't help feeling drawn to this rabbi and his open, friendly gaze. She waved her hands, looking for words. "Mitch was supposed to be in college."

"I heard. He is also studying now. Other lessons."

"All his friends think he has been kidnapped or taken into a cult." Carlie sat with her arms folded across her chest, her gaze steady.

"Carlie, I am not a guru," Rabbi Nachum said, and there was a twinkle in his eyes. "I'm only a poor rabbi. Sometimes students come to me. Always of their own free will. I would be wrong to turn them away, wouldn't I?"

Carlie sat in stony silence.

"Have you met Mitch's friends? Tal and Halle and Richard?"

"We met Miriam and her family for *Shabes*."

"Miriam? What is their last name?"

"Sarodi. But—didn't you arrange it?"

Rabbi Nachum drew back, startled. "I? No. I don't know the people."

"But I thought . . . ," Carlie stammered. "My aunt thinks . . ."

"Ah, she thinks I have arranged a *shidech* for your cousin, to hold him here." He gave a laugh, then he frowned. "I know there are groups that do this. Believe me, I had nothing to do with this meeting. And your cousin—is he ready for marriage?"

"No way!" exclaimed Carlie.

The rabbi laughed heartily, clapping his hands together. Then he asked, "How is your aunt? Mitch told me she wasn't feeling well. Is she coming to see us here at the *yeshiva*?"

"I don't think so, Rabbi Nachum. She . . ."

"I see. She believes we are the enemy."

Carlie faced the rabbi squarely now. "We want Mitch to come home with us," she said.

His heavy eyebrows shot up. "Does your aunt think I am keeping her son here against his will?"

"She thinks you have ways, yes, of persuading people."

"Mitch is free to leave," said Rabbi Nachum. "Surely, you can see that."

"Why do you want him here?" Carlie felt a rush of emotion. "It's breaking up our family. My aunt is so upset, crying. My uncle wants Mitch in the business. We're a family," she said heatedly.

Rabbi Nachum sighed and pushed back his chair, nodding sadly. "Ah, what can I say? Everyone looks for his purpose in life. If Mitch has found it here, how can I tell him he has to leave? And if he has found a way here to reach toward God, who am I to send him away? The soul takes what it needs. Right now, your cousin needs nourishment. If we can provide it—"

"Why you? Why here?" Carlie said. "There are thousands of Jews in L.A. Hundreds of synagogues and classes. Why can't he go there?"

Rabbi Nachum held out his hands, empty. "Ask him."

"I will." Carlie's heart pounded, but she met Rabbi Nachum's gaze without flinching.

Carlie didn't want to like Halle. She didn't want to be charmed by the baby, Ephraim, patting the table in front of his high chair and grinning, calling out, "Hi! Hi!" She didn't want to feel so swiftly drawn into Halle's warmth, her sudden confidences.

"Could you give me a hand, Carlie? Sometimes I think I wasn't cut out for this at all—and the baby's jumping inside!" Halle laughed while she stirred a large pot of fruit for jam.

"What can I do?" Carlie asked, glancing around the kitchen with its wild array of food, toys, sweaters, books, and utensils.

"You can feed Ephraim, if you would, please."

Carlie could not remember when she had ever fed a baby before. She could not remember feeling this sudden urge to coo, to wipe his face, to soothe his clothing, hold him close. She could not remember having met a child as gentle and sweet as little Daliah, who patted her arm and smiled and brought her a cookie.

By the time Mitch got to Halle's house, Carlie had been there for an hour, had heard all about Halle's courtship, her decision to "make aliyah" with Richard, the fights with her in-laws about leaving America, the high price of food in Israel, the impossible red tape that made every official task a torment.

Halle masked nothing, neither her passion nor her problems. Carlie liked her instantly.

"My mother," Halle said, patting her round belly, "worries all the time about my having so many children. We don't practice birth control, you know."

Carlie felt flushed. "How many do you want?"

"As many as Hashem will give me!"

"I was an only child," Carlie said.

"I have only one brother, Tal. Mitch's friend. Does Mitch want children?"

Again, Carlie felt dumbstruck. "I—I don't know. We never talked about that."

"So, how about you? Do you have a boyfriend back home?"

"Not really," said Carlie.

"Have you met Miriam? Yes, of course you have—you were there for *Shabes*. Jerusalem is like a small town." Halle laughed. "Everyone knows everything about everybody."

"We were there," Carlie said. "It was very nice."

Halle peered at Carlie. "Did you like Miriam?"

"Yes. I did." She hadn't wanted to like Miriam, but something about her—an openness and sweetness—had disarmed Carlie completely. "Her family was very nice to us, except for the grandfather," she said. "He kept staring at my aunt, as if—well."

Halle nodded. "The grandfather is from the old school. Very strict. Miriam's father is much more modern. He understands that people cannot live in a cocoon, that girls have to go out and meet people, have different experiences."

"Mitch is different when he's with them. He's so serious."

Halle laughed. "Well, he was probably nervous, too." She pulled a pile of diapers out of a dryer and began folding them with swift, efficient movements. "Look, any group has its own lingo. Of course Mitch is different with them. One gets swept along."

Carlie nodded. She recalled being in ballet school, the things she talked about with the other girls—costumes, performers, the merits of various ballet shoes. There was an attitude, even a language, that everyone expected and nearly everyone shared.

There was a small commotion as Richard, Mitch, and little Dov all trooped in together. Swiftly Halle touched her hand to her mouth, murmuring something. She saw Carlie's glance and flushed slightly. "I am always grateful," she said softly, "when they are home safe."

Carlie nodded, feeling a flash of envy. Never had she seen anyone so radiant, so happy. Yet Halle went on, her eyes lowered. "We can't let the children out alone, you know. It's not like in the States. We used to play out in the neighborhood when we were kids. Things were—different."

"I understand," Carlie said soberly. She thought of the San Fernando Valley with its pleasant streets and children out on their bikes.

"It's hard," Halle said. "But it's worth it. To be living in Israel, I mean." She smiled. "Pardon me, I'm not really proselytizing."

"Of course you are!" Mitch exclaimed, grinning. "You can't help it, you and Richard. It's your life."

"I suppose that's so," Halle admitted. "Well, when you

find what you love, you want to share it. Isn't that so?"

"Not necessarily," Carlie said. She was surprised at her own vehemence. "I love dogs, but I wouldn't bring you one and insist that you keep it."

"It's not the same," said Mitch. "We are talking about spirituality."

"Loving an animal is spiritual, too," said Carlie. "Some people get close to God through nature." She felt her pulse racing.

"That's true," Richard said pleasantly. "We are always accused of trying to indoctrinate people to *our* way. There's a lot of competition, a lot of fighting, even in religion."

"*Especially* in religion," Carlie exclaimed. "Look at all the wars, the crusades, people getting killed in the name of God." She felt Mitch watching her; he knew she was talking not to them, but to him.

Dov ran up to his father; Richard tucked the wriggling little boy under his arm and continued. "You're right. And lots of people drop out of religion because of that. Trouble is, it's not the religion that's responsible for those abuses. It's people—imperfect people hiding behind a perfect ideal."

"Come now, to the table," Halle called. "No arguments during lunch." They joked and talked about neutral things. After lunch Richard went back for a class. Mitch, Halle, Carlie, and the children went for a walk around the neighborhood, with tree-lined streets and substantial apartment buildings. It was like neighborhoods everywhere, Carlie thought.

But a woman limped up to them. She stood looking at Carlie, her face a study of confusion. "Where is the office?" she asked in English strangely broken. "The office?"

Carlie shook her head. She glanced down. On the

woman's arm a dark number was tattooed. She looked away.

Halle spoke softly to the woman in Hebrew, then German.

The woman murmured, backed away, hurried on.

"Poor soul," Halle said. "Did you see her number?"

"My cousin, Utz," said Mitch, "has a number on his arm."

"Have you been to *Yad Vashem*?" Halle asked Carlie.

"No," said Carlie. "What's that?"

Mitch said, "Museum of the Holocaust."

"Monument to the murdered six million," Halle said harshly. "When I see a person with a number tattooed on their arm, I realize again why we have to hold on, no matter what."

Carlie sighed. "Is it because of the Holocaust that you want to live in Israel? To be safe?"

"No. We're not safe here, as you can see." Halle called to Dov, who wandered ahead. "Dov! Come back here to Mama!" She turned to Carlie. "The country is in chaos most of the time. We've had four major wars with the Arabs. For years we have lived with rebellion. But it's *ours*."

"The Arabs says it's theirs."

"Whose side are you on, Carlie?" Mitch exclaimed.

Halle pulled Dov close to her side. "Look, this land is a gift," she told Carlie. "We have an obligation to it."

Carlie said, "You mean, the promised land. From the Bible." Her head was aching; she wanted to flee from this talk.

Halle persisted. "Yes! Take Hebron. The Palestinians want to rule it now. It's one of the terms of the peace accords. But Hebron has been ours since the time of Abraham. Abraham bought it—the first known deed in history—paid for it. Why should we give it away?"

"For peace," Carlie said. "I saw Rabin and Arafat on TV, shaking hands for peace on the White House lawn."

"Yes. We all saw it," Halle said. Her face was pained. "I wonder what it took," she said vehemently, "for our prime minister to shake that hand that was up to the elbow with Jewish blood."

"Arafat says they have changed," Mitch said. "The Palestinians say they want peace now."

"Ha! I'll believe it when the attacks end. Look, I have a son. I don't want him to go to war! I don't want him crippled or killed. Of course a life is more important than land. But if we give them the land, what guarantee do we have that they really mean peace? Or do we show weakness, and then they want more and more, until they even take Jerusalem?"

Halle pulled Dov toward her with such intensity that the boy squirmed and broke loose from her grasp. "Let me go!" he cried.

Halle sighed and tried to smile. "You see, it's not so easy. This land is—it's more than a piece of property. It's like a piece of our soul. I know we can't continue to rule the Arabs. It doesn't make sense. They want to be free of us, and we want to be free of them. So we try to separate, and we hope and pray we can do it in peace."

Carlie felt Daliah's hand in hers. The child skipped beside her, smiling. And Carlie felt ashamed of her own ignorance and blithe acceptance of a life without such burdens. Here, all but the children bore the scars of war. Anxiety brought a certain shrillness to people's voices, a tension to their bodies. It showed.

"Come," Halle said, obviously trying to lighten the atmosphere. "Enough talk. Let's go to the shops."

Mitch moved close to Carlie, matching his stride to hers. He smiled. "All this talk about war and peace, politics and religion. Home will seem pretty tame after this."

Carlie nodded, envisioning home, astonished that already she missed it. How could Halle and Richard leave the United States? How could they simply transplant themselves and endure all this trouble? She glanced at Halle's face, once more serene, glowing. We're different, she thought. I couldn't do this. I'd die of homesickness.

CHAPTER 14

MITCH INVITED MIRIAM to go with him and Carlie to the Biblical Zoo, which exhibited all the animals mentioned in the Bible. She had too much schoolwork, she said. He called the next day and the next. Miriam was out, her parents said. Could he come over and visit? Not now, said her mother. Tomorrow? Maybe.

The next morning, early, a message came, brought by a man on a bicycle. Mitch's name was written on the envelope in old-fashioned penmanship. Mitch read the message, stumbled out onto the porch, and read it again:

> Mitch Green, sir, we are sorry to say we cannot let you come here. We do not mean you any harm, but it is better you do not come. Nobody has any bad feelings to you, but this is how it must be.
>
> Thank you. Abraham Sarodi.

Mitch stared straight ahead; his mind felt blank. He read the note again. He ran to the telephone, grabbed it, and dialed.

He heard Mrs. Sarodi's lilting, "*Shalom*."

Mitch broke out in a sweat. He spoke, mustering the Hebrew words to make polite conversation—how are you? How is the family? How is your daughter, Miriam?

"*Tov, tov meod, boruch Hashem,*" Mrs. Sarodi answered, everyone was well, thank God.

He was stuck. What could he say now?

"*Adon Sarodi ba bayit?*" Is Mr. Sarodi at home? Yes, that was the correct procedure; after all, it was the father who had written him the note.

He came on the line, grunting, curt. "Yes! Mitch Green? You got my note. I'm sorry . . ."

"Is something wrong, Mr. Sarodi? Is Miriam all right? Is she ill?"

There was a pause. "No."

"Well, I thought—I got your letter. I just wanted to talk to Miriam."

"It is not possible," said her father.

"But—what is it? Please tell me, Mr. Sarodi. Please." He heard his voice crack; he felt like a fool.

"It is a great difficulty, Mitch," said the father, his tone strained now, as if he were lifting a heavy object. "I like you. Miriam, too. But this thing—a boy and a girl like you two—it is not what we want. You do not understand these things. You are young and you are from America."

Perspiration ran down along Mitch's sides. Everything was a blur.

"I don't understand, Mr. Sarodi. Maybe if I could come and talk to you in person. . . ."

Mr. Sarodi said, "We talk now, on the telephone."

"I don't understand what's going on, Mr. Sarodi."

"It is nothing going on—only that Miriam's grandfather

sees that this is not a right, a good—*shidech* for Miriam."

"*Shidech*?" Mitch knew the word—marriage match. "Mr. Sarodi, Miriam and I are just friends. We're too young even to think about . . ."

"You do not understand these things, how it is by us. Miriam talks now always about going to University or into the army. It is not our way. Miriam's sister married when she was eighteen. Her husband, Shuka, you met him, he is the grandson of a famous rabbi from Poland, who was the son, himself, of a very great sage, the family name we know since the year 1600. Do you understand? They were *tsadikim* of the highest order, and in our family, too . . ."

"What are you telling me, Mr. Sarodi?" Mitch felt his legs shaking, his chest aching. "That I'm not good enough for Miriam? I know I'm not learned—I'm still learning. I'm only a . . ."

"For Miriam—maybe you can understand this, Mitch—we want a man who is—*frum*. How you say it? Religious. Observant. I mean, from birth. From *before* birth. Do you understand?"

Things were choking him—phrases, ideas, lies. He could barely get the words out. "They told us here in school," he said, "and Miriam said it, too, that beside a *ba'al teshuvah* not even the wisest sage can stand. What about that?"

"Ah, that is true," said Mr. Sarodi, chuckling slightly. "Very true. But it does not mean that this is the best for our daughter."

Mitch heard nothing more; maybe he hung up first. He didn't know. Maybe he even slammed down the receiver. He wasn't sure.

Outside, Mitch felt assaulted by the cold morning air, as

if he'd been struck in the chest. Hypocrites! Lousy hypocrites! What right had they to keep him and Miriam apart? That grandfather, old devil! Old tyrant! Mitch beat fists against his thighs. He rushed along the street, kicking a bent trash can so that it clattered and rolled, and a skinny cat leaped forth with a yeowl. "Go to hell!" he screamed out in a rage.

A woman hurried past, eyes straight ahead, face set in consternation.

Mitch slowed his steps. He took several deep breaths, the way his basketball coach had taught him to do when he was injured or out of control. Oh, Coach! He wished for the feel of that large, steady hand on his shoulder, that earnest, friendly face. Oh, God. Never had he felt so forsaken or so stupid.

Why had he expected things to be any different here? All those stories, the family feeling, the kindness, the food heaped high on his plate—it meant nothing at all.

Now, what would he tell his mother? She'd get that lock on her face, *I told you so!* Her features would sharpen. She'd talk and talk until he'd go crazy wanting to scream at her, but he'd stand there and take it—*You and your ideas, you thought with all their prayers and their talk, these people were different; well, let me tell you, people are the same all over. If you're not one of them, you don't belong, and they never let you forget it. Good thing you found out now, before you got trapped. You can come home and it will be just like before. Nobody will say anything, you'll see your old buddies, pick up next semester at UCLA, you can get your own apartment—oh, Mitch, I'm going to call your father and tell him you're coming home with us!*

He walked faster, as if he were in a hurry to get somewhere, while it struck him that he had noplace to go. He was stuck, like a rat on a treadmill, running nowhere.

He thought of the people in Miriam's family, their history. Nothing in his past could compare to those saints who walked two thousand miles to Jerusalem, who struggled through all those years of poverty and abuse and called it all worthwhile, because they were living in the holy city. Who was he that he should imagine himself standing in their place?

Maybe if his mother hadn't looked so flashy; maybe if Carlie hadn't talked so much—no. It was not their fault. He was the one lacking.

He was just another spoiled American kid, trying to look good. If things got too tough, he knew, he could turn around and go back anytime. He had a safety net.

He saw a middle-aged couple walking hand in hand. He could tell they were married, by the easy way their steps were in rhythm. He tried to imagine walking with Miriam years from now, but he could get no further than this moment, his anger and his longing, remembering all the times he had walked beside her, wanting her so fiercely that he could hardly speak. If he had touched Miriam, if he had kissed her, if he hadn't been so horribly frustrated all the time, maybe now he'd know whether it was really love. But if it wasn't love, why did he now feel so terrible, so empty? How did one know the difference between desire and true love?

Mitch walked on until he came to the Wall, where the early morning worshipers stood with their prayer shawls and *tefilllin.* He had read about one old man who had not missed a single morning since 1967, when the Wall was reclaimed after the Six-Day War. Then, seasoned soldiers, men who had never been religious, called it a miracle. They pressed their bodies against the Wall and prayed.

Devotion. This was what he lacked, and Mr. Sarodi and the grandfather saw it plainly. He was like a cardboard person, one-dimensional, lacking depth. He knew it. Guilty! he screamed within himself. He stood gazing at the Wall. It seemed wrong, in this mood, to approach it. One serves God with joy, not with weeping. But then, what are all those tears that people shed at the Wall? In confusion, he walked back to the *yeshiva.*

Guy was at the mirror, trimming the ends of his mustache with a small pair of scissors. Josh sat on the floor, reading, his back against the wall.

"What's up?" Guy turned, his mouth twisted, words muffled.

"Nothing."

"You look like you swallowed a fish. Raw."

"Miriam's father said it's off. I'm not *frum* enough."

Guy whirled around. Amazement and anger distorted his face. "What?"

"We've heard this before. We fall in between the cracks. Too holy for our secular families, too ignorant for the really religious. . . ." Mitch held out the letter to his friend.

"Hypocrites!" Guy exclaimed, glancing at the note.

"Who's under the gun now?" David came in, his hair still wet from the shower.

"Tell him," Guy said.

Mitch sat down on his bed, his head in his hands. "Sarodi canceled me. It's the grandfather. He thinks I'm not good enough, not religious enough."

"Does the grandfather run that family?" David demanded.

"Apparently so."

"It is the old way," Guy said soberly. "What are you going to do?"

Mitch looked up. "What can I do? I'm not going to crash their house! Anyway, they are right." He lifted his hands, fingers outspread. "I have nothing to offer. No wisdom, no heritage."

"You've got a lot to offer," Josh said.

"But aren't you going to talk to Miriam?" Guy said. "Doesn't she have anything to say about it?"

"This isn't the Middle Ages," David added.

Mitch rose. "Look, I can go to Miriam and make a big scene. I can get her all upset about this, maybe even make her defy her parents—for a while. In the end . . ." He sat down again, then flung himself back against the pillows. "Nothing changes."

Josh stood up. "Maybe something good will come of it," he said seriously. "Maybe everything happens for the best."

David gave a laugh. "Our philosopher, our *tsadik*. I think you should at least talk to Miriam."

"Yes," said Guy. "Maybe she doesn't even know about the letter."

"I'll think about it," Mitch said.

"You coming to class?" His roommates stood at the door.

"No. You go ahead."

Alone, Mitch felt the isolation. Just a few hours ago his life had seemed full of promise. Now he could think of nothing that he wanted to do, no place he wanted to go. Everything seemed irrelevant and dead.

He glanced at the nightstand where he kept the velvet bag with his *tallit* and *tefillin*. He had missed the morning prayers, because of Miriam. Now he picked up the bag, fingering the soft velvet. A subtle fragrance clung to these objects, a faint presence that implied more than one could see or touch.

Mitch unfolded the large shawl, held the cloth to his lips for a moment, then laid it over his shoulders. Like a small tent, the shawl enfolded him. The world outside seemed to recede. All that he needed of reality was here and now.

He remembered a story he had heard about a Jewish boy who, having entered University, found a conflict between the ancient traditions and the new sciences. The boy went home for vacation, spouting off all his newfound knowledge, spending the entire afternoon in heated denunciation of the old ways. But as it grew dark, the boy got his prayer book and hastened to his devotions. What are you doing? asked the father, perplexed. I thought you just told me how outmoded we are, and now I see you are ready for the afternoon prayers. The son looked at his father, astonished. I know I said all those things, he declared, and they may be true, but a Jew has to *daven*—a Jew has to pray.

Mrs. Sarodi answered the door. The moment she saw him, her face changed. She turned red, then pale. She stepped back into the room, her hands in the air as if to hold him off, and she called without turning her head, "Miriam!"

Miriam's voice rang back, questioning, what is it?

The mother did not answer, but stood looking at Mitch, slowly shaking her head.

Miriam appeared. She looked frail and young in her school dress, a long blue jumper and white blouse, and a blue beret.

Mitch stood there awkwardly, holding out his hand, then letting it drop to his side. "Hello, Miriam."

"Hello, Mitch. You got my father's letter, didn't you?"

"Yes. He told me that your grandfather does not want you to see me."

"It is true," she said in a high voice.

"How do you feel about this?"

"I feel the same," she said, still in that strange pitch.

"How could you?" Mitch exclaimed. He hated the pleading tone of his voice, was powerless to change it, for his heart beat like a hammer, and every muscle in his body felt strained to the breaking point. "Miriam, we were getting to know each other; I thought you liked me. You even said so. Didn't you?" he demanded.

"I like many people," she said simply, half turning away.

He wanted to reach out and grab her arm, shake her, force her to respond.

Suddenly her father appeared, his walk determined, almost truculent. "Miriam, you have to leave for school, don't you?"

"Yes, Papa."

"Then go."

"Wait a minute, Mr. Sarodi," Mitch said. "I came to talk to Miriam. Is she a child, or a slave in this house?" he added recklessly.

The father turned to his daughter, pointing. "Go, Miriam." He murmured something more in rapid Hebrew.

Swiftly, without another glance, Miriam took her schoolbag and went out.

Abraham Sarodi turned to Mitch. "Maybe Miriam did not tell you," he said. "But she is—she is with someone else.

A young man she has known for a long time."

"But . . . but . . . ," Mitch stammered. "Miriam invited me to begin with. If she was seeing someone else . . . I thought . . . Miriam phoned me. She asked me . . . "

"Miriam has been interested in this young man for a long time," her father said. "Many months. We know the family. First we thought that this boy was not . . . well, now, we are thinking about it more, he is a fine boy, from a fine family."

The words came out before Mitch could think. "I see. After me, he looks good."

"Mitch, do not make this so hard; we like you," said Mr. Sarodi, but as he spoke he began to lead Mitch out the door, down the walk.

His mother hired a car to take them to Tel Aviv. Everyone would know they were tourists, Mitch thought. Israelis never hired a car. He glanced at his mother, impeccably dressed in black slacks and a plaid blazer. Carlie, too, looked like someone in an advertisement in her red turtleneck sweater and jeans. Her hair was long, very blond. He wondered whether she did something to it to get that color, but it was only an idle thought. His mind's eye pictured Miriam, her blue schoolgirl jumper; her dark, wavy hair.

She had waited for him on the street, stopping him as he hurried past. "Mitch! Wait."

"You're not supposed to talk to me," he muttered.

"Please. Do not be angry with me."

He looked at her. Tears stood in her eyes. "I don't understand," he said. "What happened?"

Miriam looked down. She swallowed hard. "Grandfather is so furious," she said. "It has gone on too long, he said, this—you and me. It is his way. The old way. When girl and boy see each other six, seven times, they decide yes or no. If they don't want to marry, it is over."

"But, Miriam, we never . . ."

She held up her hand, as if to push him away. "It was a big fight. Even Uncle Shlomo came from Jaffa, and they all talked and shouted. My father thinks there is nothing wrong with—being friendly. He says, like Abraham *avinu*, we should show hospitality and be kind to people, and that you and I are friends. Grandfather and Uncle Shlomo, and also my mother, shout that it is nonsense! No friendship like this—I am already a woman, they say, and you are a man."

Miriam's breath came in sharp gasps. Her cheeks were flushed. Mitch moved toward her. She drew away. "I cannot go against them, Mitch." She opened her hand, and Mitch saw the silver and turquoise pendant. "I will give this back to you," she said. "It is not right that I take it now."

He turned away. "Forget it, Miriam. It's yours. I made it for you."

"No. I cannot."

"I won't take it!"

"Yes. You will." She hung the chain over the spike of an iron fence. "When I go," she said, "you take it."

"I won't."

But when Miriam was out of sight, Mitch had gone back to see his pendant, his work of art, still hanging on the fence. Now he felt it in his pocket and clenched his hand around it.

"It's over," he said softly.

"What?" asked his mother.

"With Miriam."

"Over?" Carlie echoed.

His mother laid her hand on his arm. "I'm sorry, Mitch." She looked strained. "What did she say? Was it us? Something we did? I tried hard, Mitch, not to say the wrong thing. I didn't want to embarrass you."

"You didn't. It's okay."

"Then what happened?"

"I don't really want to discuss it," he said. "It just won't work out. We're too different."

"I could see that," said his mother.

"Please," said Mitch. He felt Carlie's shoulder against his. Her presence seemed to fill every space around him. He sensed her embarrassment.

"Mitch," she began.

"What?"

"What was the reason? I thought—Miriam told me she might even come to visit us. I liked her. I thought . . ."

"Whatever you thought, forget it," he said abruptly.

The three of them sat in the car, pretending to look at the sights. Carlie and his mother gave him an occasional nervous glance. He could just see their minds working. *Now he'll come home. He'll be too embarrassed, too upset to stay. He'll realize this business isn't what it's cracked up to be.*

The car took them into the bustle of Tel Aviv, its shops and apartment houses, past the *shuk*, the open-air bazaar where throngs of people bartered and shopped.

"Oh, I want to go there!" Carlie called out.

"Driver, stop! We'll meet you back here," Vivian said, "in about half an hour."

"Very well, Missus," said the driver. He got out, lounged against his car, looking after them with an amused expression.

They walked among the stalls, hung with bright fabrics, T-shirts, beads, carved wooden camels and donkeys, produce piled high. Carlie bought a large T-shirt with a Coca-Cola emblem in Hebrew. "It's for Uncle Harry," she explained.

"He'll love it," said Vivian.

Mitch wished he had noticed the shirt. Why hadn't he thought of giving his father a gift? Especially that Coca-Cola shirt; his dad had collected Coke memorabilia since childhood. "It didn't cost anything," he had once told Mitch. "I had no money, but I wanted to collect things, like all kids do. Maybe now," he always said, "they're worth something."

Mitch watched Carlie, the lightness of her step, her smile as she tried to communicate in English with the merchants. He felt heavy, lost. What about tomorrow? Next week? When would those words of Miriam's and Mr. Sarodi's stop rattling through his mind?

His mother took his arm. "Mitch, I'm sorry you're unhappy," she said. "I know you're upset."

"It's okay, Mom."

"But this is the best thing that could have happened to you. Someday you'll realize that."

"I'm okay, Mom. Really." How could it be the best thing? He'd been hurt and humiliated. Of course, he didn't want to get married. If it had been different, and Miriam's family had tried to pressure him into marriage, he'd have broken it off, fast! Was it love that made him so miserable now, or pride?

He moved to a counter of trinkets and picked up a Bedouin silver jewel box. In his little workshop he had started a wall hanging of beaten silver and copper. The materials lay there now, waiting for him. He had spent many nights sketching, first trees, then people, stones, buildings, finally setting it aside, unresolved. The feel of the mallet in his hands, the resistance of metal, the marks of his hands, his tools—all held out promises, still unresolved.

Idly Mitch picked up a large grapefruit, pressing it in his hands. The produce woman yelled out in Hebrew, "Stop that! You think this is your girlfriend? You buy, then you squeeze!"

Carlie laughed. "I think I know what she said."

Vivian took both their arms, walking between them. Something in her expression boasted to passersby, "My two children! My lovely, nearly grown-up children."

"When I was seventeen," she said, "I was in love with a boy who broke up with me because I wouldn't . . . ," she hesitated, "go to bed with him. I cried for three days. He started going with another girl. She was class secretary, very popular. All senior year I realized I could have gone to the prom with him and been the envy of all the girls, but I . . ."

"You had your principles," Mitch said, kissing her cheek. "If you'd married him," he said, "you wouldn't have had me."

She smiled. "That's right." She let go of his arm, but kept Carlie close. "This thing with Miriam. Breaking up. Someday you will thank your lucky stars."

Mitch sighed.

"Because these people are fanatics. To belong in their group, one has to give up all one's individuality."

"That's not true, Mom," Mitch said. He quickened his steps. His mother came after him.

"It is true. Let me tell you something. Your grandma Rose was born orthodox. *Frum*, as they call it."

Mitch stopped and whirled around. "What? Grandma Rose?"

"Oh, yes, they were orthodox. They were so pious that Rose wasn't even allowed to go to school."

"Why didn't you ever mention it?" he cried. "What's wrong with this family?"

His mother brushed him aside. "Girls didn't need to be educated, they said. It was in Poland, a little *shtetel*, those villages that the present generation likes to idealize."

"She never told me," Mitch said. "Why doesn't anyone . . . ?"

"They were dirt-poor. Rose had to learn how to stitch lace, for sale in the local shops. Rose begged to go to school. They laughed at her. Why should a girl know how to read? To cook and sew is enough, and to make babies. They were planning to marry her, at sixteen, to a man of thirty-nine. A widower with four children, the oldest was twelve."

Carlie had stopped, too. The three of them stood in the *shuk* with people milling past. The smell of garlic and spices and fried cakes swirled all around them.

Vivian went on, her voice carrying, her stance rigid. "So Rose ran away and married the first guy who came along. She thought he was smart and dashing. What he was, was a wild man. Married Rose and starting philandering from day one. She was already pregnant."

"Grandfather Max. Mordechai," said Mitch.

"Let's go back to the car," said his mother.

"Wait! What happened?"

"They disowned her. They actually sat *shiva* for her."

"But—he was a Jew," Mitch sputtered. "Why would they do that?"

"What's *shiva*?" Carlie asked. "You guys! What are you talking about?"

"It's what you do when someone dies," Mitch said.

"We didn't, for my parents," Carlie said.

"It's an old tradition," his mother said with a shrug. "For seven days they sit on low stools and mourn. They cover the mirrors, don't cook . . ."

"But Rose didn't die," Carlie said. "She just got married."

"They cut her off because she didn't marry the man of their choice. He wasn't religious. So they cut her off, as if she were dead."

"I never knew any of this," said Mitch.

"You didn't know that Grandma Rose can't read?"

"Yes. I knew that part."

"Mitch!" His mother grabbed his arm. "These people demand conformity. They can't handle debate or any new ideas. Everything's decided by the elders, by tradition. Every aspect of life, is dictated—where you go, what you do, your life's work."

"Oh!" Mitch cried. "You mean like Dad? You mean like home?"

His mother suddenly paled, shook herself, then rushed back to the car, pulling Carlie beside her.

Slowly Mitch followed, thinking—if things had been different, and Grandma Rose hadn't married Mordechai, then he would have been *frum* from birth, as Mr. Sarodi had put it. What might it have been like to live that way, the family together in joy over the festivals, observing every ounce of the tradition, being wholly bound up in Judaism?

And if that had been the case, would he now have rebelled against it?

CHAPTER 15

OCCASIONALLY VIVIAN MOANED and turned in her sleep. Carlie sat in the large, overstuffed chair, wide awake, her diary on her knee. A small halo of yellow light fell from the standing lamp; the rest of the room lay in shadows. She wrote:

This was one of the longest days of my life. It started out cold in the morning, warmed up as we had breakfast, then we met Mitch and took the "sherut," or jitney, to Tel Aviv. Mitch finally talked his mom out of hiring a car again—the huge expense! An Israeli family would live on that amount of money for a week, he said. It was fun seeing all those people crammed together, carrying babies and bundles.

We planned to meet Halle and little Dov and Daliah at the Tel Aviv museum. Halle and the kids had spent the night with friends in Ra'anannah. We'd all go back to Jerusalem together on the bus. Another adventure—Aunt Vivian made a sour face, but she went along.

She's been making sketches. I think she would like it here if she wasn't so worried about getting Mitch home. Why am I doing this? Why am I writing trivia? Melanie would say it's avoidance. She's right.

We stopped at a Pizza Hut for pizza, no pepperoni; they don't eat meat with cheese. Mitch explained it all again. I keep forgetting. Pizza Hut looks so weird here, as if little bits of America have been dropped, like leaflets, all over the world. Coca-Cola, McDonald's, Nike shoes. People listen to American rock on their Walkmans, and for a minute you think you're back in the U.S., then you see a very wrinkled Arab leading a camel draped in bright blankets. . . . Why am I writing all this stuff?

Carlie glanced toward the bed where Vivian lay bunched into a ball, sound asleep. She looked so vulnerable that Carlie wanted to go to her, to lay a hand on her face, gently massaging away the terror. But she did not want to awaken her aunt; let her sleep, she thought.

Carlie stretched, but even that slight movement was painful, as if she had been scrunched inside a bottle for days, and everything hurt. She touched the swelling on her lip, ran her tongue over it, shuddered. She began again, bending down close to the book.

We went to the Tel Aviv Museum. After a while my eyes started to sting and I wanted to leave. But Mitch and his mom were soaking up the art, especially the Chagall, talking about style and color, and the way his figures seem to float. . . .

Carlie got up and walked to the window. The night sky was tinged with a faint lavender haze. Star light, star bright—what should she wish for? She felt a slow, deep ache beginning in her chest, spreading through her body. Her own breath was too tender, almost painful. She rubbed her fingertips lightly along her arm, up to her throat. The slight pressure of her own fingers sent waves of longing through her body, down her spine. She became aware of the fullness of her lips, of her hair, of all the places where her body touched her clothes. She wanted to cry, then to laugh.

Alive! Something shouted inside her. We're alive!

She sat down again with her diary, this time determined to finish.

Finally we met Halle and the kids. Daliah ran to us. Mitch picked her up and carried her; she loved it, put her arms around his neck. And I loved seeing him holding that little girl. It made me think about Halle's question that day: Does Mitch want children? And I imagined Mitch with a child of his own, a little baby. . . .

We all walked to the bus station, and it was packed, people pushing to get their tickets, hollering, squeezing into the bus.

Aunt Vivian didn't like it. She gets kind of claustrophobic in tight places, I think, but she didn't say anything. There weren't enough seats, so Halle took Dov on her lap, and Mitch held Daliah. I was standing up, holding on to a pole. I'd rather stand, I said, and it was true, because that way I could see everything better. We went around a corner, I sort of lurched and Mitch grabbed me and we laughed and . . .

Carlie realized she was biting the pen. Her lip hurt. She took a deep breath and continued.

At first it just sounded like a thud. I thought we had hit something, or maybe something had been thrown at the bus, or maybe a tire came off. Then everything shattered, the noise was incredible, glass breaking, people screaming. Something slammed down on my head, hard. The doors and windows were blasted out, smoke everywhere. A person fell on top of me. I must have blacked out, then I saw fire, and I heard crying. Someone pulled my arm and yelled at me to get out. I screamed back, without really knowing how I knew, that I couldn't leave, because of the crying child. I thought it was Dov. Someone yelled, "The bus could blow up at any moment!" I couldn't leave. The cries were so pitiful. I remember pulling and straining with all my strength. I remember something coming apart, pulling the child out, running through a rip in the side of the bus. I fell down on the sidewalk and I was screaming for Mitch and Aunt Vivian. Aunt Vivian came, and she knelt down on the ground, and she was sobbing, and she held me so tight, saying my name over and over again, and she said, "Carlie, darling, please be all right. Carlie, darling, I love you so!" I couldn't even answer her, I was so dazed.

Mitch lay on the ground, still holding Daliah, with Halle kneeling down over both of them, Dov still hanging from her arms. Someone came running up to us, bringing a stretcher, but all I could see was Mitch, blood running down his face, covering his chest, and he was still holding Daliah, and there was blood all over her, and her arm was bloody, and her little hand was gone.

Flashing lights. The weird zigzag screams of the ambulance. Voices cutting into air, sharp, urgent, anguished.

"Daliah! Daliah! My God, my baby, Daliah!" Halle's face was contorted. Her scream was harsh and guttural, like an animal.

"Mitch!" Carlie screamed. "Look at me, Mitch! Can you see me?"

He turned his head. "Yes. I'm—okay."

Carlie's whole body heaved with sobs. She shook like a leaf from head to toe, icy cold. Her teeth chattered; she bit her lip. Blood ran into her mouth.

Vivian was there, her face very close to Carlie's. "Carlie, honey, everything is okay. You saved that little boy. His mother wants to talk to you. She wants to thank you, darling."

Someone came to her, a woman with a cut on her forehead. The woman was trembling. She spoke in Hebrew, saying the same words over and over again, words Carlie could not understand. But she understood the pressure of the mother's hands as she clasped Carlie to her bosom, weeping.

Men and women in smocks ran forward. "Hospital." They were taken in the ambulance, flashing lights, zigzag screams, doctors rushing in, holding up IV's.

"They're taking Daliah to surgery. There's danger of infection . . . damage . . . complete . . . no chance, even if we could find it." Something else had taken hold of Halle now, a kind of numb resignation. She looked like a figure made of wax, pale and strange. She whispered, "They cannot reattach the hand. No. Of course not. But she's alive. *Boruch Hashem.*"

Patterns presented themselves, faces and voices, bright lights and dark shadows. Carlie was taken into a small room. Her hand stung. Someone gave her a shot, spoke to her, but she couldn't comprehend anything. Gradually words seeped into her consciousness. Odd words, woeful words. Daliah's hand. Gone. Mitch bleeding. Shirt ripped away. Mitch!

And suddenly he was there before her. And then she was in his arms, clinging to him, sobbing. In his arms she was safe, but more than that, she was whole and utterly content. She felt his hands on her hair, then he was kissing her face, murmuring over and over, "It's okay, Carlie. It's okay." And she knew in that moment that what she felt by his nearness was more than sisterly, more even than need, but mingled with the desire to give, to make him happy. She loved him. She loved him.

They had all been released from the hospital, even Daliah, with the huge round bandage already forming a stump. "Better for her to go home, after this shock, than to stay in a strange place. We have given her massive antibiotics.

Bring her back in the morning for us to check her over. In time, we can fit her with a . . ."

Nobody wanted to say the words, artificial hand. Such devices were for veterans or old people, those maimed in terrible accidents or wars. This, Carlie thought, swallowing hard, this is a war. I am in a war.

As in a war, news spread. Suddenly Halle's house was a command post. Richard came home from the *yeshiva*, and Tal and several other students.

She heard people talking. They were talking about her, and it sounded like someone else, someone she didn't know. "I never saw anything like it. She refused to leave that burning bus, kept screaming that a child was caught there between two seats. Can't imagine how she knew, how she had the presence of mind. . . . It was utter chaos, but she went back, yes, back into that bus and somehow—God knows how she got the strength, she pulled that little boy out of there. The metal was hot. Her hand . . ." Carlie looked down at the bandages on her left hand. It felt numb. She had seen the blisters. They had given her something, an injection. Maybe that was why she felt so strange, so lightheaded and almost elated. Empty and full at the same time; empty of thoughts, full of feelings.

The men milled about, their tension like a fine dust in the air, settling over everything. Food appeared—hard-boiled eggs, cheese, biscuits, and fruit. People ate, as at a wake. Suddenly hunger seized them, the will to life overcoming the specter of death. "Eat! Eat!" A neighbor dressed in a limp housedress, her head covered with a kerchief, tottered back and forth, insisting, "Eat! You need to keep up your strength!"

Tal brought Carlie an ice pack and laid it gently on her

face. "You have two black eyes," he said. She only nodded and let herself be tended, like a child. Somehow, speech, the very thought of forming words, required more effort than she could summon.

Reporters came to the house. Their cameras flashed. They rattled out questions. "What do you think of the peace process? Do you think we can negotiate with terrorists?"

Richard, tight-lipped and furious, cursed them and sent them away. "Leave us alone!"

Still more people appeared: Halle's mother, her expression ferocious from holding back tears. It was growing dark. The men came together at the window to say the late afternoon prayers. Carlie heard the combined murmur of their voices. She watched the shadows advancing and retreating as the men moved in prayer.

The women gathered together at one end of the room. Carlie saw Aunt Vivian and Halle in a swift embrace. Halle's mother and Vivian drew close, whispering together like sisters. And Carlie, for all the grief and shock, felt surrounded and safe, loved.

Rabbi Nachum came in the early evening. Nobody thought of leaving; their togetherness, now, was what kept them sane. The rabbi patted his pockets, as if he had lost something. He went to each person. To Carlie, he murmured, "My dear lady. You are one of our heroes." Carlie held the words close, like a warm blanket. Richard brought her a cup of tea and a biscuit and jam. Food had never tasted so good; the goodness brought tears to Carlie's eyes.

She sat back. To her surprise, Daliah came toward her, extending her bandaged arm. "Look," Daliah said. "We're twins."

Carlie held out her arms. Daliah settled in her lap, her head against Carlie's chest. And Carlie drew in the warmth and softness of the child, and the fragrance of her silky hair. "Mama is with Ephraim now," Daliah said. "Can I stay here with you?"

"Of course," Carlie murmured, giving Daliah a kiss.

The rabbi and Vivian found each other. They sat down, Vivian on the sofa beside Carlie, the rabbi in a large, battered chair.

"I am so sorry that we have to meet under these conditions," said the rabbi.

"It was good of you to come," said Vivian.

"Of course! We are a family—students and teachers. Your son is a very special young man. And now I see your niece, too, is one of those special people. We're lucky that Mitch came to spend time with us."

"It wasn't my choice, Rabbi," Vivian said. "Surely you know I've been very concerned."

"As any good mother would be. You came to visit him, to see for yourself. Many parents won't make that effort. They cut off their children. . . . Believe me, if I had a son or daughter, I would never cut them off."

"Never? Even if they—if they disobeyed? Married out of the faith, for instance?"

Rabbi Nachum wiped his forehead. "I couldn't do it. A child is a treasure, a gift from God, a precious soul. Each is entitled to its own choices."

"Many orthodox wouldn't agree with you," Vivian said.

Carlie felt Daliah's soft breathing, the warmth of her body.

"We are not all alike," said the rabbi.

"I know." Vivian clasped her hands together. "I mean to take my son back home with me," she said.

"Very well. Will he go?"

"I hoped that you would speak with him. Tell him to honor his father and his mother. Tell him how it is for a mother to lose a child."

Carlie, listening, found herself scarcely breathing, to let Daliah sleep. She had been so distant from babies and little children, from people who, perhaps, needed her. Now she fully realized what she had done. She had saved a child! She had pulled him out of that wreckage, thinking—what? Not thinking. Just feeling and doing. Maybe that was the point, the lesson to be learned, just to do it.

"But if he stays," her aunt was saying, "I will lose him!"

"To God?" The rabbi cocked his head, listening.

"Yes! I know it sounds horrible to you, because in your life God always comes first. But I live in *this* world. I'm just a mother, while you, you're a professional."

The rabbi smiled slightly. "A professional Jew."

Vivian said, "My son vacillates. You should know that about him. He tries one new thing after the other. Then he drops them. In the meantime, people can get hurt."

"Young people ought to experiment," said the rabbi.

"This is different. This is a—dark hole. Religion pulls, works on a person's fears and longings. It makes promises, incredible promises! Religion makes people feel guilty. You can never be good enough—no, and when things are terrible, why, it's only punishment for our own sins!"

Rabbi Nachum drew back. "What has happened to you?"

"Nothing!" But it was a cry of pain.

Carlie clasped Daliah close to her body. Sleep, she thought. Sleep.

"My husband has a distant cousin," Vivian said. "Utz is his name. He was a very religious man, living in Poland. Some kind of official in the synagogue—*shames*?"

"Yes. Custodian, keeper of things, of ritual objects."

"The Nazis sent him to Auschwitz. He survived because he was on the death detail. They gave him a giant shovel and large iron tongs. It was his job to pull the burned bodies—skeletons—from the ovens. They also gave him smaller tongs to extract the gold from the teeth of the skulls."

Carlie sat very still; a white mist seemed to cover her, like a blanket. Her heart pounded. She closed her eyes, as if she could shut out this horror. She did not want to know it. Uncle Utz, thin as a rail, with that thin little smile, hesitating as he took a small piece of lox onto his plate, plucking up half a bagel, taking small bites of things, then falling asleep—Uncle Utz would always suffer alone.

The rabbi's eyes were moist. "Many lost their belief because of the Holocaust."

"I never believed," Vivian said. "Not like that. I never thought that I could petition God for the things I want, or that He would rush in and save me. I knew better."

"You are right," said Rabbi Nachum. "It is a dark hole, endless paradox, uncertainty. There is so much we do not understand. It is a journey we make in the dark—physical creatures looking for pure spirit, trying to translate one realm into another. Sometimes, however"—his voice became very soft, almost like a caress—"sometimes we come close. We manage to glimpse the hem of His garment."

"Rabbi," Vivian said, "I'm a practical person."

"Yes. Of course."

"I want my son back. If he wants to come home," she proposed, "you won't stand in his way."

"Certainly not."

"That's all I ask."

"I wish you well, Mrs. Green." Rabbi Nachum stood up, sighing deeply, nodding.

Vivian stood opposite him, nodding back. She did not reach out to shake his hand.

Carlie, watching them, was aware of their conversation as one is aware of shadows moving on a screen. Too much feeling surrounded her; too much love and grief and—yes, even hope.

She only wanted to go home. In her mind's eye was the pretty house in the valley, the green front lawn and the low fence, the mailbox on the curb, the oleander bushes along the walk.

Halle came to take Daliah from her. Her hands trembled visibly. Her face was ghostly pale. For a long moment the two looked into each other's eyes, and Carlie felt completely understood. No need to say the words, to talk about her hopes for the future, having a child like this, being needed, being whole. Halle seemed to know. She gave a nod and whispered, "Thank you, Carlie. You made us all proud."

CHAPTER 16

IT WAS STRANGE, the things a bomb does that have nothing to do with detonation or shrapnel—or the aftermath—sirens, stitches, anesthetic. The bomb changed everything.

He had held Carlie close. He had felt her arms around him, and the softness of her body. When he kissed her cheek, it took his breath away and made him wonder—how can I feel like this with Carlie, when I thought I was in love with Miriam? Carlie is my cousin—are these feelings wrong? He had looked at her and seen her need, and it had made him feel tender, protective, and strong.

There was a change, too, in the way his mother looked at him. Instead of drawing nearer, she seemed to stand away, shy. Perhaps his own manhood had been proven in that terrible blast. It was he who had held Daliah close to his chest, he who had instantly shielded her with his own body, tucked her under himself the way a mother bird nests over her young. He had taken the blows of flying debris on his skull and over the ridge of his cheek. At the hospital they shaved a large patch of his hair where the stitches were fastened, resembling a zipper. It gave him a curious look, like something unfinished.

The experience of the bomb also changed his status among the students, and he felt it even when he brushed past strangers on the street. He had survived his initiation. Now he belonged.

They tried to call his dad. All the circuits were busy.

"It happens," Tal said, "every time there is a scare."

"You mean every day?"

"You can still joke," said Tal. "That's good. Here, we laugh a lot."

"I know."

After two days they got through to Mitch's dad, his mother standing in the hotel room.

"We were on that bus," his mother said. She looked very pale. Since the bomb, Mitch could see the bluish veins on her eyelids. "We're fine, Harry," she said. "Just shaken up a little. No, there are no earlier flights back. No, I haven't checked, but—what's the point? We'll finish our visit."

Finally his mother handed Mitch the receiver; her eyes lingered on his face. "Your father," she said, "wants to talk to you."

"Dad!" Mitch felt a strange jubilation. Since the bombing, he was seized with sudden bursts of energy, as now. "We're okay, Dad. Carlie's fine, too, a burn and some scratches. She pulled a little boy out of the bus. Carlie saved him! But it *was* terrible. Our friend's little girl lost her hand. Yes. *Her hand.*" He hated repeating it; his father had stammered, "What? What did you say?" It seemed obscene to repeat it.

His father's tone was bitter, heavy. "Your grandma Rose, when she heard it on the news and then we couldn't reach you—I thought she'd have a heart attack. She's in bed now. Worried sick."

"I'm sorry, Dad."

"Are you coming home now, Mitch? Mitch, listen. Be sensible. You don't belong there. It's a third world country. People are—wild. They do these things. . . ."

"Dad, there's crime in L.A., too."

"Listen to me, Mitch! For God's sake, listen, for once in your life. You don't belong there. You're one of the lucky ones, born in America. How many people would give everything they own just to set foot in the United States?"

"Like your father," Mitch said. "He gave up everything."

"Right! People sacrificed for you, so that you could have a good life. People died for you. Your own grandfather. Why go looking for trouble? Come home, Mitch."

"I'm not looking for trouble, Dad. I'm studying."

"Then come home for a visit, Mitch. Just for a few weeks."

"I'll think about it, Dad."

"Let me talk to Carlie."

Mitch handed Carlie the receiver. He watched and listened. Carlie stood with her legs crossed, her body slightly bent as she spoke to his father in a voice that was tender and low. The two of them had a certain bond; he did not know what it was.

Carlie said, "We're fine, Uncle Harry. Would you do me a favor? Would you call Melanie for me? Her number's in Aunt Vivian's book."

Carlie's hair fell over her cheek. She glanced at Mitch. He saw the blue of her eyes. He remembered her screams when she saw his injury—just superficial scratches, but he had been covered with blood. In the hospital she had run into his arms, sobbing. Now she was composed.

Carlie said, "Tell Melanie we're fine. And tell her I'm sorry. Tell her it's okay. I was wrong to get mad at her."

A pause. Carlie gestured with her hands, shook her head so that her hair waved around her face. "She'll know what it's about," Carlie said.

More words went softly into Carlie's ear; Mitch knew what they were, even though he couldn't hear them.

Mitch heard Carlie's soft response. "I'm trying, Uncle Harry."

Students came and went. It was no disgrace. It was the philosophy of this *yeshiva* to be welcoming, but never demanding.

The question was like a constant presence, a pressure on Mitch's mind and on his body. He felt the weight of it even while he slept. Why not go home? He had every reason, could explain it with impunity to anyone who asked. *I left because of my folks—they were really upset. Even my grandmother, she's in her eighties, you know.* Yes, a noble motive, sacrifice for the sake of his family.

Or for the sake of practicality. *I have to get back to school, need to get on with my life, university, a career. Oh, it was a terrific experience, taking time off like that—I wouldn't trade it for anything. But it's time to get back.* Yes, that was sensible. Anyone could understand it.

Then there was Miriam. *I got involved with a girl. Religious girl. Beautiful. But they get married really young, and, hey, I'm only eighteen years old! I've got tons of living to do before I settle down. See, they have a whole different mind-set over there. . . .*

His friends would nod soberly; it all made sense, his coming home. Ari and Jonathan and the others would clap him on the shoulder. "Glad you're back, buddy!" Then they'd make plans, and in a couple of days it would be as if he'd never left.

He tested it out with Tal. "My folks want me to come home. Especially now. They're scared."

"You have to do what you have to do," Tal said. "Nobody would blame you. I'm just thankful you weren't hurt. Nobody was killed. That was a miracle."

"We live on miracles," Rabbi Nachum said. "They happen all around us, every moment. We are thankful for the miracles."

Thankful? To lose a hand? To have to worry every time the kids walk out the door? To look over your shoulder, not for muggers or gangs, but into the eyes of people who hate you, who think it is a holy thing to kill?

Mitch could not concentrate on his studies. At night he sat up reading, unable to sleep. When he closed his eyes, he heard the tearing sound of metal and glass; he heard a screaming child and felt the warm stain of her blood on his chest.

"Take some time out," Rabbi Nachum advised. "Travel a bit with your mother and cousin. Don't worry, the classes will always be here. Maybe," the rabbi said with a sidelong look, "maybe you want to go back home for a visit. See what you left there. Make sure . . ."

"You think I should leave? In the middle of my classes?"

Rabbi Nachum squeezed his beard. "I promised your mother I would talk to you."

"It would be like giving up," Mitch said. "Letting the terrorists win. It's what they want, to drive us out."

"Is that enough reason for staying? To get back at the terrorists?" Rabbi Nachum asked.

"Maybe it is," Mitch said. "I don't know."

Only four days remained until Carlie and his mom were leaving. Probably his mother had already bought a ticket for him. She wouldn't leave such a thing to the last minute.

In the time remaining, his mother suddenly became the energetic tourist, racing through the sights. It meant, of course, that she had no intention of ever returning.

The bombing had completely unnerved her. Mitch saw her tiredness. Still, she made her voice bright and ordered a car to take them to the south.

Carlie wanted to float in the Dead Sea. Mitch waited outside the door of the small dressing hut, standing watch along with their driver, a taciturn Israeli who kept looking about, like a sentry on duty.

"You're not going swimming?" he asked Mitch.

Mitch pointed to the stitches. "No."

"He was hurt in the bombing," his mother said, her tone a mixture of pride and blame.

They watched Carlie lie back and let the Dead Sea hold her, as on a bed. She held her bandaged hand straight up, out of the water.

His mother said, "My grandfather, when he moved to Florida, used to swim in the ocean every morning. It was a ritual with him, almost like a religion."

Mitch kept silent.

"He was a real *mensch*," his mother continued heatedly. "Not one of those Jews who goes running to the synagogue every minute, praying and bending and then, outside, not giving a hoot about anyone else. My grandparents were real people. They wanted to change the world for the better."

Mitch felt the sting of it; her eyes accused him. "I want to make the world better, too," he said, but his mother turned aside.

Carlie emerged from the water. Salt lay like pale scales over her skin and on the fabric of her red bathing suit. A mermaid, Mitch thought. He felt his mother looking at him.

"Carlie, get dressed," she said abruptly. "We've got to go on."

They drove south to Masada. To the top? asked the guide, hesitant.

"Of course," said Vivian, drawing herself up. "Let's go."

They began the treacherous ascent up to the stone parapets. Carlie ran ahead, hearing the story from the Israeli guide: "Masada—here on this rock mountain was where they retreated, the Jewish Zealots. It was their last stand against the Roman army."

"When was this?" Carlie was biting her lip, looking as if she didn't really want to know this, didn't want to deal with it.

"Before your time," the guide said lightly. "King Herod had built himself this fortress here, many years earlier. When the Jews came under attack by the Romans, they fled to Masada and took refuge. There was a prolonged siege. The Romans attacked from all sides."

The guide pointed. The air was getting thin. Mitch and the others paused to rest on a shelf of land. He tried to imagine those times, the clashing of shields, catapults, the dust. Only the dust remained. It clouded his eyes.

"Finally the Romans broke through. The Jewish leader, Eleazar, persuaded the Jews to kill themselves rather than fall into the hands of the Romans. It was a mass suicide. Nine hundred and sixty men, women, and children. Two women and five children survived by hiding in a cave."

Mitch glanced at his mother. Anger lit her eyes. She looked at him. "I don't see the virtue," she said, "to self-destruction."

"They were martyrs, madam," said the guide.

They reached the top, went like sleepwalkers through the ruins of rooms, baths, walkways, piles of charcoal, where belongings and lives had been burned black.

"My grandparents," Vivian said fiercely, as if there had been no interval at all, "used to hold meetings in their apartment on Amsterdam Avenue."

"What kind of meetings?" Carlie asked.

"Political," Vivian said. She folded her arms over her chest. "The point is, we don't have to put on different clothes or separate ourselves just to be good Jews. We're better off keeping a low profile, fitting in."

Mitch looked out over the vast expanse of desert down below, to the hazy horizon. Just so had his ancestors stood, watching for the Roman legions. He said, "Is that why Dad changed our name? So we could fit in?"

"You don't understand," his mother said. She looked from him to Carlie. "I was just a little kid in the fifties, but your father—he was older. He was affected by the quotas, the remarks . . ."

"What quotas?" Carlie asked.

"Colleges had their quotas of Jews. It's true! You kids are used to affirmative action and all that. Back in the fifties Jews couldn't even get into the L.A. Country Club. Some resorts advertised 'Christian clientele only.' Your dad didn't want to have to buck all that. Why should he?"

"So he changed his name," Mitch said, "to sound less Jewish."

"So what? He had to make a living!"

"He ran away from it."

"That's all you know, Mitch!" She drew back. "Let's not do this. Let's not fight."

"Okay." He felt drained. They came down the face of the rocky cliffs. Mitch felt exhausted from the climb and from the other battle that was being played on this dead battlefield. He wished he knew what it was that pulled him back to ancient ties. Was it God he yearned for, or was it this land? Or were the two, for him, indistinguishable?

Mitch sat in a torn overstuffed chair long past midnight, reading about wars and exile, riots and revolution. Why did every free country begin with revolution?

He had never cared about history. Now, he clung to the words. *When the death camps of Europe were liberated after the Holocaust, the Jews had no place to go. Their homes had been destroyed. Palestine was their hope. But Palestine was under British rule. The Arabs feared that the returning Jews would soon outnumber them. They convinced the British to limit Jewish settlement to a mere trickle. The Jews in Palestine were outraged—let my people in!*

Mitch gazed at the grainy photographs, mostly of gaunt young men with deeply passionate faces, their eyes dark and often furious. *Back in the thirties and forties they blew up bridges and supply depots; they carried on a continuous guerrilla warfare against the British occupation forces.*

The words of the freedom fighters blazed out from the pages of the old books. *Freedom is not for the meek! We will fashion this land out of sand and stone and sweat, and out of the agony of our own torn flesh.*

Mitch thought of Daliah. His heart sank.

He closed the book, opened it again to the place where the faces of the young men seemed to mock him. All were dead now. Some had been caught by the British and hanged. Some lived to become family men, generals and leaders. He read their names. Holon, Begin, Moskowitz, Bremen, Greenberg, Reznick . . .

Mitch froze. He backed up. Read it again.

Greenberg, Mordechai, formerly Max . . . early patriot, Dutch national, appeared in Israel in 1942 having survived a Nazi land mine that rendered his right hand useless and severely scarred the right side of his face. He fought with the Irgun, later joined the Stern gang against the British occupation. Killed in 1952 in a hotel fire. . . .

Greenberg. Green.

Mitch began to tremble. His own breathing sounded loud in his ears. Grandfather. Mitch gazed at the picture as if it were of the living man. And suddenly he felt catapulted into an entirely new reality. His own grandfather had fought here for this land.

Mitch looked into those dark eyes. A wild man, his mother had said. Yes, wild in his determination, in his convictions. What had happened, among his people, to turn them away from conviction? Once they'd been mavericks, and proud of it—different, chosen, unique. Now, all they wanted was to straddle the same dreary center line as everyone else—to be liked, to be average, to be anonymous.

Mitch looked again at the faces so filled with life. None of these men was anonymous. Their struggle had left its marks on them, but they had also left their marks on the struggle.

His grandfather's face was battered and scarred, one cheek and the mouth pulled down, the eye half closed. Mitch covered the scarred side with his finger. The other eye looked out accusingly. This man would do exactly as he pleased, would tell anyone to go to hell, would fight for the cause he believed in, no matter what it did to anyone else, wife, child, future. Or maybe it wasn't the cause at all, but adventure that had lured him, the chance to be completely free. How did one ever know, for certain, the motives of another person?

If his grandfather were here now, would they talk? Touch? Or would the wild man turn away with a laugh and a shrug? Would this man abandon him, too?

But his grandfather's genes were engraved in his own body. From him, maybe, came the shape of his head, the tilt of eyebrows, the size of his nose. Could visions be transmitted from one generation to another? Could dreams?

Grandfather. Mordechai. Without knowing anything about him, Mitch had taken his name. And now he knew for certain, as if it had been sworn to him, that the red tinge in his beard came from this man's genes, and perhaps also that streak of defiance, that unwillingness to let things pass, the need to be different, to run, if necessary, in the opposite direction from the pack.

Mitch glanced at his watch. Two in the morning. Noon in California.

He went to the telephone. With trembling fingers, he dialed, waited, his mind gone blank.

The telephone rang and rang, and Mitch almost hung up. But his father answered, breathless, as if he had hurried in from the back room. "Windows of the World!"

Liar. Cheat. Why did you lie to me? Why didn't you let me have my grandfather? The accusations rang in Mitch's head. But his tongue felt thick in his mouth. He could not speak.

Silently Mitch set the receiver down. And he thought of something Josh had said, that maybe everything happens for the best. Everything had to happen exactly as it did, he thought, to bring me to this moment.

He thought of Miriam. With her and her family, it was easy to be caught up in the world of Torah. Like a roof, their piety covered him, too. But that was not the right way. Change had to come from within him and by his own effort. Like his grandfather, he had to make his own choices and, finally, stand alone.

He took the book containing the photograph of his grandfather. He held it in both hands, like an offering. In his room he placed the book by his pillow and, still in his clothes, Mitch lay down beside it and slept.

CHAPTER 17

EARLY, THERE WAS a thumping on the door. Carlie sprang up out of bed and ran to open it. "Mitch! What's wrong?"

"Where's my mother?"

"She's in bed. What's the matter with you?"

"Mitch?" Vivian's feet were already in her slippers, robe pulled close around her body. "What happened?"

Mitch strode into the room, wearing his jeans and an old black T-shirt with the logo NIRVANA. The shirt looked odd with the thin white fringes hanging at his waist. Carlie almost laughed at the contrast of beard and old running shoes. Mitch confronted his mother.

"Why didn't you tell me the truth about my grandfather? Why did Dad lie to me?"

"Sit down, Mitch. What's wrong with you?" Vivian pushed the hair from her eyes. "I told you he was a socialist."

"I mean Mordechai. He didn't die that day on the dock. He survived and came to Israel. He's a hero! Look!" Mitch held out the book. "This is him. His picture. Mordechai Greenberg."

Carlie went over to see the picture, her heart thumping. She was tired of the yelling, the accusations. If only they could have a single day together without fighting—one fine day.

"I didn't know he was famous," Vivian said. She peered at the picture. "He looks dreadful."

"Why did Dad tell me he was dead?"

"Oh, Mitch." Aunt Vivian looked weary. She pushed back her tousled hair. "You know your father. He wanted to forget it. That's how he copes. For years he thought his father had died in that explosion. Much later they found out, quite by chance, that he had lived and gone to Israel."

"What did he do here?" Carlie asked.

"He fought for the Resistance," Mitch said.

Vivian stood up. She seemed to struggle for a moment, then she turned to face Carlie and Mitch, her expression stern. "I know that this—this glorious hero abandoned his son. He degraded his wife. He wouldn't even buy her shoes."

"Still, he was my grandfather," Mitch retorted. "Didn't I have a right to know about him?"

"It was your father's call. He was the one who suffered. Now you know. That man's values were all screwed up! He was a violent man."

"He had guts," said Mitch. "He was a fighter."

"So is your father. No glory, just taking care of everybody, working hard . . . that's a hero." There were tears in Vivian's eyes. She sat down on the sofa, her hands covering her face.

"Mitch," Carlie said, "it doesn't matter. It doesn't change anything."

"What do you mean? It means I have a stake here."

"We all do," Carlie said.

Mitch sat down on the small sofa. His tone, now, was lighter, merely curious. "Why didn't you tell about this when we were at Miriam's?"

Vivian took a deep breath, blinking away tears. "I don't know. Maybe I should have told you that night. I didn't think it would be right to undermine your father. If he didn't want you to know . . . I'm sorry, Mitch. Do you think it would have made a difference?"

"It's okay," Mitch said. "I realize that what happened with Miriam was—well, it was for the best."

Carlie glanced at Mitch. He smiled at her, and she felt flushed. Her heart raced. She wanted to talk to him alone, to really talk. She had not asked him about Miriam. Was he in love with her? Then how could the breakup have been for the best? Or was he, like she, confused about love and what is possible, even between cousins?

Maybe tomorrow, at Safed, they'd have a few moments alone together. Maybe then he would tell her.

The road to Safed wound up into the hills, circling and climbing. Carlie looked back at the rooftops and fields. The car seemed to struggle. Occasionally they passed people walking, carrying bundles. There was a steadiness in their gait, as if they expected no changes or sudden turns. Why couldn't things be that simple? Carlie sighed. She caught Aunt Vivian's eye, her quick smile.

By the time they reached the top, the car engine was hot and their driver was cranky. "Meet you later," he said. "By the restaurant."

A warm breeze billowed up from the valley. It rippled the

flags and streamers that advertised the artists' stalls. "I want to see all the shops, buy some souvenirs," Vivian said.

"What about lunch?" Mitch asked.

"I'll find something." She handed Mitch several bills. "Buy lunch for your cousin," she said.

Mitch hesitated, then took the money. "Thanks. I will. Maybe," he said, "we'll walk on down to the cemetery."

Aunt Vivian nodded. "Whatever. We'll meet back here at three."

The streets were mere dust, or paved in stone, uneven and sunken through the centuries by weather and countless footsteps. Carlie felt the warm air against her face, aware of the blue sky like a dome on this mountaintop. She breathed deeply; she felt the lightness inside her.

Stone steps led down to a small synagogue.

"You have to see this," Mitch said, pulling her inside.

Carlie's eyes widened, and she stretched out her arms, as if to embrace the charm of it, the fantasy—walls painted bright yellow and green, stained-glass windows, high-back, cushioned chairs with carved arms, fit for a king, Persian carpets, and glass cases filled with gigantic books, silver candelabra, and Torah crowns.

A chirping sound came from the ceiling. Carlie turned and saw numerous small yellow birds perched on a long rod. She pointed. "Are those real birds?"

"They live here," said an old caretaker.

"Inside the synagogue?"

"Why not?"

Carlie laughed. "Why not? Good question."

Mitch nodded, grinning. "It makes you think."

Outside again, Carlie hurried to keep up with Mitch. His

hand grazed hers. She felt the warmth of it, a burning. "Let's walk down to the cemetery," he said.

"Okay." They used to hold hands, sometimes, running to catch a bus or make a movie. His hands were large and warm.

She began. "You haven't even asked about your dog."

"Sorry. How's Arnie?"

"He misses you."

"How do you know?"

"He told me. Anyway, he sniffs your closet, especially the shoes."

"I miss him, too," said Mitch.

"Mitch, are you coming home?"

Mitch stopped, facing Carlie. He put his finger to his lips. Hesitantly, he took her hand. "Come on," he said in a light tone, as if they were children again.

And the sun dazzled Carlie as they walked; pebbles under her feet were like jewels, and she imagined sapphires and diamonds lying there—why couldn't it be?

They walked down the hillside into the enclosure marked by stones and a low line of shrubs. Grave markers lay sunken into the earth, partly buried in weeds and leaning right or left, some broken loose from their moorings, making it seem that even now they were in motion. Tree roots lay like gnarled fingers along the ground. Overhead, the branches were interlaced with vines, creating a sun-speckled ceiling, gentling the air.

"You can sit down," Mitch said softly. "Just be careful you don't sit on—anyone." He eased himself down between the crowded spaces of the dead, and Carlie sat down, too, facing him across a small patch of ground. Whoever lies here, she thought with a pang, don't worry. We come in peace. She wanted to say the words out loud, but she felt foolish, even blushing to herself.

Mitch picked up several fallen leaves, curling them between his fingers. "Here," he said softly, "time doesn't mean a thing."

"It's beautiful and quiet," Carlie said, looking about.

"When I left L.A. last summer," Mitch said, "I was pretty depressed."

Carlie, startled, only looked at him.

"I didn't realize it, but—I was sort of moving along on automatic pilot. You know?"

"I know you weren't excited about the trip to Israel," Carlie said. A pounding began in her chest. She felt on the brink of something, and she clutched her hands together, her fingers clasped onto the amethyst ring.

"I've always tried to do what they wanted, Carlie. You know that. You were there."

"I know it. But we miss you, Mitch. And your dad worries about you losing time at college."

"I was like a robot," Mitch said, "just doing what other people thought I should do. It wasn't until I came here that I felt better. Like I was finally my own person."

"I didn't know you were so unhappy," Carlie said, pushing back tears. She would have helped him, somehow, had she known.

"Remember Joel?" he asked.

"The guy who died? Sure."

"Well, it really got to me."

"I didn't know you were such great friends."

"Not great friends," Mitch said. "I never had any *great* friends. I knew Joel since grammar school, way before he got into that band he hung out with, or before he got into drugs."

"I didn't know he was into drugs."

Mitch waved it aside. "His folks told everyone he died of a heart attack. What really happened was, he OD'd. On heroin."

"How do you know?"

"Buddy of his from the band told me. They were together. It's true, I didn't hang out much with him anymore, but I liked Joel. He played guitar, wrote songs. He was going to travel all over the country, he said, join up with different bands. Of course, he never did. He died, instead."

"I'm sorry," Carlie whispered. Mitch's hands hung loosely between his knees; his head was down.

"The day after he died—did you know his folks had this service for him?"

"Did you tell me about it?" Carlie shifted uncomfortably; the ground was hard and slightly damp, and the tombstones all around offered no warmth.

"Probably not," Mitch said. He squinted, looking away from her. "In those days, I didn't tell things, not even to you. Not things that mattered."

"I see." And Carlie wondered why that hurt so much.

"Joel was cremated. The ashes were scattered at sea. All it took was one phone call, they said. His stepdad seemed so proud of that. But then I guess they needed something else, and they didn't really know what to do or where to go. I mean, Joel's mom and stepdad were regular hippies. Like from the sixties. His mom went around in sweatpants and rubber sandals, hair down to her waist. The house was a complete disaster. Nobody ever cleaned or cooked or answered the phone. They all used sleeping bags because they didn't want to make the beds."

Carlie wrinkled her nose. "It must have stunk."

"It was just so—disorganized. Total chaos. Everyone did their own thing. It was like—well, the complete opposite of Miriam's house. You know?"

Carlie bit her lip. Then she nodded. She hadn't realized that maybe Mitch wanted a different family. Maybe in a way, she thought, everyone does.

Mitch went on. "When Joel died, his mom decided to hold a memorial service for him at the beach real early in the morning. Venice Beach, down from the volleyball nets, you know, by that blue building with all the murals on it?"

"I know the place."

"So I went. I mean, he was my friend, and there was hardly anyone else going. I had to go!"

"Sure, I can see that," Carlie said. She wanted to reach out and, with her fingertips, smooth away the lines on Mitch's face. She kept her hands in her lap, the ring pressing into her fingers.

"There were just a few people, an older couple, two guys and a girl from Joel's band. It was clammy and cold. We stood around. Finally Joel's stepfather had us make a small circle. He talked about what a good kid Joel was. The girl stepped out and sang 'The Wind Beneath My Wings,' and it was pathetic, Carlie. Then Joel's mom talked, and she was crying, and she told how when Joel was a little boy he tried to jump off the roof with a sheet around him, like Superman, because he wanted to fly. And she cried and cried and said, 'Well, now I know he's happy. He's flying.' "

"Oh, God," Carlie murmured. "How awful."

Mitch went on. "Joel's mother had brought this boom box. She said she wanted us to hear Joel's last words and the voices of his friends, so she brought the tape from his phone answering machine, and she played it and . . . Carlie, it was all kinds of calls from Joel's scuzzy pals, and three calls from his *dealer*, would you believe it? He said, 'Come over to my place for cake tonight, white frosting.' Joel's folks didn't even get it."

"From his *dealer*," Carlie said incredulously.

"Wait." Mitch rocked back and forth, as if hypnotized. "Suddenly this other woman says, 'Shouldn't somebody say a prayer or something? I mean, I know Joel's father was Jewish. Should somebody say *Kaddish*?'

"Everybody acted totally confused. Then one of the guys looked at me and said, 'He's Jewish,' and they passed the prayer book to me and . . ."

"Did you know it? Could you do it?"

"I went through the book and finally I found it and I read it. Not very well. And the whole time I felt so—so mortified and embarrassed. Like I was a phony. They were trying to do something real, but it didn't work. It was just like Joel, when he was a little kid, making wings out of a sheet and trying to fly."

Mitch's face was flushed, and his voice held a different tone than Carlie had ever heard before—a mixture of shame and yearning. He did not look at her, but to a distance.

"So you felt—guilty?"

Mitch brushed his hands over his face. "I felt terrible. Empty. I didn't know it then, but I guess I was ashamed, too, because it seemed like we'd lost something. Just gave it away."

Carlie felt a lump in her throat.

"I mean, everyone has all these reasons why they don't believe in religion or ritual, dozens of reasons. I had them, too. It wasn't rational, it was boring, the people were nasty, the rabbi was a jerk. So what? Religion isn't about reasons or how other people act. It's just about—about God. Being connected to God. You know?"

"I—I guess so," Carlie stammered. She felt slightly embarrassed, sitting here talking about God, and they weren't even in synagogue. She said, "I guess I never thought much about it. Did you before you got here?"

"Maybe. I don't remember. But when I got here, I went to the Wall, like all tourists. I hadn't planned it, but I said a prayer for Joel. I'd never done that before."

"You never prayed?"

"Never on my own. This was different. Personal." He hesitated, then said, "It was like I was talking to God. And He was listening. And everything started to change for me. I started to study really hard. I found out what Jews are supposed to do, what it says in the Torah. And then, for the first time, I thought, maybe that applies to me, too. And instead of asking why I should do all those things, there was a shift."

"What changed?"

"I asked myself, why not? If God really wrote all those commandments, how can I not follow them? Nobody knows for sure, do they?

"I started doing them," he said. "Not really into it at first. But then I found myself having—well, a conversation. With God. That's what this is all about."

Carlie stared at Mitch. He had never talked this way before, never looked so passionate, almost radiant.

Mitch went on, eyes squinting against the sun. "I used to

lie awake at night so angry because your folks died, because you cried and couldn't get over it. . . ."

"I did get over it," Carlie said. "I think I did."

"Not for a long time. And I kept asking myself how things like that could happen. Poor old Uncle Utz with that awful number on his arm! And that sadness he has with him all the time. I don't know why he was saved. I don't know why all those millions of people died. Some people say there's no God because bad things happen. But I think the world is like a huge jigsaw puzzle, and we're only in a tiny piece of it. We never see the whole thing. Only God sees it all."

Carlie listened, rapt, seeing Mitch transformed. "God didn't kill my parents," Carlie said. "It was a drunk driver."

"Yes! People do terrible things," Mitch said breathlessly, emphasizing his words with gestures, strong and sure. "People can drink and drive. They can kill. That's because we have free will. God gave us free will. But He also gave us rules. And somebody has to remember what they are, and teach the people, or else it's all lost. Who is supposed to keep it for us? Isn't it you? And me?"

Carlie stared at him, scarcely breathing. "Why you?"

He smiled slightly. "Why not?"

She paused, looking all around at the tombstones, the sun filtering through the leaves, weaving patterns on the ground. They sat quietly for what seemed a long time, still wrapped in the force of their conversation and their thoughts. Then softly she asked him, "What did you mean about Miriam? That it was for the best, breaking up like that."

"With Miriam and her family," Mitch said, "it would be too easy. All I'd have to do was let myself be swept along with them, their beliefs and their ways. Such an old family, so many scholars in it! I wouldn't have to make any decisions, would I? I wouldn't really have to learn for myself."

"We thought you wanted to marry her," said Carlie. She could not look at him.

"Marry her? No—maybe after a while, I don't know. I do know that it makes it clear for me. To stay, not for a girl, not for that, but for the right reason."

Carlie turned to look into Mitch's eyes, to see them shining with certainty. "And the reason is—God?"

"Yes! It's a whole new attitude, a new life, Carlie!" he exclaimed. "I can't wait to get up in the morning. I can feel the electricity, the excitement. Wasn't it like that when you were into ballet? You went to the studio every day that summer, and you danced for hours. Didn't you love it?"

Carlie shook her head. "No. Not really. I think I was trying to really want something the way you always did. But I got bored and tired. I'm not like you, Mitch."

She got up, brushed herself off, and stood looking down at Mitch sprawled on the ground with tombstones everywhere, and new grass sprouting. Nothing seemed incongruous now, or strange. In fact, Mitch in his blue jeans, with beard and fringes and small cap on his head, looked entirely right.

Mitch got up slowly, as if he had grown taller and needed to feel his new height. He moved close to Carlie and took her arm.

"Look," he said, pointing down to the valley and up at the green hills. "Look at those trees. They shine. Look at those mountains! Just being here makes you feel so alive. When I look around I keep thinking of the words in the psalm we say every Friday night: 'The rivers will clap their hands. The mountains will sing together.' Carlie, I want to be where the mountains can sing."

Carlie scarcely moved, hardly breathed. She had never loved him so much as at this moment. "A singing mountain," she whispered. "That's so beautiful. A river that claps its hands—what else?"

" 'The trees of the forest will sing,' " Mitch quoted, " 'when He has come, when He has come to judge the earth.' "

"When will that be?" she asked. Sunlight pierced her eyes; maybe that was what brought the tears.

"Soon," Mitch said. "Maybe now, sooner."

Suddenly she felt Mitch's hands on her shoulders, and he stood before her, searching her face. "Carlie!" The joy in his voice was like something visible.

"Carlie," he said breathlessly, "stay here with me. Stay and finish high school here. There are classes in English, wonderful schools. Lots of kids do it. Oh, Carlie, it would be so great. We'll travel around together. There are trips to the Sinai; we can ride camels. We'll learn the country, the language. We'll be like we used to be, doing everything together."

Mitch stood very close, so close that in a moment she could be in his arms. Was that what he wanted? To hold her close? Did he love her? Really love her, as she loved him? She didn't know for sure; nor was it the right time to find out.

Carlie stepped back and shook her head. "I can't, Mitch."

"Why not? It's perfect! You can even stay with Halle. She'll need help with the new baby. You like her, I know you do."

Carlie looked down over the valley. She took a full, deep

breath. "No, Mitch. I want to go home. There are things I need to do there. I want to go and be a real daughter to your parents. They love me. And I love them." She tried to smile. "I'm a California girl. That's where my life is. I'd be miserable here, even with you."

"But when will I see you again?" Mitch frowned, and he looked like a little boy, perplexed and worried, like the day he came into her room with a new skateboard under his arm. Then, he had saved her. Now it was her turn.

"Look, Mitch," she said firmly, "you told us you are on a journey. Well, you need to keep on it. Don't get confused. Don't get off the track. I want to see you when you get to the end of it! I want to hear what you found out."

He looked stunned for a moment, as if he were standing on a precipice, uncertain of his footing. But then he lifted his gaze to the mountain once again, and Carlie saw that his stance was firm.

She had done it right.

CHAPTER 18

MITCH STOOD BEFORE Rabbi Nachum. He felt awkward, almost shy. "Carlie and my mother left late last night, on the one A.M. flight. My mother gave me money from my trust," Mitch said. "So I can be independent."

"That's good," said Rabbi Nachum. "She sees it your way now?"

"No. She doesn't see it. She just respects it."

"That's what counts." Rabbi Nachum pushed back his chair, stretching and rubbing his neck. It was late, and Mitch knew he would have been bent over his books for hours.

"I think Carlie got to her," Mitch said with a grin. "They had a—you know—sort of an encounter. Lots of tears and hugs and kisses."

It was the night they returned from Safed, and they stood outside the hotel, looking down past the ancient cemetery to the old city, its walls, and beyond. The light caught his mother's face, so that she seemed to glow. And Carlie said, "Mitch has to stay here, Aunt Vivian. You can see that, can't you?" And the two of them talked, almost as if Mitch wasn't there, about loving and needing and about letting go.

Rabbi Nachum said, "You have a fine family."

"A small one. All my grandparents are dead. Some crazy cousins."

"Everyone has crazy cousins," said the rabbi. "What else is new?"

"My father's father," Mitch said, "was Mordechai Greenberg. The terrorist."

"Terrorist!" Rabbi Nachum exclaimed.

"He blew up things. A railroad track. Maybe someone was killed. Did you ever hear of it? He was in the Irgun."

Rabbi Nachum blew out a deep breath. "Yes, of course I have heard the name. Amazing," he said. "So, you have roots here in Israel after all. Why didn't you say anything?"

"I didn't know it until a few days ago," Mitch said. "My father never told me."

Rabbi Nachum sat back. He nodded thoughtfully and said, "I suppose he had his reasons."

"Hatred," Mitch said. "He hated his father."

"Well. That's sad. To hate your own father. To condemn him without really knowing his motives or feelings." Rabbi Nachum gave Mitch a long look. He glanced at his watch. "It's about nine in the morning in California," he said.

"Dad! I'm glad I caught you. Aren't you about to leave for the airport?"

Mitch stood in the hall, holding the receiver close to his mouth. Shadows moved on the wall; a narrow path of light showed from the parlor. Upstairs, all was silent.

"In a few minutes," his dad said. "Where are you?" There was a shiver of hope in his voice. "Are you *here*?"

"No, Dad. I'm still in Israel. Didn't Mom tell you I was staying?" Mitch looked into the parlor, with its shabby furniture, the tables, and shelves full of books. This place, with the hum of activity by day, the nights with their long hours of reading, pondering, searching—all were like food and drink to him now.

His father said, "I thought maybe you'd changed your mind again."

"No, Dad. I feel very sure." He was part of the cycle, the eternal cycle. That was it. Through him, the cycle endured. But how could he explain this to his father?

Mitch said, "There's something I have to tell you, Dad. I've learned things about us and about your father."

"Yes, your mother told me you read about Mordechai in a book. He was some kind of a revolutionary there."

"Yes. He fought for . . ."

"You know he deserted us, your grandmother Rose and me. He never wrote." His father's voice was heavy with bitterness. "Never even let us know he was alive. Cut us off, as if we were nothing to him. Nothing at all."

Mitch moved his mouth closer to the receiver. "Dad, I know. It must have been horrible when you found out. Worse than thinking he was dead."

"Yes."

Mitch said softly, "I saw his photograph in a book. He'd been hurt pretty bad in that explosion. It showed."

"I never wished him any harm," his father exclaimed. "I never felt vindictive toward him. It was just . . ."

"It wasn't fair," Mitch said. "I wish—I wish it hadn't happened the way it did."

There was silence, a faint groan. Then his father said, "I

had to grow up alone. I grew up when I was six years old."

"That's tough," Mitch said. "But it made you tough, too."

"I had to be. There was nobody to run to. My mother was—well, you know how she is. A survivor. That's her. She worked hard. I hated to see it."

"The thing is," Mitch said, "maybe there's something in our genes. A kind of strength. Maybe it's stubbornness, I don't know, but maybe that's what helps us survive."

"Maybe," said his father.

"Once we get an idea," Mitch said, "we don't let go. Like, you built that business from scratch. Grandma Rose makes her art without even any tools or supplies—she does it because it's what she needs to do. It's who she is."

"That's right. She's always expressed herself. She's a strong woman."

"Dad, I don't want to be a quitter. I've finally found out what matters to me. And I have to do it. Like you did. I couldn't stand to live with myself if I just let it go."

Time stretched; Mitch clasped the receiver tightly, waiting. Then Mitch said softly, "I want you to be proud of me, Dad. Mom says you're a hero."

"Come on."

"Really. Look, I want to come for a visit. But not yet. I need to get more grounded. Does that make sense?"

Another long pause, then his dad sighed. "It all makes sense in a weird way. You going off. Your mother now says she's going to get back into art school. She told me on the phone already, as if it was going to be an argument. I don't mind. Why would I mind? People have to take what they need. Everyone is different. Me, all I need is my shop and a good game of golf once in a while. And my family."

"So maybe I can come home for a visit in the summer."

"That would be great, son."

"Great," Mitch repeated. He took a deep breath, was about to say the words "I love you, Dad." But it would be unnatural. He and his dad didn't talk that way.

"Take care, son," said his father.

"You, too, Dad," said Mitch.

The next morning, in the middle of a lecture, Mitch suddenly felt the aliveness, the answer. He couldn't wait. He excused himself and ran out.

Like a wild man, he acknowledged to himself, like a fanatic, he raced through the streets of Jerusalem, dodging cars on Jaffa Street, leaping past mothers with babies in strollers, past the construction crews with their cranes and hydraulic drills with their outrageous racket.

Mitch ran into the little shop, pulled on his denim coveralls, and picked up the sheets of copper and silver, his palms sliding over the sleek surfaces, his fingertips already working.

Each segment of the finished work appeared before him, the rivers twisting and dancing their way between trees, the shining leaves, and the mountains. Somehow he would find a way to give melody to the mute metals; he would convey, through the work of his hands and the longing in his soul, the sound of music. He would make the mountains sing.

It might take a long time, but he would do it.

At the airport he had given the silver and turquoise pendant to Carlie. "I love it," she said as she put it on. In her eyes was the kiss she could not give him, but he saw it. She was right, of course, in her decision. They both needed time alone, to find out exactly who and what they were. She was a healer. Maybe she knew it now. Maybe not yet, but in time she would.

She said, "I'll always wear this, Mitch. Turquoise is my favorite stone."

"I know," Mitch said. And he realized then that the pendant had been intended for Carlie all along.

Time would tell, he thought, about Carlie, about him and the paths they must follow. Everything has its own season. Nothing can be rushed. That's how it was with art, too, he thought as he set to work on this new piece. It takes time to bring the vision to the surface. It is like a birth.

Finally, it lives.